AFLP   14455

Brandt, Lyle
The Lawman: Hanging Judge

THE LAWMAN: HANGING JUDGE

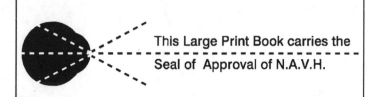

This Large Print Book carries the
Seal of Approval of N.A.V.H.

THE LAWMAN: HANGING JUDGE

LYLE BRANDT

THORNDIKE PRESS
A part of Gale, Cengage Learning

GALE
CENGAGE Learning™

Detroit • New York • San Francisco • New Haven, Conn • Waterville, Maine • London

LIBRARY OF CONGRESS CATALOGING-IN-PUBLICATION DATA

Brandt, Lyle, 1951–
    The lawman : hanging judge / by Lyle Brandt.
        p. cm. — (Thorndike Press large print western)
    ISBN-13: 978-1-4104-2624-6
    ISBN-10: 1-4104-2624-6
    1. Judges—Fiction. 2. Large type books. I. Title.
PS3602.R364H36 2010
813'.6—dc22   2010007663

Published in 2010 by arrangement with The Berkley Publishing Group, a member of Penguin Group (USA) Inc.

Printed in the United States of America
1 2 3 4 5 6 7 14 13 12 11 10

For Sam Peckinpah

PROLOGUE

The killers entered Enid, Oklahoma, from the four points of the compass. They had ridden long and hard, alone, to reach that city on the prairie and fulfill their destinies.

The riders did not know each other. They had never met and would not recognize each other's names if names were offered — which they wouldn't be. Some might have friends in common, but they'd never know it, since discussion of their private histories was strictly banned.

Four strangers, drawn together by a common cause they could not ignore.

Perhaps it was that commonality that made the men resemble one another. True, they varied strikingly in height, weight, hair and eye color, a host of individual particulars, but there was still a *sameness* to them, if they were examined by discerning eyes.

All four were seasoned murderers. They had not merely killed in self-defense or warfare, but had plotted murder in the dead of night, carried out their plans with grim resolve, and felt satisfaction when the deed was done. Lye soap could wash the blood-stains from their hands, but it could not remove the mark of Cain.

Their faces told the story. Brown, blue, green, or gray, their eyes had witnessed slaughter and had reveled in it.

There was also something in the way they moved. Mounted or walking, they might seem relaxed to casual observers, but there was a kind of tension always present in their bodies. Callused hands never strayed far from knives and pistols. They were con-stantly alert to danger, watching everything around them, seeking enemies among strangers.

The first rider arrived at noon. He'd risen early, with a long way yet to go, and pushed his chestnut mare to reach the town by lunchtime. He was tired of cooking on the trail and had enough money to dine in style for one or two meals, anyway.

Which might be all he'd need.

His name was Samuel Houston Bowers, but he wasn't using it on this trip. He would make up something for the hotel register; it didn't matter what he signed, since no one ever double-checked. To those he planned to meet, he would be simply Number Four.

The town was larger than he had imagined, as befit the seat of government for half of Oklahoma Territory. Riding in, he passed all manner of professional establishments, displaying notices for lawyers, doctors, dentists, bookkeepers, surveyors — take your pick. He saw a school, two churches, two saloons, and every kind of shop he could imagine if he spent all day thinking of goods to sell.

It made his skin crawl.

Number Four disliked cities. In fact, he hated them.

He was a country boy at heart, whose family had been uprooted from its land after the War Between the States, forced into crowded city quarters while his father looked for work and wound up slaving in a factory that killed him years before his time. His mother had to take in washing after that, for those who could afford to have it done by someone else, and when that failed to make ends meet, she'd reached "arrangements" with a list of "gentlemen admirers" who contributed to keep a roof over her head.

Sometimes, during his darker moments, Number Four considered seeking out those men and killing them, but what good would it do? When honor died, when hope was lost, the soul was dead. And only hate remained. It was a feeling he had nurtured from his adolescence, and it served him well.

Scanning the strangers all around him, strolling up and down Main Street, Number Four imagined some of them were watching him. One or two were blatant, staring at him until his grim visage made them turn away, but most were cagey, only flicking glances now and then in his direction. He could never really catch them at it, but he knew how townsfolk thought of strangers, looking down their noses at the ones who didn't fit, didn't belong.

Enid had three hotels: the Pearl, Grady's, and Soderquist's. Number Four chose Grady's for no special reason and tied up his chestnut outside, within reach of a watering trough. He took his saddlebags and Henry rifle with him as he clomped across the wooden sidewalk, shedding trail dust.

It was cool inside the hotel lobby, well out of the noonday sun. A slender man of middle age waited for Number Four behind the registration counter, smiling as if he'd rehearsed it with a mirror every morning of his life.

"Good afternoon, sir. May I help you?"

"Need a room," said Number Four.

"Of course, sir. Do you have a preference?"

"A what?"

The smile flickered a bit. "Do you prefer a room fronting the street or at the rear? Perhaps a certain floor?"

"Don't care, long as it's got a bed and piss pot."

"Certainly. In fact, sir, we have indoor plumbing here at Grady's. A commode on every floor."

"How much?"

"A dollar nightly, at the rear. One-fifty for the Main Street view."

"I'll skip the viewing bit," said Number Four. He placed a silver dollar on the counter, saying, "Stick me in the back."

"Yes, sir. If you'll be kind enough to sign the register . . ."

He was about to write "Jeff Davis" as a joke, but then thought better of it and wrote "Nathan Bedford" in a straggly hand. Something for them to ponder when his job was done, if they could ever work it out.

The clerk gave him a key, said, "Third floor rear," and smiled him on his way. The number painted on the key was 308.

Number Four counted steps as he went up the stairs, filing the final tally in his memory for future reference. He never knew when some midnight emergency might send him racing for the street in utter darkness, and it paid to memorize the exits from a new place on arrival, know how many steps it took to put him on the ground floor if the place was filled with smoke or men who aimed to kill him.

Living, in his world, meant living on alert. It had been tiring, once upon a time, but he was used to it after so many years. Self-discipline was second nature to him now.

It made him who and what he was.

Room 308 was nothing special, but he'd slept in worse. It beat the cabin he'd been living in, outside of Searcy, Arkansas, when he received the summons for his current job. The sheets and towels were clean, there was a pitcher filled with water in the wash-basin, and there were clothes hangers in a cupboard with a door that he could close to hide his things.

It went against the grain to leave his rifle and his saddlebags, but Number Four knew he would look strange carrying them through the streets. The last thing that he needed, now, was to draw more attention from the locals. Anything that made them take a second look at him was bad.

He left his things inside the cupboard,

closed it, locked the bedroom door behind him as he left, and found the indoor privy at the far end of the hall. It was a strange device, but served its purpose well enough. When he was finished there, he went downstairs and out to find the livery, walking his chestnut by its reins while wagons rattled past him on Main Street.

Boarding the mare cost him another fifty cents, but Number Four was satisfied to pay the price. He'd seen a restaurant along the way and heard his stomach growling as he passed it. Walking back to feed himself, he checked his pocket watch and found that he still had four hours, yet, before he was supposed to meet the others.

It was time enough to eat and have a look around. Specifically, to view the courthouse, where the deed was going to be done. If there was any hope of getting clear when it was finished, Number Four would find it.

And if not, at least he'd know that he had done his duty to the bitter end.

Edward McDaniel was the second to arrive in Enid, but his comrades, when they met, would call him Number Three. He'd spent ten days on the trail from Joplin, Missouri, and had killed two men along the way to reach Enid on time.

Damned fools shouldn't have tried to rob him in the first place. If they'd known their business, they'd have seen he was more trouble than the two of them could handle, and they would've known he didn't carry cash enough to make it worth the risk.

Well, they were buzzard bait by now and on their way to being bleached white bones. Their deaths were meaningless to Number Three. The only target that he gave a damn about was waiting for him at the end of his long ride.

Waiting to die.

He'd burned the note that summoned him, but he could still recall its words verbatim. They were seared into his memory, as if etched by a red-hot brand.

Nighthawk! The sepulchre has opened! Every loyal man must do his duty! Meet your three brethren in Enid, Okla., general delivery, on the deadly day of wailing week in blooming month, at the mournful hour after noon. Orders await! Fail not! By command of the dragon. * * *

For those who knew the code, the message was transparent. He must be outside the post office in Enid at five o'clock in the afternoon, on the third Monday in May.

14

Three others would receive notes similar to his, and he assumed they all would instantly obey.

There had been time for him to pack his things, give notice at the worthless job he'd held for seven weeks — almost a record — and to point his grullo gelding southward for the journey to another killing ground. He wouldn't miss Joplin and didn't really care where he was going.

All that mattered was the task at hand.

It would be murder, naturally. The Dragon would not summon him from such a distance simply to intimidate an enemy. It would be all or nothing this time.

Just the way he liked it.

Enid looked like any other town to Number Three. He had no eye for architecture, decoration, and the like. He could appreciate a good saloon, but only for its liquor and the women it employed. Churches were wasted on him, though he called himself a Christian if somebody raised the question. Stores and all the rest of it meant nothing to him unless he was shopping for specific items, such as ammunition or a pair of boots.

And what he wanted, at the moment, was a bath.

Ten days of smelling like a dusty animal

was long enough. His own smell had begun to bother *him,* and Number Three could well imagine its effect on others. While he was not overly concerned about hygiene, he disliked being filthy and would rather that the undertaker found him reasonably clean, if anything went wrong.

There was a chance, he realized, that when he left Enid he would be riding in a flatbed wagon to Boot Hill. Death was a possibility each time he took a killing job, since most men wouldn't stand and take it without fighting back. Surprise could help, of course, but if the target was important he'd have guns around him, paid to keep him healthy.

Not that it would help.

When Number Three was on a job, the job got done. He had performed at least a dozen missions of this nature for the Brotherhood over as many years, with maybe twice that many private contracts on the side. It was a fact of life that someone always needed killing — more each year, it seemed — while those willing to do the job were getting scarce.

A rancher here. A banker there. A wife who'd strayed. A husband who was standing in the way of true love's passion. Some old coot whose death would hasten an inheritance.

Come one, come all. It added up.

But there would be no paycheck for this job, beyond expenses for the trip. This one, and others like it, sprang from oaths that Number Three had taken, his abiding faith in what was right and wrong.

Some people had to die because the very fact of their existence upset nature's balance. They were worse than useless, fouling everything they touched for generations yet unborn.

He'd killed a fair number of those and would be pleased to add another to his score.

Halfway along the second block of Main Street, Number Three spotted a barber's shop that advertised hot baths. He road on past it to the livery, sparing his first thought for the tired and hungry gelding, then walked back with his saddlebags and Model 1887 Winchester repeating shotgun.

Passing on the shave and haircut, he went straight to the back room where two deep metal tubs stood waiting, situated six or seven feet apart, both presently unoccupied. They faced in opposite directions, for some reason, flared at one end for a headrest, and he chose the tub that let him watch the door.

The barber took his money, then began to ferry buckets filled with steaming water to the empty tub, while Number Three un-dressed. He placed his shotgun and his matched set of Colt Single-Action Army revolvers within arm's reach of the tub, then lowered himself into the near-scalding water one painful inch at a time.

You get what you pay for, he thought and began to relax. The barber brought soap, then left Number Three alone with his thoughts.

Just as well, being bloody and dark as they were.

His mind was no place any common man would care to go.

And those who tried were lost.

The third shooter to enter Enid on that May Monday was Darren Wallace, known to his handful of living friends as Duke. Among the riders who were gathering, he would be Number Two.

He was the youngest of the four who had been summoned, hadn't been of age to fight against the Yankee scum before old General Lee laid down his sword at Appomattox, but like every other son of Dixie, Number Two knew that the war had not ended with treaties signed in 1865. It still went on, and would continue until every damned blue-belly who had fought against the cause of liberty was punished for his sins.

These days, when full-scale battles were impractical, the punishment was dealt out to deserving subjects one by one, as time and circumstance allowed.

Despite his relatively tender years, there was no doubt concerning Number Two's ability to pull his weight. He never flinched from killing, be the target man or beast, and none of it preyed on his mind. An alienist might have said that he was born without a conscience. Certain preachers might've questioned whether he possessed a soul.

None of that meant squat to Number Two while he was riding up from Abilene, Texas, two weeks in transit with the tools of his trade. He carried a Winchester Model 1873 repeating rifle, a Smith & Wesson Schofield revolver, and an Arkansas toothpick with its thirteen-inch double-edge blade honed to razor sharpness.

Plenty of death to go around, up close or at a hundred yards.

When Number Two rode into Enid, no one on Main Street gave him a second look. Or, if they did, he didn't notice, didn't give a damn. Looks couldn't hurt him, and if some fool tried to pick a fight, why, Number Two would duck his head, decline the honor, and move on. It wouldn't matter

19

what the other bastard said.

Until the job was done.

And then . . .

His biggest problem, until recently, had been receiving decent service in saloons. Bartenders often thought he was too young to drink, and whores were prone to ask if it was his first time. He'd spent the better part of eight months working on a straggly beard, to make himself look older, and the odd shooting did wonders for the level of respect that Number Two received.

In Waco, when he'd still been welcome there, the local roughnecks had begun to call him Kid Lightning, after his fast draw. Number Two had liked the sound of that, but understood that nicknames were like brands. They worked against you when you needed anonymity.

Like now.

The most important things in an assassin's life were weapons and a ready means of transportation. Number Two kept all his hardware cleaned and oiled, ready for service at a heartbeat's notice, and he lavished equal care upon his buckskin stallion. Thus it was that after checking into Soderquist's hotel — top floor, with windows overlooking Main Street — that he made his next stop at the livery and got the stallion nicely situated. Only then did he consider eating, stepping out to have a look around the town before he met three strangers to discuss the job.

He wondered who the mark was this time. While it made no difference to Number Two, beyond details of execution, he still liked to know why targets had been chosen. What had this one done to earn the Dragon's lethal wrath?

He'd be a Yankee or a scalawag, of course. All of them were. But the specific details of his crimes might be intriguing. Number Two took more pride in his work when he was rubbing out the enemies of civilized society.

Did such a thing even exist today?

Dixie's destruction in the war, coupled with the outrages it had suffered afterward, had wiped out most of the Confederacy's charm and dignity. The glory days were lost beyond recall, in Number Two's opinion, but it still was possible to settle scores with those who'd done the damage, and with those who followed their example a quarter century later.

Number Two was not a sunshine patriot or summer soldier. He could not forget, and he would not forgive. As long as he could draw a breath and draw a bead, no enemy was safe.

The restaurant was nearly empty when he walked in off the street. The waitress was a gawky ginger girl who showed him to a corner table by the broad front window. Number Two sat with his back to the wall, so no one could creep up behind him, and ordered a steak with potatoes and beans.

While he waited, he studied his four fellow diners. An old man with a shock of snow-white hair was smiling over soup bowls at a woman half his age, hoping that she would be dessert. The other customers were loners, one a banker or a lawyer by the look of him, the other wearing twin Colts over dusty clothes.

A brother?

Number Two considered it, knowing three others had been summoned, then he let it go. His questions would be answered in another eighty-seven minutes, at the post office. Until then, nothing mattered but his grumbling stomach and his sweet anticipation of the job.

He hoped it would be something interesting, a challenge. More than one target, perhaps. Maybe a family. He'd never shot a woman or a child before, but had no qualms about it. Number Two was well aware that nits make lice.

What was it that the Holy Bible said?

Something about a father's sins passing down to the third and fourth generations of children, with punishment for all. It sounded fair enough to Number Two, who'd seen the sons of Dixie suffering his whole life long.

His meal arrived and was as good as he had hoped. He dug in, cleaned his plate, and washed it down with coffee afterward, but skipped the apple pie.

Too much of a good thing could slow him down, and Number Two reckoned that he would need all of his skill, speed, and agility before the job at hand was done.

Maybe tonight.

Number One — born Robert Adam Shelton in Acme, Mississippi, on the first day of the fight for Gettysburg — had reached Enid on Sunday afternoon, ahead of schedule. It was planned that way, allowing him to scout the town and try to spot the others riding in.

Which wasn't difficult.

It wasn't that a stranger could've glanced at them and known what they were up to, but they had a certain look about them that was common to all three. Cowboys rode into Enid looking dusty, dry, and horny. Peddlers came in looking eager, forcing smiles. Folk who were simply passing through might show some interest in the shops, but mostly they were weary, looking for someplace to spend a quiet night or two.

His fellow members of the Brotherhood looked *wary,* looking all around like outlaws on the dodge, trying to see if anyone had noticed them beyond a normal passing glance. If so, they'd be on guard and ready for the worst. In fact, there was no telling what they'd do.

And they would do exactly what he told them, when the time came. Why else were they here, if not to serve?

He tracked them from a distance, watched them settle in without making it obvious. Two of them chose the same hotel by accident, since there'd been no instruction on that bit, but Number One didn't consider it a problem. People came and went in Enid every day, some far more desperate in appearance than the men he'd waited for.

They'd drawn no serious attention to themselves, as yet.

And soon, it wouldn't matter, anyway.

The trick, as Number One was well aware, would not be pulling off the job so much as getting out of town once it was done. Orders forbade them moving on the target while he slept or carrying him off by stealth to fill a shallow grave. It was to be a public execution, carried out with flair, to demonstrate the Brotherhood's long memory and grim refusal to let old sins go unpunished.

At ten minutes to five o'clock, he stood outside the post office, a block from Enid's federal courthouse. Number One was casual, leaning against a hitching post, smoking a hand-rolled cigarette. The thumb of his left hand was hooked inside his gunbelt, with the little finger folded so that three fingers protruded, stiff and slightly splayed.

At a glance, those fingers might have formed the letter "M," perhaps an inverted "W," or . . .

He saw the others coming now. Two from the east, one from the west. None of them seemed to notice the others, but all had eyes for him — or, more specifically, the hand sign Number One displayed. When they were twenty feet or so away, all three of them mimicked the gesture with their own left hands, leaving their right hands free and dangling next to holstered pistols.

The password, next.

One of the pair on Shelton's left said, "Beg your pardon, friend. I'm looking for a Mr. Ayak, hereabouts. You ever heard of him?"

"Afraid not," Number One replied. "But

there's a Mr. Akia who runs a shop nearby."

"That's what I meant to say," the first man answered, offering his hand.

The handshake was a signal, in itself. Clutch with the thumb and little finger, while the other three pressed flat against the inside of the stranger's wrist, as if checking his pulse. Shelton repeated it twice more, confirming that the others were, indeed, the men he'd come to meet.

"I'm Number One," he said, when they were finished with the ritual, and nodded as the others introduced themselves around the small half circle. Number Three had been the first to speak, followed by Number Four, then Number Two.

No names were offered. Each man understood that if they managed to survive their mission, they would likely never meet again.

"You've seen the courthouse," Number One declared, not really asking. As the others nodded, he informed them, "That's the target, more or less."

"What's 'more or less' mean?" Number Three inquired.

"I mean we have to do the job *inside,*" said Number One.

"That should be interesting," said Number Four.

"I've got a place where we can talk about

it privately," said Number One, and he led them three blocks down Main Street to the Rosebud.

It was the larger of the two saloons in Enid, hence the place where faces were most rapidly forgotten. There were bedrooms available upstairs for hanky-panky and two card rooms in the back for private games. Shelton had rented one of those for Monday afternoon, and they were right on time. The barkeep nodded at him without studying the faces of his four companions and went back to serving booze.

They sat around a poker table with a whiskey bottle and four glasses on it. Shelton poured, first time around, and offered a toast.

"In the sacred, unfailing bond!"

"The Brotherhood!" his three companions said, as one, and drained their glasses.

As Number One refilled them, he declared, "We all know why we're here. The Dragon's found one of our enemies from bygone days. He's fat and sassy now, thinking no one can lay a hand on him. Our job's to prove him wrong."

"Be nice if we could get a look inside the place, before we start," said Number Three.

"It opens up at eight o'clock," said Number One. "Feel free to nose around. They

27

don't ask questions if you look like you've got business with the court."

"How many guards?" asked Number Two.

"Depends on what they're doing, who's on trial. At least one marshal in the courtroom, more if they're afraid of someone breaking out or making trouble. Most times, there'll be others in their office on the second floor, or just hanging around."

"How many *total?*" Number Three inquired.

"If no one's out collecting prisoners," said Number One, "there could be seven."

"Not so bad," said Number Two.

"The local law's a constable," said Number One. "He's got four deputies, two working days."

"No vigilance committee?" Number Two asked.

"Not as such. They have a system of alarms, in case the bank gets robbed. We should assume most of the shopkeepers are armed. Whether they'll fight or not is anybody's guess."

"The ones I've seen look soft," said Number Two.

"Still wouldn't hurt to have a nice distraction," Number Four observed.

"I've got one for you," Number One replied. "Tomorrow's a hanging day."

1

Jack Slade dreaded the grim routine of hanging days. Twice monthly, he did everything within his power to get out of town — pursuing fugitives, serving subpoenas, anything at all to miss the spectacle of strangers dangling by their necks.

It wasn't that he was opposed to hanging. On the contrary, Slade thought that certain people were too dangerous or too depraved to live. He had killed some of them himself, during performance of his duty as a U.S. marshal, and had few regrets.

He simply didn't like to watch the others swing.

If asked to pin it down, to explain his personal dislike of hangings, Slade might have discussed the ritual aspects, the circus atmosphere surrounding public executions, or the chaplain's smug superiority as he harangued the men about to die.

But none of that really explained it.

What Slade hated most of all about a hanging was the sound and smell of it. The brittle noise of snapping necks. The stench of bowels and bladders letting go.

But here he was, this Tuesday, standing by to watch another one. Four men were set to go at noon: one rapist, two armed robbers who had shot a constable in Lawton, and a man who'd killed his neighbor with an ax in a dispute over some geese.

Guilty as hell, the lot of them, but Slade still didn't want to watch them die.

As if he had a choice.

All marshals found in Enid on a hanging day were obligated to attend. No special orders were invoked, but there was always crowd control to think of, and the outside chance that someone might try springing one of the condemned.

It hadn't happened yet, but anything was possible.

With that in mind, Slade wore his Peacemaker and brought a shotgun with him to the courtyard where the scaffold stood and spectators were ranged behind a line of wooden sawhorses arranged to keep some distance between gawkers and the gallows.

As usual, there were some thirty-odd observers in attendance. Slade was pleased to see no children in the crowd, which happened sometimes with a weekend execution or when school was out for summer. Even now, he wondered why the women came to watch, and why some of them seemed almost excited by the prospect of a dangling corpse.

Or four.

Slade's watch told him the prisoners would be emerging from the courthouse cell block in about five minutes, time enough to get them on the platform, noosed, and ready for the drop at noon. Before they fell, Judge Isaac Dennison would have assumed his post on the small balcony outside his second-story office window, and he'd personally give the signal for the hangman to proceed.

The judge regarded it as his responsibility, had told Slade once that after sentencing a man to die, it was his obligation to attend and supervise the execution to the bitter end.

Of course, he hadn't called it *bitter.* Slade had worked that out from the expression on the judge's face, the grim tone of his voice. The deathwatch might be duty, but he didn't have to love it.

Nor did Slade.

He was positioned near the exit from the cell block when the heavy door swung open

31

and the first marshal emerged. Judd Landry, nodding as he passed Slade, followed by the four condemned inmates with clanking chains connecting them like road-gang prisoners. Another marshal, Alan Stark, brought up the rear and paused to close the door behind him, then trailed Landry and the striped suits toward the scaffold steps.

Slade glanced up toward the judge's balcony, in time to see the windows open, Isaac Dennison emerging in his funeral suit, his face deadpan.

Slade turned away from the scaffold to study the crowd.

Sam Bowers lit his cigarette with a match from the box Number One had given him last night, returned the matchbox to his pocket, and drew sweet smoke deep into his lungs. It began to calm his nerves almost at once.

Not that he needed any artificial help to carry out a killing, even when the risks were high. Not likely, when he'd taken on four men at once and walked away from it, the only one still breathing.

It was true, of course, that only two of them were armed — with knives, at that — and he'd been carrying two pistols, but that was beside the point. He was a stone-cold killer, damn it, with the emphasis on *cold*.

Two minutes, by his watch, until the bastards who'd been dumb enough to get arrested said their final words and dropped into eternity. He finished off his smoke in three long drags, getting a nice rush from the nicotine, then pitched the butt onto Main Street and walked back into the courthouse.

It was warm for May, but no one seemed to give his long duster a second glance. He kept his right hand in the pocket, reaching through where he had slit the lining for a firm grip on the Henry rifle pressed against his side. He had a live round in the chamber, with the hammer down, so all he had to do was cock the rifle with his thumb and blaze away.

But not just yet.

A broad staircase took Number Four up to the second floor, where he was told the target had his private quarters. That would be the easy way, bust in and kill him at his desk while he was signing papers, maybe drinking whiskey on the sly. But no. The Dragon wanted something showy, so they had to have an audience.

The courtroom would've been all right. He and his brethren could've walked in with the other spectators, then blazed away when it felt right. They would've had to face two marshals, that way, rather than the five he counted wandering around the place so far.

Still, five on four was nothing, when he thought about it. Most particularly when his people had the sweet advantage of surprise.

And afterward?

With any kind of luck, they'd all get out alive, but Number Four knew better than to count on it. A thousand different things could still go wrong, from misfires to a problem with the horses they'd left tied outside the lawyer's office next door to the courthouse.

Part of the escape plan hinged on their ability to spook the crowd that turned out for the hanging and to terrorize whoever might have business in the courthouse. Once the sheep stampeded, running with them ought to be the easy part.

Not getting shot would take a bit more skill.

Bowers picked out the door that he'd been looking for, lips moving as he read the name imprinted on a brass plate, mounted right around chest-high. He turned the knob with his left hand and crossed the threshold, smiling as a young man with a mop of curly hair rose from a smallish desk to greet him.

"May I help you, sir?" the secretary asked.

"I got a message for the judge."

"Sir, I'm afraid he's not receiving at the moment. If you'd care to wait —"

"I wouldn't," Number Four replied and whipped his rifle's barrel hard across the stranger's face, putting him down.

No shots before the main event, his churning brain reminded him.

He reached another door and opened it, raising the Henry as he crossed a well-appointed office. Number Four thumbed back the rifle's hammer, aiming at the broad back of a figure on the balcony.

Slade heard the first shot echo through the courtyard, coming from somewhere behind him. And *above?* He spun in that direction while the ladies in the crowd were gasping and the hangman waited for a signal, standing with his gloved hand on a lever that would spring the traps.

Slade was in time to see Judge Dennison pitch forward, back arched as if someone had kicked him from behind. His belly met the railing, and it might've stopped him going over if a second shot had not exploded from his office, ripping through the judge's back.

Slade saw the bullet exit — more precisely,

saw the plume of blood that trailed behind it from the exit wound, high on the left side of the judge's chest — then Dennison was toppling over, strong arms flapping like a rag doll's as he fell.

Just then, a shotgun blast thundered across the courtyard, and a storm of buck-shot pellets struck Judge Dennison, the railing, and the wall behind him. Slade spun to his left, raising his own twelve-gauge, and saw a shooter crouching on a roof directly opposite, pumping the lever action on what had to be a Winchester repeater, getting ready for another shot.

Cursing the impulse that had made him pick a scattergun over a rifle, Slade squeezed both triggers without really aiming, trusting the noise to distract the sniper, even if his pellets didn't reach the target. He was clawing for his Colt, eyes on the shooter, when he saw a puff of crimson and the figure fell back, out of sight.

Judge Dennison lay crumpled on the ground, already staining it with blood, but Slade knew there was nothing he could do to help the wounded man. If Dennison was dead, the effort would be wasted. If he wasn't, Slade's priority must be preventing any more shots from impacting his prostrate form.

Slade swept the crowd, seeking ground-level shooters, found none, and ran back to the courthouse. Inside, there was chaos. The echo of gunfire had set people running for exits, either to escape or get in on the action outside. Slade moved toward the stairs, dodging some who ran into his path, shoving others aside.

Upstairs, another rifle shot reverberated from the lobby's arched ceiling. A man cursed and a woman screamed. Some of the people who'd been running up the stairs turned back and scrambled down again.

Slade holstered his Peacemaker, fed his last two shotgun shells into the double-barreled twelve-gauge, and began to climb the stairs.

Number Four was fuming as he left the judge's office. Two shots from a range of fifteen feet or so, and still he wasn't certain of a kill. His second shot had punched his man over the railing, but a second-story drop was only fatal if you landed on your head — and even then, it might not kill.

Speaking of which, Bowers had nearly died himself, when Number Three cut loose across the courtyard with his shotgun. One lead pellet from that blast had nicked his hat brim, and he'd felt another whisper past his cheek. If either one had struck him in the face, he would be lying in the judge's chambers now, brains leaking from his ears.

Angry and frustrated, he'd shot the judge's secretary for the hell of it, before he left the office. One less Yankee bastard to study law and use it to deprive real men of things they'd cherished all their lives.

No bullet fired into a blue-belly or scalawag was wasted.

As he cleared the judge's outer office, Number Four saw half a dozen people running past him, toward the stairs. He snarled at them, brandished his Henry, but he didn't fire on them. He had eleven shots remaining in the rifle and would use them as required on anyone who tried to stop him on his way out to the street.

As if in answer to his thoughts, a lawman suddenly appeared before him, leveling a six-gun from the hip. He wore a white shirt with a shiny star pinned on it, and instead of simply shooting Bowers, as he should have, the lawman shouted for him to halt and drop his rifle.

Number Four triggered a reflex shot that nearly missed the lawman, barely grazing his left arm. The lawman fired his pistol in a rush and missed completely. Bowers pumped the Henry's lever action, fired again with an adjustment to his left, and got it right that time.

The bullet struck the lawman just above his belt buckle. The wounded man cried out, staggered, was falling when he fired another shot. That slug missed Number Four's throat by an inch or so and snapped his collarbone on the left side.

Bowers bellowed in pain, feeling a rush of nausea accompanied by spots swarming before his eyes. It cost him to control the Henry's swaying muzzle with his left hand, while he worked the lever action with his right. Only the lawman's greater pain prevented him from killing Number Four as the gunman advanced upon him, cursing with each awkward, shuffling step.

Afraid of missing, Bowers leaned into the shot and pressed the Henry's muzzle flush against his target's forehead. "Save a place for me in Hell," he snarled and squeezed the trigger, spraying blood and brains across the polished hardwood floor.

Each step was torture now, as he lurched toward the stairs. Someone ran past and jostled him, forcing a scream between clenched teeth. A Herculean effort kept the gunman on his feet, but how much farther he could walk was anybody's guess.

The street and tethered horses felt as if

they were a hundred miles away.

He reached the staircase, teetered on the top step for a moment, pondering a way to use the handrail while still carrying his rifle. Finally, he gave it up and leaned against the rail instead of holding it, took one step down and then another, whimpering with each new jolt.

He'd covered one-third of the stairway when another lawman faced him, standing at the bottom with a scattergun and calling up to him, "Stop where you are and drop your guns!"

"Like hell," the wounded rifleman replied, forcing a twisted grimace-smile.

Slade held the shotgun's double barrels steady on the stranger's chest and told him, "I'd rather not kill you."

That was true enough. Slade needed certain questions answered, and a dead man couldn't talk.

"No problem," said the shooter, giggling. "How 'bout *I* kill *you?*"

The rifle's muzzle wobbled toward Slade, seeming to take forever as he lowered the shotgun and squeezed its left trigger, blasting the wounded man's legs into tatters. The rifleman shrieked, dropped his piece, and collapsed on the stairs in a welter of blood.

Slade rushed him, scooped a pistol from its holster on the man's right hip, and tucked it down inside his own belt at the back. The rifleman was gasping like a stranded fish as Slade leaned over him, pressing the scattergun against his heaving chest, and asked, "Why did you shoot the judge?"

Despite his agony, the gunman smiled with bloody yellow teeth and said, "Wouldn't you like to kn—"

The right side of his face disintegrated as he spoke, and Slade recoiled from the bloody explosion, ears ringing from a gunshot behind him and below. He rolled in that direction, saw another shooter twenty feet away, across the courthouse lobby, pumping a live round into his Winchester's chamber.

Slade fired the shotgun's second barrel without aiming, as he rolled aside and drew his Colt. The rifleman was running by then, with no trace of a wound to retard his progress. Slade glanced back for a heartbeat at the dead man on the stairs, beyond all questions now, then rose and raced off in pursuit of his killer.

Slade didn't know if the backup gunman had meant to kill *him* or had aimed for his wounded comrade to ensure his silence, but the presence of a third shooter told Slade that the attack had been well organized and planned out in advance. It hadn't played out as a jailbreak, since there'd been no bid to liberate the convicts on the gallows, so he knew the shooters meant to kill Judge Dennison.

Had they succeeded?

Were there more shooters around the courthouse, even now?

Slade didn't know and *wouldn't* know until he'd finished running down the rifleman who'd missed him by a hair, mere seconds earlier. If he could take that one alive, answers might be forthcoming. If he had to kill the gunman . . .

There was still the shotgunner he'd seen and fired on from the courtyard, if someone had spotted him and managed to prevent him from escaping. If Slade's shotgun blast had missed the sniper's vital organs. If the shooter hadn't scrambled to the street immediately and escaped.

Too many *ifs*.

He concentrated on the runner, weaving in and out among the frightened bystanders who milled about the courthouse lobby. Slade was forty feet behind him when a gunman slammed his rifle's stock into an old man's face and leaped across his victim's falling body, through an exit to the street.

Damn it!

Slade sprinted in pursuit, shouting at everyone in front of him to clear the way. He reached the doorway, started through it, and a rifle bullet struck the doorjamb, spraying jagged shards of wood into his face.

They missed his eyes, and Slade, cursing, lunged through the doorway, sprawling belly down onto the dusty wooden sidewalk.

Duke Wallace knew he'd missed the lawman with his last shot, but he didn't give a damn, as long as the near miss slowed his pursuer and gave him a chance to reach the horses tied next door.

Escape was all that mattered to him now.

He didn't know if Number Three and Number Four had nailed the judge as planned, but Number Four was dead for sure and couldn't be compelled to answer any questions from the law. Wallace had done his duty on that score, and could defend himself if a tribunal was convened to question his behavior.

First, of course, he'd actually have to get away.

He reached the street, saw Number One already there beside the horses, one foot in the stirrup of his saddle as he braced to mount his roan gelding. Duke's buckskin and the others' horses waited for their riders to appear, shying a little at the sounds of gunfire, but not panicking yet.

Someone was shouting after Number One and running toward the horses, from across the street. Another lawman, damn it, waving a long-barreled pistol as he ran, big belly wobbling over the front of his trousers.

Kid Lightning saw Number One turn, draw his own piece, and both men fired together. One of the horses, a grullo, reared up as the constable's bullet tore into its buttock, lunging away from the pain and pinning Number One between its weight and his roan. Number One's shot went wild, smashing a window on the far side of Main Street.

Number Two glanced back along the sidewalk, couldn't see the marshal who'd chased him out of the courthouse, and returned his full attention to the lawman who was bracing Number One. He sighted down his rifle's barrel, squeezed the trigger, and felt something close to exultation as his bullet slammed into the lawman's chest.

By that time, Number One was in his saddle, wheeling toward the open street. His slumped posture suggested injury, but Number Two had no time left to think of anybody else.

If he was going to get out of Enid in one piece, the time to go was *now.*

He started for the horses, made three strides, then crumpled as an agonizing hammer stroke slammed his left leg, behind the knee. Gasping, he lost the Winchester '73 as he fell, vaguely aware that it had spun beyond his reach, over the lip of the sidewalk.

Cursing with fluency that would've shamed his sainted mother and the pastor of his childhood church, Duke Wallace dragged himself across the sidewalk planking with his left hand, pushing with his good leg, while his right hand drew the Schofield pistol from its holster. In his fevered mind, two words repeated endlessly, suppressing any conscious thought.

No quarter!

He would not surrender, would not ask for mercy, and would grant none to his enemies. Whoever wanted him would have to *take* him, and if he was still alive when he ran out of bullets, Number Three would use his Arkansas toothpick to gut the enemies who came within arm's reach.

He rolled into a doorway, saw a horrified shopkeeper staring down at him through glass, and drove the man back with a gesture from his six-gun.

Come and get me! thought Kid Lightning, and the words spilled over through his clenched teeth.

"Come and get me, Marshal!"

Slade crept forward, inching toward the doorway where his quarry lay concealed. A crimson trail led to the alcove, confirming Slade's take on the source of his voice and his glimpse of the staggering body in motion.

He had the man pinned down, but waiting was a problem. On one hand, the shooter might be strong enough to force his way inside the shop whose doorway sheltered him. Or, failing that, he might stay where he was and keep Slade at a distance while he bled to death.

And that would never do.

Slade needed *someone* to question about the attack on Judge Dennison, if only to satisfy himself that all the plotters had been laid to rest. Now, out of four gunmen that he had seen, Slade knew that one was dead and one had ridden out of town, hunched over as if gut-shot. That left two, both wounded by his gunshots, one of whom was presently beyond his reach.

Which made the shooter in the alcove

even more important.

"Come and get me, Marshal!" he called out, again.

You asked for it, Slade thought and started creeping to his right, as quietly as possible across the wooden sidewalk's planks. He reached the edge, rolled over it, and lay prone in the dust of Main Street.

Now, the hard part.

Pushing with his knees and elbows, Slade began to crawl along the street, trying to stay below the gunman's line of sight as he drew level with the doorway where his prey had gone to ground. He did his best to minimize the scraping sounds his boots and body made as he proceeded, hoping that excited voices from the street around him would distract the man he needed to surprise.

Slade knew that he was in position when he'd halved the distance from his starting point to the three horses tethered outside Amos Walling's law office. There was a small shop in between that building and the courthouse, where the gunman hid, but for the life of him Slade couldn't think of what it sold or who the owner was.

Focus!

Because he'd crawled in from the shooter's right, Slade would present a left-hand profile when he rose to face his adversary. That meant he would have to turn ninety degrees to use his pistol, giving his opponent two or three seconds to aim and fire while he was rising.

Would it be enough to finish him?

No other option, Slade decided, and was braced to make his move, when suddenly a shot rang out nearby, accompanied by crashing glass.

Slade jerked upright and found his quarry half turned in the doorway, on one knee, angling his six-gun through the shattered glass door of the niche where he had hidden, squeezing off a round into the shop beyond. Before Slade could fire, maybe wing the shooter and disarm him, a muzzle flash inside the shop marked the finishing shot of the skirmish.

Slade's quarry toppled over backward, pistol spilling from his hand, and sprawled across the sidewalk, twitching. Another heartbeat put Slade at his side, noting the steady pulse of blood that issued from the shooter's ventilated chest. The man was clearly dying, eyes already slipping out of focus, but his right hand still went groping for the big knife on his hip. Slade clutched his wrist and stopped the move, with no effort at all.

"I had to do it, Marshal," someone told Slade, from behind the shattered door. "He could've come in any second. Hell, it wasn't even locked."

Now that Slade saw him, he recalled the shopkeeper, had seen him countless times and must have spoken to him, but couldn't pull his name out of the air. It didn't matter, as he turned back to the nearly dead man sprawled before him.

Bending close, still mindful of the knife, Slade asked him, "Can you hear me?"

No response.

"Who are you?" he inquired. "Who sent you here?"

Nothing.

"I need to know —"

The gunman shuddered once, from head to toe, and blew a crimson bubble from his open lips. Just that, and he was gone.

"Damn!"

Now, he had only one hope left.

And that was dashed when Slade got to the courthouse, just in time to see Judd Landry and a man he didn't recognize depositing a body on the sidewalk, near the courthouse steps. They'd obviously brought it from the building due east of the courtyard where the gallows stood, and one look at the corpse told Slade it was the rooftop sniper he had blasted with his shotgun, while Judge Dennison was tumbling from the balcony.

Three dead, and one long gone.

"You hit him, Jack," said Landry, "but he wasn't done fighting. I had to finish him."

Slade saw the bloody shirt, tattered where his buckshot had torn through fabric, into flesh, but his was clearly not the fatal wound. A black hole in the dead man's cheek, an inch below his left eye, seemed to stare at Slade.

"You finished him all right," Slade granted. "He say anything at all?"

"He cussed me pretty good. Nothing apart from that."

"Okay."

"Were you expecting something?"

"Hoping," Slade corrected him.

"For a confession?"

"Something. Anything."

"No luck with this one, then."

"One of them got away," Slade said.

"Well, damn it! I was hoping that we'd got 'em all."

"Not quite."

"You get a look at him?" asked Landry.

"Only from behind, as he was riding off. I missed my chance to drop him."

"Hey, it happens," Landry sympathized.

Slade had dreaded bringing up the subject, but he had to ask now. "What about the judge? I saw him hit, and —"

"He was breathing, last I heard," Landry replied. "The bailiffs ran him over to Doc Hauser's office."

"How'd he look?" Slade asked.

"Not good."

Slade was already moving as he said, "I need to see him. Find out if he knows what this was all about."

Landry's voice followed him across the street.

"Don't get your hopes up, Jack."

2

Dr. Gustave Hauser's office was across the street from the courthouse and one block west. Slade found a crowd gathered outside, spilling over the sidewalk to the street, and pushed his way through to the door, where one of the town's constables stood blocking the way.

Slade recognized him as Tom Embry, read the mingled fear and anger on his face, and stepped around him. Embry caught him by the sleeve and told him, "Marshal Slade, he looks real bad."

Slade nodded, disengaged himself, and went inside. He followed muffled voices and the clink of instruments along a short hallway, into Doc Hauser's back-room operating theater.

The sight before his eyes froze Slade on the threshold.

Judge Dennison lay on his back, stripped naked and covered with blood. Doc Hauser and his nurse, Hattie Dufresne, were doing something to their patient's left leg, likely struggling to stanch the flow of blood from buckshot wounds.

Slade circled wide around the operating table, feeling bitterly ashamed to see Judge Dennison like this, yet unable to look away. It struck him that he had seen better-looking corpses.

Hauser noticed Slade and told him, "I could say it looks worse than it is, but I'd be lying."

"Will he make it?" Slade inquired.

"Can't say, yet. One slug drilled him through and through. He's got another in his back, but I can't work on that until I stop the bleeding from his legs. What happened out there, Marshal?"

"Two men caught him in a cross fire," Slade replied. "A rifle and a shotgun."

"What, a jailbreak?"

"Doesn't look that way."

"Jesus!" Hauser glanced at his nurse and said, "Pardon my French."

"I've heard worse," Hattie answered, concentrating on her work.

Slade asked, "How long until you know if he's . . . if he'll . . ."

"At least an hour, likely more," Hauser replied. "If you're inclined to wait, there's something that might interest you."

"What's that?" Slade's mouth was desert dry.

"A note. It fell out of his jacket while we were undressing him." The doctor vaguely waved a bloody hand in the direction of a corner where the judge's ruined clothes lay in a rumpled pile.

Slade saw the note lying on top, stooped down, and picked it up. Blood spatters on the paper were already drying to a rusty brown, but he could read it all the same.

Beware! The silent Brotherhood remembers! All your sins shall be revealed and punished! There is no escape! Make peace with God, thou infidel! Flee if you will, but there is no escape! *Sic semper tyrannis!* Traitors die, and so shall you! * * *

"Sic semper tyrannis?" Slade read it aloud.

"In Latin, 'Thus always to traitors,' " the doctor translated. "You've heard it before, I suspect."

"Sounds familiar," Slade granted. "But —"

"Booth spoke those words, after murdering President Lincoln."

"Oh, right. And the link to Judge Dennison is . . . ?"

"He could probably tell you," Doc Hauser replied, while he stitched one of Dennison's wounds. "As to whether you'll ever be able to ask him, I promise nothing."

"You want to be a little optimistic, Doc?"

"Optimism, is it? Well, I've seen worse, Marshal."

"Did they make it?"

"Not as I recall."

Slade nodded, muttered something about having work to do, and let himself out past Tom Embry and the milling crowd of townspeople. A couple of them shouted questions at him, but he kept walking as if he hadn't heard.

The note he carried folded in his hand was still damp with the judge's blood. It made Slade's fingers feel unclean, but he clung to it, almost crushing it. Questions crowded his mind.

How long ago had Dennison received the threat?

Why was he carrying it on his person?

Had he shared the note's contents with anyone else?

What in hell did it *mean?*

The reference to "sins" being revealed and punished indicated something from the judge's past. And that, in turn, reminded

Slade of how little he knew about his employer's background. They'd never discussed any personal subject at length, but he'd have to start looking at Dennison's history, now, if he hoped to catch the gunman who'd escaped and anyone who stood behind him.

How else could he find them and prevent yet another attempt on Judge Dennison's life?

May not be necessary, said a small voice in his mind. *He hasn't pulled through this one, yet.*

Cursing under his breath, Slade jogged back to the courthouse to begin his search.

Number One wasn't gut-shot, as Slade had surmised, but he reckoned his damned ribs were busted. Not cutting-your-lung-open busted, but still bad enough that it hurt every time he drew breath or shifted in his saddle.

If it hadn't hurt too much to laugh, he might've found it funny. In the midst of all that killing, bullets flying everywhere and a lawman coming straight at him, it had been a damned horse — and a comrade's horse, no less — that wounded him. What were the odds?

Pretty damn good, from where I sit, he

thought and grimaced, cursing, as his gelding lurched a bit beneath him.

Galloping away from Enid had been hell, between the sharp pain in his side and fear that he'd be shot out of his saddle any second. He'd been braced to take the bullet, but it never came, and when he stopped to check his back trail — turning in the saddle hurt too much, forget about it — it appeared no one had followed him.

Not yet, at least.

He'd ridden westward out of town for two reasons. First, going eastward would have meant passing the courthouse and the lawmen who were scouring its grounds for targets. Second, heading in the opposite direction from his final destination would, with luck, confuse any pursuers.

He was simply looking out for Number One.

Or plain old Bobby Shelton, as he was now and would be until the next time he was sent to run an errand for the Dragon.

If there was a next time.

Turning homeward, finally, he wondered whether they had been successful. He'd been stationed in the crowd below the gallows, saw that Number Two and Number Four had both scored hits, but then the judge had fallen from his balcony, a lawman near the gallows started firing back at Number Two, and there was no way Shelton could perform his duty as the third man in a triple cross fire. Hoping that the judge was dead or dying, he had run, self-preservation kicking in, and left the others to their fate.

It's not my fault, he thought. But would the Dragon buy it?

There'd been no plan or intention for the four of them to leave as one. They weren't a holdup gang and had no hideout where they could relax and divvy up their loot. It was a case of each man for himself after the job was done, and Devil take the hindmost. Even if the law caught some of them and made the captives talk, they couldn't point a finger at the Dragon, didn't even know one another's names.

As for the Brotherhood . . . why, it didn't exist.

There'd be no repercussions over losing track of his companions, but it would be quite a different story if the judge survived his wounds. In that case, with the raid a failure, retribution might be coming Shelton's way.

In fact, he could count on it.

If there was one thing the Dragon valued over all else, it was discipline.

Speaking of which, Shelton was wondering if he had discipline enough to ride around the clock, or if his roan could carry him that long without a break somewhere along the way. He'd camped out overnight, riding to Enid, but he didn't relish sleeping on the ground or lighting a campfire that might draw U.S. marshals in like moths to flame. That said, the trip back home was going to be longer, thanks to his diversionary tactics and the pain that made him hold his mount's pace to a walk.

See how it goes, he told himself.

He had at least four hours yet, before nightfall. Call it fifteen miles closer to home by the time it was too dark for Shelton to see. There'd be no moon to speak of tonight, so he might have to stop, after all.

But no fire.

And if the hunters came sniffing, he'd let the night cover him, hope for the best. If they found him, he'd fight to the death and try to take some of them with him.

He thought about the others, wondered whether they were still alive and if they'd managed to get out of town. He knew that Number Two had saved his own ass, coming out of nowhere when the constable was drawing down on Shelton and the jostling horses spoiled his aim. Then there'd been more gunfire and Shelton hadn't seen what happened next.

He'd been too busy making tracks.

He wished the others well, then put them out of mind. There was no more that he could do for them, alive or dead or sitting in a prison cell. Each one of them had done his part for Destiny.

Tomorrow, if it came, would take care of itself.

The undertaker had a full house by the time Slade got to his establishment. There were six dead, in all: three gunmen, two deputy constables, and Judge Dennison's clerk. Slade hadn't known the city lawmen well, except to nod in passing on the street, but Jason Bean, the clerk, had been a likeable young man with wedding plans.

His June bride would be weeping now and trying to make sense of what had happened.

Slade was doing that himself, minus the tears.

The undertaker, Angus Crick, showed Slade his standard solemn face and said, "A sad day, Marshal. Any further word about the judge?"

Slade felt like snapping at him, telling Crick that Dennison was still beyond his reach, but it seemed churlish and he settled for, "Still hanging in there."

"Praise the Lord!"

"It couldn't hurt," Slade said. "I need to see if any of the shooters carried something to identify him."

"Certainly," Crick answered, nodding. "If you'll follow me? We've just begun the preparations. Still disrobing, if you will."

"Whatever's in their pockets ought to get me started," Slade replied.

He had already checked the horses the three dead men had left behind, pawed through their saddlebags, and found nothing but trail food, extra ammunition, bits of cooking gear, and clothing. None had carried any documents or letters.

Hell, Slade didn't even know if they could read.

The undertaker's workshop was the next thing to a slaughterhouse. Crick had one operating table, or whatever it was called when corpses were the patients, and his surplus clients were lined up shoulder to shoulder on the canvas-covered floor. He'd taken Jason Bean first, leaving the lawmen and their former adversaries resting side by side.

Crick's two assistants, pale types like their boss, were starting on the younger constable, unbuttoning his shirt and trousers, when Slade walked in. They glanced up at him briefly, then went back to work.

"I'll check these three," Slade said, and crouched beside the nearest gunman, careful not to kneel in blood.

It was the man who'd fired a shotgun at Judge Dennison as he was falling from the balcony, his shirt soaked through with crimson drying to the shade of rust on old scrap metal. He was naturally unresisting, and the body hadn't stiffened yet, less than an hour after death.

Slade checked his pockets, a distasteful chore that offered no rewards. The man had died with seven dollars on him, plus a jackknife, a tobacco pouch and rolling papers, and a pocket watch that bore no personal inscription.

Slade moved on. The next corpse in the lineup was his adversary from the courthouse stairway, face-shot by his own ally, who lay beside him now in death. The second shooter's pockets yielded several dollars' worth of change, a pencil stub, a well-used handkerchief, and a white matchbox that bore a red inscription reading SOUTHERN STAR.

On a whim, Slade put the matchbox in his own shirt pocket and was shifting toward the third corpse when he noticed something odd. The face-shot gunman had his sleeves rolled up above his elbows, and the inside of his right forearm was marked by . . . what?

Not scars. Not warts or moles.

Blue-ink tattoos.

Three symbols in a row, rising midway between the wrist and elbow. Little stars . . . or were they asterisks?

Slade studied them a moment longer, then turned back to the first shooter's corpse. It was a long shot, maybe far-fetched, but if he was right . . .

Slade fumbled with the buttons of the right-hand cuff, got them at last, and pushed the sleeve up elbow-high. Nothing. He was about to shrug it off, then took it just a smidge farther and tried the left arm.

There they were.

Slade would have bet his next month's pay that different tattoo artists had inscribed the marks on each man's arm — the ink seemed slightly different, the placement obviously so — but it was difficult to tamper with a simple asterisk. You couldn't make it smile, sprout wings, or tell a story.

Moving to the shooter who had died outside the shop on Main Street, Slade went for his arms first and was not surprised to find three asterisks tattooed across the inside of the man's right wrist. By that time, Slade had palmed the note Judge Dennison was carrying when he was shot and matched its cryptic signature against the three tattoos.

Which helped him not at all.

The third stiff's pockets gave up no more in the way of clues to personal identity than had his two companions. A little spending money, more tobacco, and a corncob pipe were all the man had carried, in addition to his weapons.

Nothing of value, but the note and the tattoos would get him started, if and when Judge Dennison was capable of speech.

Slade left Crick and his two apprentices to tend the dead and started back toward Dr. Hauser's surgery.

"I've done all I can do," said Hauser, when he met Slade in his waiting room. "It may be all that *anyone* can do."

"You got the slugs out?"

"Finally," the doctor said. "And cleaned the wounds as best I could. Hell of a job, when someone's hit that many times."

"How many?" Slade inquired.

"Two rifle shots and seven buckshot pellets. Every one through fabric, so you've got *that* in the wound, along with lead and anything he rolled around in, falling like he did."

"What are his chances, then?"

"Son, I'm a doctor, not a fortune-teller. He lost blood, and plenty of it. He's in shock, and now we have to think about infection. I've got no drugs to fight that, if it happens. Hell, they don't exist."

"Well, do you *think* he'll make it?" Slade demanded.

"I've been known to place a bet," Doc Hauser said. "On this one, I'd say even money is the best you're going to get. Don't be surprised if we lose him."

"Doc, no offense, but is there anybody else who'd have a better chance of saving him?"

"I'd give him three-to-two odds if we had him in the fancy hospital they've got in Oklahoma City. But that's two days bouncing in a wagon, with the flies and God knows what else, by which time *they* likely couldn't help him, either. Son, I'm what you've got."

"Like I said, Doc, no offense intended."

"None taken. You want the best for him, like everybody else."

Not everyone, Slade thought.

"One other thing. I've got a clue that might identify the man who got away,"

65

Slade said, stretching the truth a bit.

"Then I'd go after him," Doc Hauser said.

"Thing is, I won't know if the clues mean anything until I've shown them to Judge Dennison."

That put a frown on Hauser's face. "You want to talk to him."

"I do."

"Right now?"

"As soon as possible. If he . . . goes . . . and I haven't had a chance to ask him, at least one man who's responsible for this will ride off clean."

"At least one? You think there were more involved than those — what was it? Four or five?"

Slade nodded. "I suspect someone planned this and sent them here. It's tied in with this thing I need to ask the judge about."

"Marshal, the man's as close to death right now as he will ever be, short of the grave itself. You start to question him — assuming he can even *hear* you, much less answer — it could push him on across."

Slade took the folded, bloodstained paper from his pocket, opened it, and passed it to the doctor. "This is what I need to ask about," he said.

Doc Hauser read the note, face blanching. At the end of it, he muttered, "Jesus Christ!"

"There's more," Slade said. "All three of them laid out at Crick's are wearing tattoos of the same three stars."

"What's it supposed to mean?" Doc Hauser asked.

"That's what I hope the judge can tell me," Slade replied.

" 'Your sins shall be revealed and punished,' " Hauser read aloud, before he handed back the note. "I hope this isn't one of mine. Go in and see him, if you need to, but remember that he hasn't got much left. A seizure now, or any little thing at all, and he's a goner."

"Thanks, Doc."

"Don't thank me," Hauser said. "I plan to wash my hands like Pilate, then I just might have a drink or three."

Slade passed into the operating room, where Dennison now occupied a narrow bed on wheels, against one wall. He didn't know how Hauser and his nurse had shifted Dennison off the operating table, and Slade didn't let it steal his train of thought.

He stood, then knelt beside the judge's bed, saw eyelids flicker when he spoke Dennison's name. After a long moment, the eyes came into focus, more or less. The sound that issued from the judge's lips was indecipherable — maybe simple respiration, possibly a hiss or sigh.

"Judge," Slade began, "three of the men who did this thing are dead. One got away. I need your help to run him down and find out who's behind it."

Dennison blinked at him. Were his eyebrows moving, too, or was that Slade's imagination? Either way, he forged ahead, taking his shot.

He raised the note and held it close enough for Dennison to read, if he was capable of focusing his eyes and mind on anything right now.

"I need to know who sent this to you," Slade explained. "The men we bagged had little stars like this" — his finger tapped the lower right-hand corner of the note — "tattooed inside their arms."

No doubt about it, then. The judge's eyes and nostrils flared at Slade. He tried to speak, but only made a raspy, breathless sound of stuttering that reached Slade's ears as "kuh-kuh-kuh."

Slade leaned in closer, was about to ask again, when Dennison's eyelids descended, breaking the contact between them. Waiting long enough to verify that Dennison was still breathing, Slade rose and left the operating room.

Doc Hauser met him near the door, a glass of amber fluid in his hand.

"The way you look," he said, "I'm betting Isaac couldn't help you."

"That's a bet you'd win."

"Too bad," said Hauser. "I'd have liked to see the other bastards swing."

Slade sat with Marshals Landry, Stark, and Williams in the office they all shared, one floor below Judge Dennison's chambers. Two other marshals, Toby Dean and Clint Van Cleef, were standing guard over the judge at Dr. Hauser's surgery.

Slade had begun their meeting with the blood-flecked note, watching it pass from hand to hand as each man read it, scowling, sometimes cursing softly.

"And the three dead shooters all have tattoos of these same three stars?" asked Stark.

"Stars, maybe asterisks," said Slade.

"What's that?" asked Landry.

Williams told him, "It's a symbol used in writing, usually for a footnote. Sometimes when you're leaving out some letters."

"Why would anyone do that?" Landry inquired.

"They may not like to write a curse word, for example," Williams said. "Instead of writing *shit,* they'd write the *s* and *t,* with asterisks in place of *h* and *i,* to clean it up. It's also used to hide a name. Like if you've got a witness you're trying to protect, you might use asterisks, in place of his last name, in your reports."

"How come I never heard of this?" asked Landry.

"Guess I spent more time in school," Williams replied.

"Or stayed awake in class," said Stark, smiling.

"And then, there's sacred names," said Williams.

"What's that?" Slade asked him.

"Some folks believe it's blasphemous to write God's name on paper, so they use an asterisk instead of *o,* or maybe just three asterisks in place of letters."

"So the stars or asterisks on this note could stand for a name," Slade said.

"It's possible," Williams agreed. "A short name. Maybe just initials. Anyway, whoever wrote it must've thought the judge could work it out."

"But did he?" Landry asked. "I mean, if he knew someone planned to kill him, he'd have told us, right? He'd send one of us out to grab the prick and haul him in, instead of waiting to get shot."

"It's not a crime to send a letter," Slade observed. "Even a threat against the president's just words on paper. You'd have thought they'd change that, after Lincoln, but it's still not grounds for trial."

"He could've warned us, anyway," said Landry. "So we could've kept an eye out for the shooters in advance."

"He could have," Stark said, "if he took it seriously."

"If he didn't take it seriously, why'd he keep the note and carry it around with him?" Slade asked.

And got no answers.

Finally, Landry suggested, "Then it must be something personal, you know? Something *private* he didn't feel like sharing with us."

"Even at the risk of getting killed?" asked Williams.

"Maybe," Landry said. "Hell, I can't read his mind."

"Well, then, there's this," Slade said, and tossed the SOUTHERN STAR matchbox out to the center of the table. "One of them had this, for what it's worth. I don't know what it means, but it's the only name I found on any of them. If it *is* a name."

"It is," said Stark.

"You recognize it?" Slade asked, sharply.

"Not the matchbox, but the Southern Star is a saloon in Last Resort. I had a couple drinks in there, about six months ago."

"What's Last Resort?" Slade asked. "A town?"

Stark nodded. "Yeah. Some crazy names they give them, huh?"

"Where is it, Alan?"

"Eighty miles or so northwest of here," Stark answered, with a frown. "You think it means something?"

"I think," Slade said, "it's all I've got."

Dusk was approaching by the time Slade got his packing squared away. He needed food for two days on the road, and water enough for himself and his horse if they failed to discover a stream on the way. A change of clothes and boxes of spare ammunition completed the list.

In that vein, Slade included twelve-gauge buckshot cartridges to feed the Winchester repeating shotgun he'd appropriated from one of the shooters who had wounded Judge Dennison. A scattergun was handy, sometimes, and it would be nice to have one that held five rounds, as opposed to two.

With any luck, he'd have a chance to use it on the men who had conspired to kill his boss and wound up murdering three decent

72

men in the process.

Despite the anger churning in his gut, Slade wasn't going on a vengeance ride. One thing Judge Dennison had drilled into his head, when Slade had been commissioned as a marshal to pursue his brother's killers, was that duty took priority over emotion. As a U.S. marshal, he was bound to bring the plotters back alive for trial, if that was possible.

But if they happened to resist . . .

We'll see, Slade thought, and even as the words formed in his mind, he knew his ride to Last Resort might be a waste of time.

What did a matchbox prove? Suppose it *did* come from the Southern Star saloon in Last Resort, and one of Dennison's would-be assassins *had* stopped there to wet his whistle or his dick. So, what? That didn't prove the plot against Judge Dennison was hatched there. It was mere coincidence.

Yet Slade's own words to Alan Stark came back to him.

It's all I've got.

He had to do *something.* Slade felt as if he'd lose his mind, sitting around Enid, waiting to see if Dennison would live or die. He needed to be moving, seeking, hunting those responsible.

And if he failed, at least he would have

tried.

It was too late to leave that evening, and Slade still had one stop to make before he started on his ride to Last Resort. He hadn't seen as much of Faith Connover as he would've liked to, since his last long trip away from Enid, and Slade knew he had to say good-bye, at least, before he went off hunting for Judge Dennison's surviving enemies.

He'd been honest with Faith about what had happened, his last time away, explaining how the Bender family — deranged mass murderers and worse — had captured him, how crazy Kate had tried to make Slade be her love puppet before a young Cherokee warrior intervened. And while Faith told him there was nothing to forgive, her attitude toward Slade had been reserved since then, to say the least.

Slade couldn't blame her. Hell, he didn't even trust *himself,* but something told him that he couldn't just ride out tomorrow morning without stopping at Faith's place to say . . . something.

In case that's all there is, he thought. *In case I don't come back.*

3

Bobby Shelton's plan to ride on through the night had failed. Pain and fatigue had ganged up on him, but he still managed to rise at dawn and drag himself aboard his waiting roan.

He knew the way, from where he'd spent the night without a fire to keep him warm, and if he slipped into delirium or dozed off in the saddle, Shelton thought his horse could likely find the Dragon's spread without his guidance. It was born and raised there, after all, a native of the hallowed soil.

Shelton had practiced what he meant to say, using the gelding as his captive audience until he had the snags untangled, but he knew it shouldn't *sound* rehearsed. He had to be concise, straightforward, and above all sound sincere.

If he could fake that, he was home and dry.

Landmarks guided him over the last five

miles or so. A giant willow standing on its own. Two rounded hills resembling a prostrate woman's breasts. A line shack where the Dragon's outriders could shelter if the weather turned against them unexpectedly.

And finally, he saw a couple of those riders bearing down on him, with rifles drawn and resting on their saddle horns. He knew the rifles would be cocked, fingers inside the trigger guards as they closed in.

At fifty yards they recognized him, put the Winchesters away, and made small talk until he broke it off, informed them that the Dragon was expecting him. They didn't offer to escort him, knowing he could find his own way, and they didn't ask about his hunched and slightly twisted posture in the saddle.

Had they even noticed he was injured? Would they care?

Shelton rode on and saw the ranch house fifteen minutes later, picking up his pace a little for the home stretch, even though it pained him. Someone in or near the house would spot him and announce him to the Dragon well before he reached the long front porch and started to dismount.

No one came out to greet him, though. They let him struggle off the roan — no easier than mounting, even with the aid of gravity — and tie it to a hitching post before one of the Dragon's servants ambled out to usher him inside. Nothing about the house had changed while he was gone, of course. Paintings of vanquished heroes vied for wall space with the mounted heads of animals. Dark wood was everywhere. Lamps held the shadows more or less at bay.

The houseman led him to the Dragon's library, with books lining three walls, more paintings on the fourth. These were of battles: Chancellorsville, the Wilderness, and Malvern Hill. Shelton wondered why only Union victories were shown, but he had never dared to ask.

The Dragon came to greet him. Tall, broad-chested, square-faced, smiling, with a glass of whiskey in his clutches that precluded shaking hands.

"Bobby," he said. "You made it."

"Yes, sir." Wincing as another stab of pain caught up with him.

"But not unscathed, I see."

"It's nothing much, sir. Cracked a couple ribs, I think."

"During the action?"

Shelton nodded. "Yes, sir. Just a stupid accident."

"I'll have it seen to. First, though, your report."

"Yes, sir." Shelton swallowed hard, his mind racing. "We met up like you planned and had a look around the courthouse. Talked it over there, amongst ourselves."

"Was everyone on time?" the Dragon asked.

"Yes, sir."

"Of course they were. Go on!"

"They had the hanging set for noon, like usual." Shelton pressed on. "I got the other three in place and went down to the court-yard, by the scaffold."

"With a clear view of the balcony," the Dragon coached him.

"Yes, sir. Anyhow, they brung the four men out that was supposed to hang, and once they're up the stairs, here comes the judge."

"You had a clear view of him?" asked the Dragon.

"Sure. There's no doubt it was him, sir."

"Good. Go on."

"Well, Number Four was going in to take him from behind, and Number Two was on a roof across the way. He had a clear shot past the gallows. I was down below, amongst the townsfolk. Number Three was in the courthouse, covering the marshals."

"And?" The Dragon was excited now.

"It started out just fine," said Shelton.

"Number Four got off two shots. Looked like he hit, both times. He knocked the judge over that railing, spoiled my shot" — fudging a bit, why not? — "but Number Two hit him with buckshot there, while he was falling."

"Yes? What then?"

"Um . . . well, sir . . . That was when a marshal over by the scaffold opened up on Number Two and knocked him over, out of sight. Then, them that come to see the hanging started running ever' which way, goin' crazy. There was no way I could get up on the judge to take my shot, so I . . . um . . ."

"Ran away?"

"Retreated to the horses, sir. We had it all planned out, just like you said."

"And Number Two was shot."

"Yes, sir. I saw him take the hit and fall back."

"What about the others, Bobby?"

"Well, I know that Number Four got *in* the courthouse, but I never saw him come back out. My guess would be the marshals got him. By the time I reached the horses, Number Two caught up to me, but there were lawmen everywhere. I dropped one" — piling on the fudge — "but then a couple of the horses shied and squashed me in between 'em. I got mounted anyway and rode out under fire."

"And what of Number Two?"

"I don't know where he went, sir. First, I hit the lawman, then got squashed. Next thing, I'm mounted, and I couldn't see him anyplace."

"Where would he go?"

It hurt to shrug, but Shelton managed it. "Beats me, sir."

"So, a mystery." The Dragon stared him down for several seconds, then allowed himself to smile. "Oh, well. We knew there would be casualties. What matters is that your team did the job."

"Yes, sir."

Another pause, before the Dragon asked, "There's no chance that the target's still alive?"

"I don't see how he could be. Hit three times at least, once with a shotgun. Falling off that balcony and all."

"I hope you're right, Bobby," the Dragon said. "For all our sakes, I hope you're right. Now, go see Kane about those ribs."

Slade's relationship with Faith Connover had been complicated from the start. Unknown to Slade, she'd been his brother's fiancée when Jim — not *just* a brother, but

Slade's identical twin — had been murdered as part of a land-grab. Jim's death had brought Slade to the Oklahoma Territory in search of vengeance, and against all odds he'd stayed to hunt Jim's killers as a U.S. marshal working for Judge Dennison.

When that was done, Slade realized the lawman's mission suited him, and he could think of nowhere he preferred to be.

In part, at least, because of Faith.

Slade knew it had been eerie for her, in those early days, talking to a face that mirrored Jim's, while picking out the differences in their personalities. Neither one of them had expected affection to fill in the void of their mutual grief, but it had.

And now, Slade thought he had spoiled it, albeit through no intent or real fault of his own.

He couldn't blame Faith for reacting as she had and wondered if the wise thing might have been to keep her in the dark, but silence had felt like a lie that would fester between them. He'd made a choice, and now he had to live with it.

Damned if you do, damned if you don't, he thought.

The key word being *damned.*

Faith's spread lay some two miles outside of Enid. It was out of Slade's way, to the north, but he could stand the detour. He'd already missed his chance to track the shooter who'd escaped, and his hope — such as it was — lay now in tracing one of them back to the town of Last Resort.

As Slade approached Faith's house, he hoped that name would not turn out to be prophetic.

Faith surprised him, coming out to meet him on the front porch, looking daisy fresh as ever. Slade considered staying in his saddle, talking down to her from there, but he decided it would be bad form. He wouldn't ask to go inside, would tell her time was short, but they could still talk face-to-face.

"The news got here ahead of you," she said, by way of greeting. "How's the judge?"

"Alive," Slade said, "for what it's worth. Doc Hauser says it could go either way."

"And how are you?"

"Came through without a scratch, as usual."

"Did you?"

Her eyes searched his and seemed to plumb Slade's soul.

"You know me," he said and wondered whether that was even true.

Faith let that go and said, "I understand one of them got away."

82

Slade nodded. "I may have a lead on that. Or, maybe it's a wild-goose chase. I have to run it down, whichever."

"Can you tell me where you're going?"

"Sure. Some town I never heard of, two days east of here. They call it Last Resort."

"What takes you there?"

"Probably nothing," Slade replied. "A matchbox with the name of a saloon. One of them had it in his pocket. Alan — Marshal Stark — says it's in Last Resort. For all I know, there could be fifty joints with the same name, scattered from here to California."

"And what's the name?"

"The Southern Star."

Faith shook her head. "It doesn't ring a bell."

Slade smiled. "You don't spend much time in saloons."

"That's true," she said. "But Last Resort . . . I've heard something, if I could just remember what it was."

"Don't let it trouble you. I'll be there soon enough."

"And home again, safely?"

He nodded. "That's the plan."

"Be careful, Jack."

"I always try to be," he said, regretting it at once.

"More careful, then. We almost lost you, last time."

Slade wondered if Faith's *almost* meant he still had a chance, but fear prevented him from asking.

"Well," he said, "I'm burning daylight. I just wanted to stop in and say hello, good-bye, whatever. Let you know I'm thinking of you."

"Likewise," she replied. "We should sit down and talk when you get back."

"Sounds good," he lied, already dreading it.

As he was turning toward his dun mare, Faith came off the porch, caught his left arm, and rose on tiptoes to surprise him with a quick kiss on the cheek.

"I mean it about being careful, Jack," she said.

He nodded, had to speak around a hard lump in his throat to say, "I hope to see you soon."

"I'll be here."

Slade glanced back once, as he rode away, and found Faith staring after him. He smiled, knowing she couldn't see it from that distance, clinging to a shred of hope.

William Joseph Dixon was a man of sub-stance, any way you sliced it. He stood six foot five without his boots and tipped the scales around three hundred pounds. His square head, crowned by wiry salt-and-pepper hair, sat atop broad shoulders on the barest vestige of a neck. His broad chest strained the shirts he wore, while corded muscles in his massive arms threatened the sleeves. His voice, though generally mild, was like the grumbling of a bear inside its winter cave.

Big men weren't particularly rare in Oklahoma Territory or the West at large, but big, *rich* men were something else. Dixon liked to pretend he was indifferent to numbers, but in fact he knew his net worth to the penny. When the banks had closed on Friday last, he had possessed $6,453,189.34 in cash, plus real estate and other property valued in excess of $2,000,000.

William Joseph Dixon had *arrived,* as Eastern snobs were prone to say.

His holdings presently included a twelve-thousand-acre farm planted in cotton, a stable of prize thoroughbreds, and roughly half the shops in Last Resort, together with its restaurant, saloon, hotel, and weekly newspaper. His influence was felt in every corner of the town. When he said, "Jump!" the yokels asked, "How high?"

Well, some of them.

Admittedly, there were some rough spots that still needed ironing out, in town and elsewhere, but Dixon had plans. Big ideas.

It was hard to believe, looking back, that he'd come West twenty years ago with next to nothing, twenty dollars in his pocket and the clothes he stood in, looking for a fresh start in the wake of war and occupation by a horde of savages who'd turned his family's legacy and reputation into trash.

The bitterness still dogged him, as it would until the day he died, but getting rich meant getting *even,* and he wasn't finished yet, on either score.

Not by a long shot.

He'd been expecting word from Enid all that afternoon. Not trusting Bobby Shelton as his only pair of eyes, Dixon had sent a second man to shadow him — strictly as an observer — and report back what he'd seen. The day was wearing on, and Dixon was becoming restless, when his houseman came to tell him that he had another visitor.

"I thought you'd be here earlier," he told the wiry man who stood before him, five foot six if that and maybe half of Dixon's weight.

"I couldn't get out right away," his spy explained. "After the big excitement, they were watching anybody leaving town."

"All right. Tell me."

"Six dead, three of 'em ours, Boss."

"And the *other* three?"

"A couple of town constables. The judge's clerk."

"You're telling me that Dennison is *still alive?*"

"Was when I left. Hurt bad, but hanging on."

He still might die, thought Dixon, but it wasn't good enough. Not by a damn sight.

"Very well," he said. "What happened?"

"Well, sir, it all happened pretty much the way you planned it out, but there was marshals ever'where around the courthouse. One of 'em I seen killed two of our men. May have killed a third one, but I couldn't say for sure. They were inside the court-house, then, and I was on the street."

"I don't suppose you caught his name?" asked Dixon.

"Sure did, Boss. Jack Slade."

"Good work. What about Shelton? How'd he do?"

"Well, now, I ain't no tattletale."

"Remember what you *are,* then. That's an order!"

"Yes, sir. He was there, all right, running around and looking after things. Once all the shooting started, I saw Bobby skin out of the courtyard where they hang 'em, headed for the horses. One of the constables threw down on him and Bobby fired a shot or two but missed him."

"So, he *didn't* drop the lawman?"

"No, sir. That was one of ours I never seen before."

"I see. Thank you. Go get some grub, if you've a mind to."

"Thank you, sir."

When he was gone, Dixon turned toward an open doorway on his left and said, "You heard that?"

Jesse Stoner, Dixon's foreman, stepped into the parlor with a frown etched on his stubbled face.

"He lied to you."

"In part, at least," Dixon replied. "I can't fault him for getting out of town. There's nothing else he could have done. But now, the constable . . . that's something else."

"You want me to get rid of him?" asked Stoner.

"That's a bit extreme, I think," said Dixon. "He performed his duty to the best of his ability, under the circumstances, and we still may hear that he succeeded. On the other hand, I can't forgive the lying self-promotion."

"How about a session with the blacksnake?" Stoner asked.

Dixon allowed himself to smile.

"Sounds reasonable," he replied. "Oh, and before you go, we have that other little problem to discuss."

Long rides were wearisome, but they allowed Slade to collect and sort his thoughts, work through ideas and problems without any need to make an instant choice concerning anything.

With eighty lonesome miles in front of him — a full day in the saddle, give or take, before he laid his eyes on Last Resort — Slade felt that he could let himself relax a bit.

Not much, perhaps. But some.

Riding was watchful business, too, staying alert for snakes, storms, bandits, or what have you. Reaching the end of the trail meant staying alive and fit to travel.

Slade wasn't sure what he should make of his last conversation with Faith Connover. She clearly wanted to say more, and Slade felt he was bound to listen, even if the outcome went against him. In his mind and heart, he owed her that, at least. And if she still wanted to talk, at least there was an implication that he had a fighting chance.

Unable to determine any more on that

front by himself, Slade turned his thoughts back to Judge Dennison and the attempt to murder him. Whether the judge survived his wounds or not, Slade was determined that the men responsible for the attack would pay for it. If he could bring them in alive for trial, their penalty would hinge on whether Dennison recovered.

Attempted murder meant a term in prison.

Murder meant the rope.

But if Slade found the people he was seeking and they didn't like the prospect of a trial, if they resisted or attempted to escape, then *he* would be the one to mete out justice.

If he lived that long.

Slade knew that he was handicapped by ignorance this time. He didn't know the would-be killers' motive, even with a written threat in hand. It seemed to be revenge — the reference to "sins" was clear enough on that — but rising from what circumstance? How long had the assassins or the men who hired them brooded over their abiding grudge?

Judge Dennison was fifty-eight years old. He'd been a lawyer since his early twenties, and a judge since he was thirty-five or so, based on the rare comments he'd made to

Slade concerning his background. Dennison was a private sort of man, who shied away from stories where he played a leading role, preferring to cite parables from history or scripture when the need arose.

Slade hadn't thought about it much before the gunmen turned Enid into a shooting gallery, but now he realized that he knew next to nothing about Dennison's background or private life.

What *did* he know?

Born in Connecticut, during October 1833. Judge Dennison had studied law in New York City, practiced there, and joined the Union army as a first lieutenant when the war broke out in 1861. Left military service as a colonel, four years later. Named to fill the federal bench at Enid during 1888, two years before Indian Territory became Oklahoma.

Too many gaps, Slade told himself.

In any life spanning fifty-eight years, there was ample time and occasion to make enemies. Lawyers were magnets for grudges. They sued people, foreclosed on property, soiled reputations, collected large fees. Judges, likewise, sent people to prison or put them to death.

How many times had Dennison been threatened during his career? Would he remember all of the occasions, even if he had been strong enough to speak? How many prisoners or friends and relatives of men he'd hanged now wished him dead?

Slade's problem wasn't finding out *if* Dennison had enemies, but rather narrowing the field. And he was starting off without a single name, much less a list of suspects.

Just a matchbox, for whatever that was worth.

But when a long shot's all you have, you play it. Slade's life as a gambler had taught him that. The only other course of action was to fold his hand and let the plotters slip away, unpunished.

"Over my dead body," Slade informed his mare.

The horse ignored him, plodding on toward Last Resort.

What kind of name was that, to give a frontier town? Not quite the worst he'd heard — *Gehenna* took the prize for that — but it was still a hopeless kind of name, suggesting that the founders who had chosen it were weary, broken down, and close to giving up their last hope of success.

In fairness, Slade knew he would have to see the town before he judged it. Maybe it deserved the name it had been given. Some towns, he'd discovered, were like people, blessed — or cursed — with personalities that seemed to dictate what became of them in the long run, whether they prospered or dried up and withered on the vine.

Dusk caught Slade on the open prairie, and he started looking for a place to camp. A half-mile deviation from his course brought him shelter in a copse of trees fed by a small but steady stream of clear, cool water. There was ample grass to feed his mare and cover for the small fire he would build for warmth.

So far, so good.

After he'd eaten, double-checked the tether on his horse, and spread his bedroll, Slade turned in. He kept his six-gun close at hand, his rifle and the captured shotgun resting on the ground to either side of him. Imagining a small alarm clock with the hands fixed rigidly at five o'clock, Slade closed his eyes and drifted off to sleep, hoping he wouldn't dream.

The seven men who came for Bobby Shelton at the bunkhouse dressed identically, from the white hoods that hid their faces to their red-and-white-checked shirts and denim jeans. All wore six-guns on their hips, one in a lefty's rig. None of them spoke, and Shelton asked no questions.

What would be the point?

He knew the men behind the masks. Knew where they'd come from, anyway, and who had sent them, even if he couldn't call each one specifically by name. The lefty might be Johnny Sloane, or he might not. What difference did it make?

They weren't his friends tonight.

They were the Dragon's soldiers.

Shelton, who had worn the same costume on numerous occasions, met the party stoically, removed his gunbelt — wincing at the stab of pain from his taped ribs — and offered no protest when one of them produced a rope and slipped a noose over his head. Shelton's relief at seeing that they hadn't tied a hangman's knot was fleeting, there and gone.

They led him from the bunkhouse to the yard, where two more hooded soldiers waited, holding torches. Those two led the way as Shelton's escorts marched him off into the night, using the rope around his neck as if it were a leash, and he their dog.

His mind was racing, searching for a way to save himself if they had come with killing on their minds. Of course, they wouldn't do it in the bunkhouse, where there'd be a mess to clean up afterward. Whether they shot, stabbed, hanged, or burned him, they would do it at a site where they could leave his corpse as buzzard bait.

And as a lesson to the rest.

Pleading would do no good, even if Shelton knew why he'd been singled out for punishment. Clearly, it had to do with his foray to Enid and the ambush of Judge Dennison. But *what,* exactly?

Had the judge survived somehow? Was that it? If the Dragon learned that Shelton's team had failed, he might punish its leader, expiate his rage with Shelton as the sacrificial goat.

It wasn't strictly fair, but what did fairness have to do with life in general, much less the workings of the Brotherhood?

Nothing.

They marched him for two hundred yards or so through darkness interrupted only by the flutter light of torches, until suddenly a giant oak tree loomed before them. Shelton knew where they were, now; he'd ridden past the same tree countless times, working around the spread or running errands for his boss.

The Dragon.

At the tree, they found a tenth man waiting. This one wore a black hood and a kind of robe to match. The robe had flaring sleeves and hung below his knees, where denim pants and dusty boots were visible. A skull-and-crossbones was embroidered on the robe, above its owner's heart.

Shelton was pretty sure the robed man must be Jesse Stoner, but the voice that issued from behind the jet-black mask confused him. It was harsh, raspy, and pitched lower than Stoner's normal speaking voice. A trick, perhaps, but once again, it made no difference.

Shelton was facing judgment, and it didn't matter who pronounced it. The decision was the Dragon's. There was nothing he could do but take it like a man.

"Brother Shelton," the black-masked man began, "you have been judged by a tribunal of your peers and found guilty of practicing deception in performance of your duty."

Shelton found his voice at last. "Deception? What deception?"

"You reported to your betters that in Enid, after execution of your mission, you disposed of a lawman."

Shelton grimaced. He felt his stomach twist, his scrotum tighten, as his lie was publicly revealed.

"I shot at him! He dropped!" Shelton replied, almost beseeching now. "I thought —"

"And even now you lie," the black mask

cut him off. "One of your brothers shot the lawman and paid for it with his own life. You only live today because of him, and still you try to rob him of his dying glory."

Hot tears stung his eyes. Shelton said nothing in response, biting his tongue to keep from making matters any worse.

"Your punishment for lying to the Dragon was assessed at fifteen lashes. Five more will be added for your lies to me. What else have you to say?"

"No . . . no . . . nothing, sir."

"Prepare the prisoner for punishment!"

The white-masked men on either side of Shelton gripped his arms and marched him toward the oak tree, shoved his face against the trunk, and used the rope already noosed around his neck to tie him there. Shelton would not have run, but he supposed the rope would also hold him upright when the whipping started, if his knees gave way or he blacked out.

Was there a way to *make* himself black out? Holding his breath, perhaps?

When he was bound, one of the men returned and slit his best shirt up the back with a sharp knife, then pulled the ruined halves away to bare his flesh and the white tape encircling his rib cage.

"Twenty decent lashes," said the black-masked man. "No shirking, now."

Behind him, Shelton heard a rustle whisper as the man holding the bullwhip limbered up. He braced and waited for it, but the first stroke still surprised him with its agonizing bite. He clutched the oak and bit his lip to keep from screaming, tasted blood, and lost it by the third stroke, writhing like a scalded animal and crying out to Jesus, to his mother, to the Dragon for forgiveness.

Somewhere in the midst of it, perhaps he *did* pass out. The next thing Bobby Shelton knew, he lay on soft, cool grass, surrounded by his tormentors. His brothers.

"Take him back to the bunkhouse," the black mask said, "and get one of the darky women in to tend him. Then come back here double-quick. We've still got other business to discuss."

4

Slade woke a full hour before the sun rose and decided to be on his way. He had jerky for breakfast, made sure that his mare quenched her thirst at the spring, then broke camp, saddled up, and rode on.

His late start out of Enid yesterday meant Slade would not reach Last Resort until mid-afternoon, unless he ran his horse into the ground. Despite his sense of urgency, he knew that it would do no good to lame or kill the animal in a misguided bid to shave an hour or two from his journey.

The matchbox was a shaky piece of evidence, at best. On top of that, it had no more than six or seven matches in it when its owner died. Slade didn't know the shooter's smoking habits, or how many campfires he had lit since picking up the matchbox, but he realized the dead man might have carried the Southern Star's advertisement for some length of time.

Would anyone in the saloon remember him? Perhaps.

At least Slade wouldn't have to settle for describing the dead gunman. Enid's photographer in residence, Jake Fly, had snapped pictures of all of the assassins, individually and together, lined up at the undertaker's parlor. In his saddlebag, Slade carried facial close-ups of the three, to help jog sluggish memories in Last Resort.

It might turn out to be a waste of time, but what else did he have? Sometimes, even a hopeless task beat sitting on your hands and killing time.

Or letting *time* kill *you.*

Dark velvet night was fading into gray by the time Slade had traveled two miles from his camp. Another half hour brought pale rosy light to the east, delineating a horizon that still bore no trace of a town.

Slade tried to picture Last Resort, thinking of other towns he'd visited while he was gambling for a living, then while he was serving warrants for Judge Dennison. There was a certain sameness to them all — saloons, hotels, shops, churches, sometimes schools. It would be easy to conclude that if you'd seen one frontier town, you'd seen them all.

But there were always differences, as well.

Some of them obvious, others more subtle, and a few buried so deeply that you had to dig for them, maybe risk getting buried yourself.

Towns had secrets because *people* had secrets. It wasn't just poor folk or those living outside the law. Everyone, without exception, had something that he or she was ashamed of, afraid to make public for fear of embarrassment, social exclusion, or even arrest.

Slade had discovered some of Enid's secrets, working for Judge Dennison, although most of them weren't serious enough to rate a trial. He knew a few men who were stepping out on faithful wives and one or two wives who were not so faithful after all. He knew that Enid's town drunk was a minister, way back, but hadn't figured out what sent him reeling from the straight and narrow path into a whiskey bottle.

And Last Resort would have its secrets, too.

Did they include conspiracy to kill a federal judge?

Slade didn't know yet, but he meant to find out, if he could.

Or, maybe, die trying.

That wasn't in his plans, but Slade knew it was possible each time he woke up in the morning, buckled on his gun, and pinned his badge onto his vest. He'd known folks who might try to kill him just *because* he wore the badge, even if Slade had no thought of arresting them. Some viewed all lawmen as their mortal enemies — and usually with good reason.

Still, he wasn't riding into Last Resort with any preconceptions. For all Slade knew, the shooter with his face blown off in Enid could've spent one night in town, or passed through in an hour on his way to somewhere else. Stop off to get a drink, light up a smoke, and stick the matchbox in his pocket.

Nothing to it.

On the other hand . . .

He might learn something just from watching faces when he showed the photographs around the Southern Star, or somewhere else in Last Resort, like the local sheriff's office, if there was one. Anybody who had seen one of the shooters, even briefly, could increase Slade's store of information, possibly direct him to another source.

And if they shied away or lied to him about it . . . well, in that case he'd learn something, too.

■ ■ ■ ■

Daybreak meant milking cows, collecting eggs, and feeding chickens, all before Colin Jackson thought of sitting down to his own well-earned breakfast. There was no respite from work around the farm, but Jackson didn't need an easy ride. He didn't mind the grueling work at all.

Because the farm was *his.*

The Federal Homestead Act guaranteed his claim to one hundred sixty acres of land, as long as he improved it and filed the necessary paperwork, including an application and a deed of title. No one could deny that Jackson and his family had made improvements to their property — building a house and barn, tilling the soil that had lain fallow prior to their arrival — and he'd filed the papers as required.

Case closed. Except, not quite.

There'd always be some folks — *white* folks, in his experience — who wanted all their neighbors to resemble them, to talk and think like them, to close ranks against "strangers" and "outsiders" if they broke the mold. Jackson had learned that lesson back in Arkansas, where he'd been born a slave, to parents who were also slaves. The war had stricken off their chains, but simply stepping out of shackles didn't mean a man was *free.*

Jackson was twenty-six years old when freedom took him by surprise, already mated to his Mayzie, though their master wouldn't authorize the sacrament of marriage for his "nigras." After Appomattox, during what the whites called Reconstruction, Jackson was allowed to work for pay, rent land, and even vote — but exercising any of those new rights had a price attached. Beyond the ballot box, where white men on both sides clamored at Jackson, telling him to vote their way, it seemed that there was damned little protection from the same men who had chained him as a slave and sent him out to work for nothing in their fields.

At last, with three children to feed and Mayzie's widowed mother making up a family of six, Jackson had known what he must do. The only way to *really* shed his chains was to uproot his brood and take them off to someplace where there never had been slaves. Someplace where they could put down roots in free soil and grow strong together.

Someplace like the Oklahoma Territory.

He had been a long time making up his

mind, and longer still making the move, but they were here now, and he meant to stay. No matter what his adversaries said or did.

Because if Colin Jackson ran *again,* his heart told him he'd never stop. He could flee all the way to California, then jump in the ocean and start swimming, but he'd never find a place where he could truly be a man.

He'd always know that he had run away, one time too many.

He greeted every sunrise with a sense of apprehension, but he also nurtured hope. Maybe *today* would be the day that he was left alone to live his life in peace. Or, if not, maybe it would be tomorrow.

All he had to do was stay alive, to wait and see.

But in the meantime, as he went about his early morning chores, he kept a rifle constantly within arm's reach.

He might be hopeful, but his mama hadn't raised a fool.

"I see him," Happy Beauchamp said. "Look over by the barn."

"That's him, all right," said Zack Bodeen. "Big nigger actin' like he owns the place."

"Reckon he *does,*" said Jesse Stoner.

"Anyway, he *will,* unless we talk him out of it."

"Let's get to talkin'," Virgil Blankenship suggested.

"First things first," Stoner replied.

He pulled a black hood from his right hip pocket and drew it on over his head, adjusting the oval eyeholes for clear vision. The hood billowed and depressed in time with Stoner's breathing.

Stoner watched the others don white hoods and draw their chosen weapons. All of them were dressed alike for raiding, with the same checked shirts and jeans they'd worn to punish Bobby Shelton. Uniformity boosted morale, was good for discipline, and guaranteed that any witnesses could not identify a specific raider by distinctive garb.

When all of them were ready, Stoner led them at a plunging gallop toward the Jackson homestead. He'd been ordered by the Dragon to make sure the squatters learned their lesson this time, even if it was the last thing that they ever learned on Earth. If time allowed, they could move on and hit the second family of blacks who'd put down roots a mile or so away.

The order had been music to his ears.

Stoner was happiest when hurting others, staring into eyes half glazed with pain and begging for an ounce of mercy. He was duly grateful that the Dragon and the Brotherhood allowed him opportunities to quell that hunger.

Like right now.

"He's seen us!" cried Ben Mason, riding hard on Stoner's left. "Lookit him go!"

Stoner saw Colin Jackson running toward his house and knew he'd get there well before the riders swarmed into his yard. He also saw the long gun Jackson carried, and wondered if Jackson had guts enough to use it against white men.

Only one way to find out.

Stoner squeezed off a shot from his long-barreled .44 pistol, knowing the range was all wrong and the bullet was wasted. It made Jackson pick up his pace, though, and kept him from pausing to aim as the raiders approached.

Strategy.

A moment later, they were in the yard, all whooping rebel yells and firing at the house, pocking its door and walls and window shutters with their bullet holes. A rifle shot came from the house, too late, as they circled around behind the barn, but Stoner had his answer now.

Jackson would fight.

Which would make taking him out all that

much sweeter.

Behind the barn they dismounted and left Danny O'Keefe complaining that he didn't want to hold the horses while the rest of them had all the fun.

"Just do your job," snapped Stoner, "or you'll wind up hugging an oak tree!"

O'Keefe was quiet then, while Stoner split his raiding party. He sent Jeff Tibbs, Ben Mason, and Virgil Blankenship around the north side of the barn, while he led Zack Bodeen and Happy Beauchamp in the opposite direction. Their instructions were not complicated: find a way inside the house or flush the Jacksons out into the open, where they wouldn't last a minute under fire.

The simple plans were always best.

Another moment and he had a fair view of the house, but Zack and Happy couldn't see around him, standing bunched together at the southeast corner of the barn. It didn't help having three men in place, if only one of them could fire safely.

"I'm breaking for the chicken coop," Stoner informed his men. "Both of you cover me. When I'm in place, Zack, make a run for the corral. We'll cover you, and then we'll have triangulated fire."

"Won't put us on the inside, though," Beauchamp observed.

"Let's take it one step at a time," Stoner replied. "You ready? Right, then. *Go!*"

He heard a rifle's crack from the direction of the house, then Zack and Happy were unloading, silencing the lone defensive gun. Stoner slid into cover with a sturdy structure screening him from Jackson's fire.

No great surprise, it smelled like chicken shit.

And Stoner realized that he was huddled in the sun, without a hint of shade.

So what?

If he was stuck there long enough to get a sunburn, chances were that he'd be dead. But Stoner didn't reckon that was in the cards.

He was a born winner.

The losers were about to feel his wrath.

The first shots, coming from a distance, put Slade on alert. Their speed and numbers told him that it wasn't hunters, not unless they'd found a bison herd nobody else had seen in seven years of scouring the plains.

So, trouble, then.

Slade got a fix on the gunfire and sent his mare in that direction, bending low over the saddle horn to lessen wind resistance as she ran all out. They climbed a gentle slope, crested a rise, and Slade reined in to eye the spread laid out in front of him.

Faces were hopeless at a quarter mile, but Slade saw four men firing toward the farmhouse, while two others made a run around in back. A seventh had been left behind the barn, minding their mounts. Strangely, all of the gunmen seemed to have white heads.

Some kind of masks?

Slade wasted no time puzzling over it. Drawing his Winchester, he urged the mare downslope into a trot that soon became a gallop. Looking for the best way in, he circled toward the east end of the house, well out of rifle range, to swing around and meet the flankers at the rear.

They saw him coming, one of them stooping with cupped hands to give his friend a boost onto the roof. Slade wasn't sure if they could see his badge, what with the hoods and all, so he announced himself.

"U.S. marshal! Lay down your guns."

Instead, they raised them, drawing down on Slade. He fired a quick shot toward the taller of the two, then jerked the mare's reins hard and vaulted from his saddle. On the drop, his free hand yanked the lever-action shotgun from its saddle boot.

Slade dropped his rifle where he stood and slapped his mare away, trusting her to return upon command. Slade's adversaries fired on him as soon as he was clear, but found him crouching where he'd stood upright a moment earlier, the shotgun at his shoulder, rifle lying in the dust.

Slade hardly had to aim with the Winchester '87, at a range of thirty feet. Again, he fired at the taller man first, a fist-sized clump of buckshot pellets hammering the target's chest and hurling him to earth.

The second shooter reconsidered his position, turned, and started running while Slade pumped the shotgun's lever action. He was fifty feet away when Slade's next shot lifted him off his feet and punched him through a sloppy forward somersault.

Two down, with five remaining.

Slade cocked the shotgun, scooped up his rifle, and moved past the cooling bodies, toward the northwest corner of the farmhouse. He was almost there, slowing his pace, when a window shutter swung open beside him, to reveal a black man staring over rifle sights.

"Who'n the hell are you?" the rifleman demanded.

Slade half turned to let him glimpse the badge. "A U.S. marshal," he responded. "Here to help."

Bright eyes in the dark face examined Slade for several heartbeats longer, then the gunman grunted, grabbed the open shutter, and stepped back to slam it shut.

Okay, then.

Slade moved on and reached the corner of the house, craning around to scan the battlefield. From his position, he could only see one shooter, standing at the northeast corner of the barn, firing a rifle toward the front of the farmhouse. Between shots, he'd glance toward the roof, waiting for his companions to appear.

Slade thought of shouting out another warning, then decided it would only give the front-yard shooters time to flank him, maybe catch him in a cross fire. Grim-faced, he set down the shotgun and raised the rifle to his shoulder.

Fifty feet or so, an easy shot, with no need to allow for windage. Slade eased back the rifle's hammer with his thumb, lined up his sights, and held his breath while he squeezed the trigger.

Down range, his target was pumping his own rifle's lever action when Slade's bullet ripped through his chest, slamming him back against the barn's north wall. From there, he puddled down into a slouching heap, slack fingers cradling the useless rifle in his lap.

And that left four.

Slade grabbed his shotgun, edged around the corner, and advanced toward the farmyard.

"I don't *know* who he is, Mayzie! A marshal's all he said. A white man with a badge. No mask."

"Where did he come from, Colin?" Mayzie asked.

"I got no time for questions now," he answered gruffly, instantly regretting it. Instead of an apology, he added, "Get back with your mama and the children, now. Stay under cover like I told y'all."

Mayzie backed off slowly, glaring daggers at him as she went, but Colin had no time to think about her wounded feelings. They could all be dead within the next few minutes, and it wouldn't mean diddly if she was mad at him or not when they were killed.

Bullets were still slapping against the house as Colin reached the window where he'd fired his first shot at the raiders. That had been a wasted effort, but at least he'd shown them that they couldn't just walk in and have their way.

At least die fighting, when it's time to go.

He risked a peek through the gun slit he'd cut in the shutters, planning for a siege and dreading it at the same time. It wouldn't be so bad if he'd had time to get his womenfolk and kids away to safety, but the enemy always tried striking at a man's weak points. It was too late to spare them now, but he could still defend them to his dying breath.

And what about the marshal? Where *had* he come from? Was it mere coincidence, him passing by just when the raiders struck? Or was he one of them?

It wouldn't be the first time Jackson had seen lawmen working hand in hand with terrorists. In Arkansas, it had been understood that white folks chose the sheriff and he served *their* needs, enforced *their* will where racial matters were concerned. White men with badges typically downplayed disputes among nonwhites, ignored white-on-black crime completely, and came down on blacks who insulted a white like the pure wrath of God.

Was it the same in Oklahoma Territory?

Jackson hadn't thought so, but his only interaction with the law so far had been his registration of the claim to his homestead. No marshals were involved in that, and he'd filed no complaints about the threats he had received since settling on the land. In part, his silence came from thinking that the law would let him down.

And, on the other hand, he took a certain pride in taking care of things himself.

See where that leads, he thought and ducked back as a bullet struck the shutters, inches from the open gun slit. Jackson ducked back, crouching, clutching his Winchester hard enough to numb his fingertips.

"You want me, boys," he whispered to the enemy, "come in and get me. If you dare."

Sprawled behind the Jacksons' chicken coop, Jesse Stoner heard gunfire behind the house and hoped his men had found a way inside. That hope was dashed when the initial rifle fire gave way to shotgun blasts, then silence.

None of Stoner's men had brought a shotgun with him on the raid.

After squeezing off a couple more rounds from his own Winchester, toward the house, he heard another rifle's crack and scooched around to look in the direction of the barn. A dusty boot was visible, protruding at the building's northeast corner, leaving no doubt that its owner had been shot.

Goddamn it! What in hell was happening?

The sun had risen higher in a clear sky since they rode into the farmyard. Stoner squirmed beneath its glare, sweating inside his muslin hood. The chicken coop would cast no cooling shadow over him for hours, yet.

If he survived that long.

One of his men was clearly dead or badly wounded, and he figured that the other two who'd run around behind the house were also gone. Why else would there be silence now, where they'd been meant to wreak havoc? Cursing, he scratched Tibbs, Mason, and Blankenship off his mental list.

That still left Happy Beauchamp at the southeast corner of the barn, and Zack Bodeen in the corral. Danny O'Keefe was lost to him, no way for Stoner to communicate with him behind the barn. He was considering some way to signal Beauchamp, maybe send him back to fetch O'Keefe, when Stoner heard an unfamiliar voice raised from somewhere behind the house.

"You in the yard!" it said. "My name's Jack Slade, and I'm a U.S. marshal. Lay your weapons down and step into the open with your hands raised."

Happy Beauchamp gave a whoop of laughter, called back to the farmhouse, "That's a good one, nigger! Sure as hell won't help you, though!"

The strange man's voice replied, "Three of your friends are dead, already. I'd prefer to take you in alive, but it's your call."

That sent a chill down Stoner's spine, despite the heat that baked him where he lay. The sweat beading his face felt clammy, and it stung his eyes.

He gambled, shouting to the unseen stranger, "How do we know that you're who you claim to be?"

The voice came back at him, saying, "You'll see my badge when you step out, unarmed. Until that happens, we're done talking."

Zack Bodeen fired off a wild shot toward the corner of the house where Stoner thought the voice had come from, but it didn't even hit the building, much less the supposed lawman. An eerie silence fell over the homestead after that, lasting for several minutes, leaving Stoner's jangled nerves on edge.

A scraping, dragging sound distracted him, and Stoner risked a glance around the chicken coop that showed him Zack Bodeen, intent on belly crawling closer to the house. It was a risky proposition, but if he could cover just a few more feet unnoticed, he could likely rise and sprint to the front porch, beyond the reach of Colin Jackson's guns.

And then?

Stoner couldn't begin to think of what might happen next.

He braced himself to cover Zack or nail the so-called marshal if he showed himself, but Stoner had no targets. As Bodeen jumped up and rushed the house, Stoner was rapid-firing toward the shuttered windows, wondering how many rounds he had left in his Winchester.

And then *another* shot rang out from God knows where, and Zack seemed to trip on something Stoner couldn't see. He tumbled, rolling in the dirt, and didn't rise again.

"Zack! *Zack!*"

Shouting his friend's name, Happy Beauchamp broke from cover, loping toward the house and firing as he went. He didn't seem to have a target when he started, but a flicker of movement at the southeast corner of the farmhouse told Stoner their unknown enemy had worked his way around in back, to hit them from the other side.

His nerve broke, then. Gasping for breath inside his stifling hood, he bolted from behind the chicken coop and sprinted for the barn as if his life depended on it.

Which, apparently, it *did.*

He left Beauchamp to face the marshal or whoever it might be, heard rifles spitting back and forth at one another in the yard, and then another joined the chorus, firing after *him.* Bullets were snapping at his heels when Stoner reached the barn, but cover didn't slow him down. He ran until he met Danny O'Keefe, still holding the horses where Stoner had left him.

"What the hell?" O'Keefe demanded.

"Saddle up!" Stoner replied. "We're getting out of here."

"The others — ?"

Stoner thought of Happy Beauchamp, knew he couldn't take a lawman *and* the Jacksons on his best day.

"Dead!" he snarled.

"Jesus! Well, what about —"

"We take the horses," Stoner told him, thinking of the Dragon's brand on each of them and sick of the debate. "Get in the saddle *now!*"

Danny obeyed him, finally. Stoner reached out to take the reins of two riderless horses, leaving three to his companion. Then, without another backward glance, he spurred his gelding northward.

Even in his panic, he was thinking. They could lay a false trail, then turn back toward home.

And it was *home* that worried him.

The Dragon hated to receive bad news.

■ ■ ■ ■

The gunman charging from behind the barn was fast, determined, but his fury spoiled his aim. Slade went to meet him, crouching underneath the hurried fire, then dropping to one knee and lining up a shot that drilled the shooter's chest.

The hooded man lurched backward, almost falling, but he caught himself somehow, using his last reserves of strength to raise his rifle one more time. Eyes glittered feverishly through the round holes in his mask.

Slade aimed between them, fired again, and saw the hood balloon behind his target's head on impact. This time, Slade's opponent dropped without resisting gravity. His mask blossomed with crimson, and his hooded skull produced a squelching noise on contact with the ground.

Slade heard a shout, somewhere behind the barn, and ran in that direction, rifle at the ready. He was too late, though, and saw the last two shooters galloping away, already dwindling, trailing dust and extra horses in their wake.

Slade whistled for his mare, but with no thought of chasing them. He needed answers from the man who'd braced him in the farmhouse window, earlier, and it was possible the dead would tell some stories, too.

Slade's mare arrived and whickered at him. He picked up her reins and led her back to the corral, hitching her loosely to the fence. By then, the black man who had drawn down on him stood framed in the farmhouse doorway. Other faces, frightened, clustered in the shadows just behind him.

"I believe it's over," Slade informed them.

"Maybe so," the homesteader replied. "For now."

Slade thought a proper introduction was the place to start. "Jack Slade," he said. "We met a while ago."

The black man almost smiled at that. "I'm Colin Jackson. That's my family, inside. I guess maybe we're in your debt."

"I don't keep score," Slade said. "You know your visitors?"

"Night riders," Jackson said, and spat into the dust.

Slade glanced up, squinting at the sun, and said, "They ran a little late."

"Sometimes they switch around, you know? Don't want the people they're intimidating to feel safe by night *or* day."

Slade took a peek beneath the bloody

mask of the last man he'd shot and knew he'd have a hard time recognizing what was left, even if they had been old friends.

With Colin Jackson trailing him, he walked back toward the body at the northeast corner of the barn, unmasked it, and asked Jackson, "Do you recognize him?"

"Might've seen him sometime, on a trip in town. I wouldn't swear to it."

The dead man wore his sleeves rolled up. Slade's eyes were drawn inexorably to the three blue asterisks tattooed inside the left forearm.

"Well, now," he said. "What have we here?"

5

A walking circuit of the house confirmed what Slade already knew. All five of the gunmen he'd shot bore the same asterisk tattoos on their arms. As with the shooters back in Enid, the positioning varied from man to man, but each of them was marked.

Slade had unmasked the other three, as well. When he removed the hood from number four, Colin Jackson observed, "I know that one, for sure. He works for Mr. Dixon."

"Who might that be?" Slade inquired.

Jackson was on the verge of answering when both men were distracted by the sound of hoofbeats rapidly approaching from the south. They turned to see a lone rider whipping his horse into a lather with one hand, clutching its reins and a repeating rifle in the other.

Slade readied his Winchester, thumb on the hammer. Jackson saw the move and said, "Don't want to shoot him, Marshal. That's my neighbor, and about the only friend I've got on Earth right now."

Despite that warning, Slade stood ready, just in case. When the approaching rider was a hundred yards away, Slade saw that he was black and let himself relax a bit.

Not all the way, by any means, but just enough.

The new arrival reined in and dismounted in a swirl of dust, eyes flicking back and forth from Slade to Jackson and the unmasked body lying at their feet.

"Colin, I heard the shooting," he declared. "Got here as fast as I could saddle up, I swear."

"And I appreciate it, Martin," Jackson said. "You would've been right useful, if the marshal hadn't happened by, ahead of you."

The winded rider turned, noticed a second body lying several yards away. He seemed about to move in that direction, but he caught himself and swung around toward Slade.

"Marshal, you say?"

Slade told the man his name and watched him studying the badge, as if he couldn't quite believe it.

"This is Martin Abernathy," Jackson said. "He's got the homestead south of mine.

Same problems with the white folks, too."

"You want to fill me in on that?" Slade asked.

Jackson frowned thoughtfully and said, "You want to talk, we may as well get in, out of the sun."

Jackson led them into his house, with Abernathy next in line, Slade bringing up the rear. Slade gave his eyes a moment to adjust, counting two women and three children in the farmhouse living room. They all seemed to know Abernathy, nodding to him, while they stared suspiciously at Slade.

"This is my family," said Jackson, moving down the line. "My wife, Mayzie."

"Please to meet you, Marshal," she said, in a tone that was less than convincing. She turned to the older woman beside her. "My mother, Ruth Little."

"Marshal." Frank suspicion was etched on her dark, weathered face.

"Ma'am, I'm sorry for what you've been through."

"Well, I reckon we're lucky you came when you did," she allowed.

"I coulda helped," said Martin Abernathy, from the sidelines.

"I've no doubt of it," Slade told him, bent on keeping peace. At least, for now.

"My children," Colin Jackson said, con-

125

tinuing the introductions. "Matthew is our oldest."

"Please to meet you, mister," said a solemn boy, approximately ten years old.

"And then, the twins, Peter and Paul."

"Well grounded in the scripture," Slade observed, eyeing the silent twins.

"You might say that," Jackson acknowledged. "Martin's left his brood to help us out this morning, and I hope it doesn't cost him."

"Don't you worry," Abernathy said. "They never hit both spreads at once, and what I seen outside, they were a might shorthanded when they left."

"You've faced this kind of thing before?" Slade asked.

"We've had some visits," Jackson said. "This is the worst, so far — for here, at least. Before, they never tried to —"

Jackson seemed to realize what he was saying with the children close at hand and stopped himself. Slipping an arm around his wife's shoulders, he said, "Mayzie, don't you suppose it's time to rustle up some breakfast for the young ones?"

Putting on a smile that didn't reach her eyes, she answered, "I believe we all could use some."

"I already had some eggs," said Abernathy,

126

"but if you was to insist —"

"You know I will, Martin," she said, with more sincerity behind the smile.

Herding the children toward the kitchen space, Jackson's wife and mother-in-law left the men to their bloody business.

"We ought to move those bodies," Jackson said, to no one in particular. "The kids have seen enough already, for one day."

"Around behind the barn all right, for now?" asked Slade.

"Should do," Jackson replied. "I'll waste the whole day planting 'em . . . unless you want to take them with you, into town?"

"I could, if you've got five spare horses," Slade replied.

"Looks like I'm digging, then. One thing a farm can always use is fertilizer."

Stepping back into the sun, they started dragging corpses from the places they had fallen to the west end of the barn. They formed a rough line there, shoulder to shoulder, one still hooded, while the others turned their faces to the sun.

"I guess it doesn't matter if they burn some," Jackson said.

"They're burning down in Hell, right now," said Abernathy, glaring at the bodies.

"Could've been me and my family, lying there," said Jackson. "Or, more likely, cooked inside our house."

"It wasn't in the cards today," Slade said.

"Guess not. Let's get washed up and see what's on the stove."

"I need to hear your story," Slade reminded him.

"I don't mind telling you," said Jackson. "You're the only one amongst us doesn't know it, as it is."

When they were settled over breakfast plates, Jackson began his tale. "I don't know if you've been down South much, Marshal. I don't hear it in your voice."

"I passed through, here and there," Slade said. "New Orleans, mostly."

"Well, you may've noticed that the Dixie white folks have a certain way of thinking, where the coloreds are concerned."

Slade nodded understanding.

"Truth is, most of 'em still don't believe they lost the War Between the States. As far as slavery, they gave it up on paper, but since then they're tryin' every way they can to make things like they used to be."

"How's that?" asked Slade.

"Law says they can't have slaves, all right? It doesn't say a sheriff can't arrest you and a judge can't find you guilty of something you never did. Once that's out of the way, you get a choice: pay up a fine you can't afford or work it off. The sheriff farms his convicts out and gets a bonus from the bosses using 'em."

"That's not the only way of makin' slaves," said Martin Abernathy, cutting in. "Most places in the South, now, black men have to have a job, or they get locked up quick as vagrants. Now, to prove you've got a job, you have to sign a contract with the boss man. Buried in the middle of the fine print, it'll say you have to pay 'expenses' as you go. Could be for cotton seed, some tool the foreman claims you broke, whatever. And the boss man owns the store where you be sent to buy your food and clothes. Likely, he owns the shack you live in, charging rent. End of the month — and I mean *every* month — you owe the boss more money than you earned. Of course, you can't leave till you've paid it off, or else you get arrested as a thief."

"That's peonage," Slade said, using a term for backdoor slavery that he'd learned since putting on a badge for Isaac Dennison.

"That's life, below the Mason-Dixon line," said Colin Jackson. "If the boss man and the overseers and the sheriff aren't enough, they've got no end of men like those out by the barn. I grant you, now, they dress a little fancier down South. Some of 'em got these fancy robes, put bedsheets on their horses when they roam around at night. But underneath those hoods, they're all the same."

"The Ku Klux Klan," said Slade.

"Some call it that," Jackson replied. "Others say it's the White League or the Silent Brotherhood. Whatever name you put on 'em they're floggers, lynchers, back-shooters."

"You got away, though," Slade observed.

"We up and ran, the lot of us. Both families together. Sheriff Behan back at home's got no pull in the Oklahoma Territory, and we've got the Homestead Act behind us. All we want now is some space to breathe and grow."

"But someone wants you out?"

"Whole lot of someones, more than likely," Abernathy said, with certain bitterness. "But if you trace it back, the word comes down from Mr. Dixon."

"Never heard of him," said Slade.

"You will," said Jackson, "if you spend an hour in Last Resort. He owns half of the town, at least, and land for miles around. A good ole Southern boy, is Mr. William Joseph Dixon, out of Mississippi, Alabama, someplace where they still fly rebel flags above Old Glory. He loves coloreds *in their place,* which means workin' for him getting next to nothing for their trouble."

"Just like home," said Abernathy.

"So, you're saying those are Dixon's men outside?" asked Slade.

"You won't find nothin' on 'em that'll prove it," Abernathy said, "but you won't lose a penny if you bet that way."

"First time his people came to see us," Jackson said, "they didn't bother wearing masks. I know his foreman when I see him, but the others come and go. He's got at least a couple dozen gunmen workin' for him on his spread, hangin' around in town."

"What did they want?"

"Oh, nothin' much. Give us a couple dollars on the acre for our land, and we can either move along or go to work for Mr. Dixon, pickin' cotton. I reminded them about the law. Man tells me we're a long, long way from Washington."

"Do you know anything about the tattoos on their arms?" asked Slade.

"I seen a couple like 'em," Abernathy answered, "back in Arkansas. I won't say they were absolute the same, but pretty close."

"Who wore them, there?"

"Ku Klux."

"I understood the Klan was broken up, some twenty years ago."

Jackson and Abernathy smiled at that. Slade's host sipped coffee, then replied, "That's what they *say*."

Slade's mind was churning now. Why would the KKK, or even former members of that secret band, try to assassinate Judge Dennison? Was it a mission from their "silent brotherhood," or were the former Klansmen hiring out as mercenary executioners?

"Sounds like your Mr. Dixon's worth a closer look," he said.

"You look too close," Jackson advised, "may be the last that anybody sees or hears of you."

"I'll take my chances," Slade replied. "Whoever sent those men, I owe him one."

"I need to thank you once more, Marshal," Jackson said, as he watched Slade preparing to depart. "We *all* thank you."

"Let's call it even, for the breakfast," Slade replied.

"I don't think so."

"You want me to," Slade said, "I'll send the undertaker out from Last Resort to fetch your visitors. Save you the sweat of digging graves."

"They won't be much to look at, by the time he gets here," Jackson said.

"They weren't much, going in," said Slade. "I'll make it clear that I did all the shooting, in pursuance of my duty. There'll be no comebacks against you from the law."

"It's not the law that worries me out here," said Jackson. "Sheriff Evans won't set foot outside of town, unless he gets a prod from Mr. Dixon. Or, he wouldn't when I went to him about the threats and all."

"You're clear on this, regardless," Slade assured him.

"Not with Dixon. This is only gonna make him madder than before. Two of his men come back without the other five, he'll want to pay us back. You, too."

"With any luck," Slade said, "he'll start with me."

"Maybe. But I'll be sleepin' with my rifle, just in case."

"It couldn't hurt."

Slade mounted up, waved to the children watching from the doorway of their threatened home, and started off once more toward Last Resort. He had another three, four hours on the trail to think about what he'd learned from the Jacksons and their neighbor.

William Joseph Dixon.

No, it didn't ring even the smallest bell. Which didn't prove a thing, of course. There must be big and little men all over Oklahoma whom he'd never met and never would. Their fame, if any, could be localized, a matter of geography.

Or of deliberate secrecy.

Twenty minutes shy of noon, Slade spotted Last Resort on the horizon. As he closed the distance, it took form, but he saw nothing to distinguish it from any other frontier town. Most had their big men in command, although "big" was a relative term. Some were tough, some were rich, some were both. In any case, they made the big decisions, pulled the strings, because others submitted to their will.

Dixon, he guessed, was such a man.

But he was still *only* a man.

And Slade would bet his last cent that the Big Man wasn't bulletproof.

No one made any show of watching Slade as he rode into town. He saw the sheriff's office on his left, decided that could wait, and rode on to a hotel called the Empire Arms. Being the only one in town, Slade reckoned it would have to do.

Slade took his saddlebags and long guns with him to the registration desk. The young clerk looked askance at so much hardware, until he'd had time to note Slade's badge, and even then his smile was tentative.

"Good day, Marshal. How may we serve you at the Empire Arms?"

"I'm thinking of a room," Slade said.

"Of course! We do have several vacancies at present."

"It's my lucky day."

The clerk surveyed a rack of keys and said, "I have one on the second floor, two on the third, one on the fourth."

"I'll take the second," Slade replied, thinking its window would allow the shortest drop if anything went wrong.

"Just as you wish, sir. We charge fifty cents per night, all services included."

"What would those be?" Slade inquired.

"Well . . . um . . . the maid, clean linens, towels, and the amenities."

"Are those *indoor* amenities?"

"Not yet, sir. But the plumbing is on order, I assure you."

"Right, then. When it gets here, let me know."

Slade gave the clerk a dollar, with a warning that he might be staying longer than two nights, received his key, and made his way upstairs. His room was at the back, its window overlooking the "amenities" — a plain one-holer in a fenced-off yard.

Slade took Fly's photographs out of his saddlebag and slipped them carefully into an inside pocket of his vest. That done, he locked the room, descended, and began to walk his mare down to the livery.

He drew more glances now, but still no overt scrutiny. Towns had a certain stake in keeping track of strangers, as he realized, and there was nothing sinister about the looks that Slade attracted, moving down the street.

Not yet.

He wondered whether that would change, after he started dropping names. Smart money said that when he tossed a pebble in the pond, it wouldn't take the ripples long to spread.

And he was anxious to begin.

Slade walked back two blocks from the livery to reach the Southern Star saloon, nodding respectfully to those along the way who eyeballed him. It was early for wholesale carousing, but most saloons opened in time to serve drinkers who needed a jolt at the top of their day, and the Southern Star was no exception.

As he entered through the swinging batwing doors, Slade counted heads. One bartender, two middle-aged devotees with their feet up on the rail, and three men at a table in the southwest corner, playing cards. The cardplayers stopped betting long enough to check him out in passing, while the standing drinkers tracked his mirror image in the glass behind the bar.

"Help you?" the bartender inquired.

"Beer," Slade replied. "Maybe some information with it."

"Information about what?" the barkeep asked, while he was filling Slade's beer mug.

Slade swiped a hand across the bar to make sure it was dry, then took the photos from his pocket, laid them out, and asked the bartender, "You recognize these fellows?"

Barely glancing at the photographs, the barkeep answered with a question of his own. "Should I?"

Fudging the truth for all he knew, Slade said, "One of them used to be a customer. Maybe all three."

"Mister, I don't —"

"It's Marshal. And you need to have a look before you start denying anything."

That put some color in the barkeep's cheeks, but he complied, seeming to study each of the three faces in its turn.

"They don't mean anything to me," he said, at last.

"You're sure?"

"I said so, didn't I? Hey, what's the matter with them, anyway?"

"They're dead."

"Guess you're not looking for them, then," the barkeep said.

"Not them," Slade answered.

"What's that mean?"

"Somebody sent them on a shooting job, in Enid. As you see, it didn't go so well for their side. Now, I'm looking for the ones who gave the order."

"Doesn't sound like anybody I know."

"And you don't remember any of them drinking here?"

"They aren't locals. You know, we get a lot of drifters passing through, stop in to wet their whistles. That's what a saloon is for. I don't bother with faces, if their money's good."

"Makes sense," Slade said. "Would there be anyone in town who does tattoos?"

"Tattoos, you say?" The barkeep's face took on a pinched expression. "Like, *tattoos?*"

"You got it."

"Nope. Nothing like that I ever heard about. We got a Chinaman in town, does laundry. No tattoos. No, sir."

"So, that's a *no,* then?"

"Yes, sir. I mean, no."

Slade thought he might as well turn up the heat.

"Well, then, maybe you've seen people around town who might *have* tattoos?"

"Drawing a blank on that one, Marshal. Sorry."

"Nobody among your regulars?"

"None I can think of."

"Maybe just a small one, on the inside of an arm? Three little stars, for instance?"

"Sorry. No."

Slade sipped his beer and said, "You won't mind if I ask your customers."

"Why bother them? They ain't done nothing wrong."

"I'm not arresting them," Slade said. "Just making friendly conversation."

"Doesn't sound too friendly. Shootings, dead men with tattoos."

"Did I say that?"

"Say what?" the barkeep asked, too hastily.

"That any of the dead men in these pictures had tattoos?"

"You musta done."

Slade shook his head. "Try harder."

"Look, you show me dead men, then you ask about tattoos. What else am I supposed to think?"

"You own this place?" Slade asked.

"Uh, no. Just manage it."

"So, who's the owner?"

Grudgingly, the barkeep answered, "Mr. Dixon."

"Mr. *William* Dixon?"

"Right."

"How would I get in touch with him?"

A shrug. "Ride out and see him at his place, I guess. I don't go lookin' for him. When he wants to see me, he comes in."

"No special day or time?"

"Nothin' like that."

"Okay, then."

Slade finished his beer, then went to interrupt the card game. The three players glowered at him while he introduced himself, looked at his three death photos, and denied knowing the men whom they depicted. Slade let it go at that, thinking he'd pushed it far enough for now, without asking the three to bare their arms.

"Nice town you've got here," he remarked, as he retrieved the photographs.

"It's nice and quiet," said the dealer.

"Like to see it stay that way," the player on his left remarked.

"Something we've got in common, then," Slade answered, as he turned away.

"What brings you here?" the dealer challenged him. "Looking for ghosts?"

"Something that creeps around at night," Slade told him. "But my money's not on ghosts."

"You never know what's waiting for you in the dark," the dealer said.

"In my experience," Slade said, "it's usually cowards."

He left them chewing over that and pushed back through the swinging doors. Outside, late afternoon was working its slow way toward dusk.

Slade realized that he was hungry and remembered riding past a restaurant on his way into town. It stood another block due west, almost across the street from his hotel.

He was two doors from the tantalizing smell of beefsteak on the fire when someone called out from behind him, " 'Scuse me, there. Would you be Marshal Slade?"

Slade turned, his right hand dropping naturally to the curved grip of his Peacemaker, and found himself facing another lawman.

"Whoa, now!" said the stranger, raising empty hands. "I don't mean any harm."

Slade placed him somewhere in his later forties, gray hair showing underneath his hat and deep lines etched into a face that had absorbed more than its share of sun and alcohol. A slightly tarnished star, inscribed SHERIFF, perched on a barrel chest above an even larger stomach. Slade smelled sweat and stale tobacco from six feet away.

"Would you be Sheriff Evans?" Slade replied.

The sheriff frowned at that. "I don't believe we've met," he said.

"And yet, you're calling me by name."

"Oh, that's no magic trick," Evans admitted. "We keep track of strangers here in Last Resort, for everybody's good. Joe Eddie, over to the Empire Arms, sends word whenever anybody new checks in."

"I'll have to thank him."

"Doesn't tell me how you knew *my* name," the sheriff probed.

Slade thought of Colin Jackson, but wasn't about to cite him as a source. "You know," he said. "Word gets around. What can I do for you, Sheriff?"

"That's my question," said Evans. "Is there anything that *I* can do for *you?*"

"Well, if you want to talk right now," Slade told him, "you can come along and watch me eat."

That said, he turned and moved on toward the restaurant, feeling the sheriff staring after him. Another moment, and the local lawman caught up. He followed Slade into the restaurant — labeled the Southern Belle — and trailed him to a corner table, by a window facing on the street.

While Slade studied a menu on the wall, a waitress wearing calico and dark hair tied back in a bun approached them, smiling wide to cover both potential customers.

"Good afternoon, Sheriff . . . and Marshal. May I bring you something?"

"I just bet she could, eh, Jack?" the sheriff leered, making Slade wonder if he'd had a shot or two of courage at his office, prior to coming over.

"Ma'am, with my apologies for any imposition, I believe I'll have the T-bone steak with beans and fried potatoes. And some coffee, if you don't mind, just to keep me fortified."

Her smile had faltered for a second, but it came back now — at least, for Slade. "My pleasure, Marshal," she replied, then turned with stony eyes to say, "Sheriff?"

"Just coffee," Evans groused. When she had left to place the order, he leaned forward, elbows on the table, telling Slade, "We like to have a little fun sometimes, you follow?"

"Fun for who?"

The sheriff rocked back in his chair, studying Slade as if he represented some new species that had suddenly appeared from nowhere.

"All right, so you're not one of the boys," he said. "What can I do for you?"

"That ought to be my question, Sheriff, since you came to me."

The moment of confusion clearly irritated Evans, but he shrugged it off. "That's right," he said, recovering. "Well, like I told you, we keep track of strangers here in Last Resort."

"Especially those with badges, I suppose."

"We don't like rude surprises, Marshal. People get . . . upset."

"How often does that happen?" Slade asked.

"Almost never."

"So, maybe you're overdue."

Through clenched teeth, Evans said, "You wanna tell me what you're doing here, or is it meant to be some kind of mystery?"

"Lawmen solve mysteries," Slade said. "Or, they're supposed to, anyway. I'm working on one now."

"In Last Resort? I'm not aware of any unsolved crimes."

"Then it's my duty to report one," Slade replied. "This morning, riding in, I met a gang of hooligans with masks on, raising seven kinds of hell."

Evans seemed paler now, despite his burnt-in tan. "With masks, you say?"

"Well, more like hoods. And they were all dressed just alike. I found that strange."

"Not necessarily," said Evans. "Some spreads, hereabouts, prefer their hands to wear a certain style of clothes."

"Like uniforms?"

"That's the idea," Evans agreed.

"I'd think the hoods would interfere with cowboying."

"Oh, that was likely just a prank. What were they doing, anyhow?"

"The term we use in court would be attempted murder."

Evans swallowed his reply as the waitress arrived, delivering Slade's meal and two large mugs of coffee. When she'd left again, he asked Slade, almost whispering, "Attempted *murder?* Who is it you claim they tried to kill?"

"Myself, for one."

"Marshal, it's possible that you misunderstood —"

"Sheriff," Slade interrupted him, "when someone points a gun at me and pulls the trigger, I don't call it a misunderstanding. And it's sure as hell no prank."

145

"Well, now, I'd like to help you find these boys, if what you say is true. But I should warn you that my legal jurisdiction doesn't stretch beyond the town limits of Last Resort."

"No problem," Slade replied. "My guess would be they're lying where I left them."

"Wha— ? You mean . . . Jesus, you *killed* them?"

"Five of them. A couple got away, but I'll catch up with them later. Right now" — Slade took the photos from his vest and handed them to Evans — "what I need is information on these three."

Holding the photos gingerly, the sheriff asked him, "More dead mean?"

"Dead as it gets."

"Why are you showing these to *me?*"

"I'm checking leads. One of them had a matchbox from the Southern Star. And what's that all about?"

Now Evans looked confused. "What's *what* about?"

"The Southern *Star,* the Southern *Belle.* Who's all nostalgic for the land of cotton?"

"Mr. Dixon owns the Star and Belle, along with other things. I guess he likes the names."

"And he's a son of Dixie, is he?"

"Plenty of us are," Evans explained. "You

146

likely don't remember how the South was made to suffer, during what some call the Reconstruction. Decent people lost their homes and land, lost damn near everything. Some who fought back were killed or sent to prison."

"And, I'm guessing, some got rich," Slade said.

"Damned scalawags and carpetbaggers, sure. Lots more gave up and left, to find someplace where they could live the way they wanted to. It's like —"

"A Last Resort," Slade said.

"You're catching on." Evans returned the photographs. "I've never seen those men before. They're dead, and anyway, whatever they were up to —"

"It's outside your jurisdiction?"

"What's *inside* my jurisdiction, Mr. Slade, is this town and its people. I'm entrusted with their safety, and I won't see them harassed."

"You choose a strange word for a criminal investigation, Sheriff."

"What's the so-called crime?"

"Conspiracy to kill a federal judge, for starters. And this morning's incident tells me your problem's bigger than I thought."

"I haven't got a problem," Evans said.

147

"But *you* may have one, if you're not careful."

"Sheriff, if you believe that local badge of yours will keep me from the men I'm hunting, you should reconsider. While you can."

Evans got up and left without another word.

Slade found his steak was cooked just right.

6

From the Southern Belle, Slade walked three blocks westward to Last Resort's church. It was Southern Baptist, but Slade didn't suppose he could give William Dixon the credit for that one.

At least, he hoped not.

The front door of the church had been propped open and was held there with a stone roughly the size and shape of a large man's skull. Slade thought of John the Baptist, how he'd wound up headless thanks to Salome, and wondered if the stone was meant to be an icon for the faithful.

Once again, he hoped not.

Despite its coat of white paint and its relatively dark interior, the church held mid-day heat inside. Its air was stagnant, even with the front door open wide. Slade crossed the narthex, peered into the nave through yet another open door, and saw no one. He was turning away when a shadow detached itself from the wall to his left and took on human form.

"May I help you, Brother?" asked the shadow man.

As he emerged into the sunlit narthex, Slade saw that the speaker was a thin gray man, dressed all in black except for a white shirt whose collar needed washing. From the getup and the Bible clasped before him in both hands, Slade took it that he was the minister.

"Reverend," he said. "I'm Jack Slade."

"Hiram Locke," the preacher said, removing one hand from the Good Book long enough give Slade's a damp squeeze. "What brings a U.S. marshal into Last Resort, if I may ask?"

"Two days ago, some men tried to assassinate Judge Isaac Dennison in Enid. At least one of them was here a short time earlier."

"Indeed?"

"No doubt about it," Slade replied, stretching the truth to suit his mood. "In fact, I now have reason to believe they have — or had — friends living here."

"When you say *had* . . ."

"I mean three of the four are dead. One got away. I'm tracking him and those who sent him."

"Well, that's certainly disturbing, I must say." The pastor raised his Bible chest-high, seemed about to fan himself with it, then reconsidered. "I can't honestly imagine anyone in Last Resort who would involve themselves in anything like that."

It was Slade's cue to palm his photographs and hold them up in front of Locke's long face. "You wouldn't recognize any of these boys, then?"

Locke swallowed audibly, then shook his head. "Most *definitely* not."

"No matter," Slade replied. "I don't imagine they were much for praying."

"These are the —"

"Shooters from Enid. Right."

"God rest their souls!"

"I guess that's possible," Slade answered. "But they weren't asking forgiveness when they died."

"I won't pretend to know a stranger's heart, Marshal."

"Pastor, I wonder if you might know anything about a group of men I met today, outside of town."

"It's possible, of course."

"We weren't exactly introduced, but I've been told one of them worked for someone by the name of Dixon."

"*William* Dixon?"

Slade shrugged carelessly. " 'Dixon' was all I heard."

"Was there . . . some difficulty with these men, Marshal?"

"You might say that. They tried to kill me and some other folks besides."

"Good Lord! But you're intact, I see."

Slade nodded. "More than I can say for them. It all worked out. For me, at least."

"Well, I suppose you'd have to speak with Mr. Dixon personally, if you feel there's some connection —"

"Does he have an office here in town?"

"Why, yes."

"And where would that be, Pastor?"

"I believe that he does business from the Southern Star. When he's in town, that is."

"Okay. That ought to get me started."

"Marshal, may I ask how many men were killed this morning?"

"Five. Which makes it eight, so far."

"That's dreadful. Simply dreadful."

"I have hopes of bringing in the rest alive," Slade said, then shrugged again. "But I leave that to them."

"You have a grim profession."

"Feels more like a calling, sometimes," Slade replied.

"Well, if there's anything —"

"In fact, there is," Slade interrupted him.

"Do you know anything about tattoos, Reverend?"

"*Tattoos,* you say?"

"So far, the dead men all had little stars tattooed on one arm or the other," Slade explained. Was that a little twitch from Locke's left arm or his imagination? "Oh, and all the ones I met this morning dressed alike, in red-and-white-checked shirts, blue denim pants, and muslin hoods."

"How extraordinary!"

"I'd have thought so, too," Slade said. "But now it's looking like a local style. Well, Pastor, thanks for all your help. Maybe we'll meet again."

"Perhaps," Locke said, a beat behind the conversation as Slade left the church and moved on down the street.

His next stop was the barber's shop, selected on the theory that most local men would visit on occasion, while a stranger passing through was also likely to desire a shave, haircut, or one of the hot baths a window placard advertised. As Slade entered, the barber occupied a chair, rising with a herky-jerky motion that suggested a game leg.

"No waiting, mister. Oh, that's *Marshal.* Sorry. Step right up."

Slade told him, "I'm afraid that all I need

right now is information."

Shutters dropped behind the barber's pale blue eyes. He was a nearly bald man, pushing fifty years of age but not the kind who ran to fat. He stood a bit lopsided, favoring the left leg as if it was slightly shorter than the right.

"I normally do shaves and haircuts," he replied.

"The men I'm looking for would need them, sometime or another."

Cautiously, the barber scanned the street through his tall windows. "You're not from around here," he observed.

"No, sir. I rode over from Enid."

"Having trouble there that leads to Last Resort?"

"I think so," Slade acknowledged.

Lowering his eyes to Slade's shirt cuffs, the barber said, "I need to see your arms."

Suppressing the impulse to smile, Slade unbuttoned his cuffs and raised the sleeves to his biceps, rolling each arm in turn to let the barber see both sides.

"That good enough?" he asked.

"I reckon so. Get in the chair and let me drape you. Make believe I'm working while we talk."

Slade hung his Stetson on a peg beside the door and sat down in the barber's chair.

Before the barber draped him with a sheet and fastened it behind his neck, he shook Slade's hand.

"I'm Jabez Washington, Marshal. And it's good to see you."

"Jack Slade, Mr. Washington. Now, about that business with my sleeves . . ."

"I had to check you for tattoos, of course."

"Three little stars?"

"The very same. You know the bastards, then."

"Not well enough. Four of them tried to kill Judge Dennison in Enid, two days back. One got away."

"The others talk?" asked Washington.

"Only to Jesus or the Devil."

"Three less of 'em, anyway." The barber sounded mad enough to spit.

"Eight less," Slade said, correcting him. "I met another gang this morning, tearing up a homestead west of town."

"One of the colored families?"

"You know them?" Slade inquired.

"I know *of* them," the barber said. "They're not my customers, but every now and then they come in town to get supplies. 'Course, anyone can tell you where they live and shovel horseshit about why they shouldn't be here."

"So, the town's against them?"

155

Washington considered that, his scissors here and there around Slade's head without removing any hair.

"I wouldn't say the town at large," he answered, finally. "More like, it's split. We've got some decent people here, Marshal, in spite of everything. But Mr. High-and-Mighty Dixon, now, he hates the colored like a plague, unless they're working in his fields for next to nothing."

"That's a name I've heard before," Slade said.

"You'll hear it everywhere in Last Resort," said Washington. "He owns the hotel, the saloon, the restaurant, and maybe half the other shops. He lives outside of town on Little Dixie — what he calls his spread — but pulls the strings on those he owns."

"Would that include your sheriff?" Slade inquired.

"Town pays his salary, but if you told me he was getting scraps from Dixon's table on the side, I wouldn't be surprised. I've never seen him lift a finger when the Little Dixie gang is liquored up and raising hell."

"That's good to know," Slade said.

"So, *eight* of them are really dead?"

"So far. I missed a couple at the farm this morning, but I want them, too, if I can find out who they were."

"Smart money says they work for Dixon. He's hell-bent on running out the colored families, or getting them arrested so that he can pay their fines and have them picking cotton for him, like the old days."

"Old days?"

"Sure. His daddy was a big-time Mississippi planter when the war broke out. Three sons went off to fight the Yankees; only one came back. Next thing they know, it's like the world's turned upside down. Black folk can vote, whites have to pay them for their work. What will they think of next?"

"And Dixon didn't like it."

"Like it, hell! From what I hear, he fought against it like the war had never ended. Led some kind of so-called 'brotherhood' to terrorize the coloreds and whatever whites tried helping them to get along. The members all had those tattoos. The way I understand it, Dixon ran out twenty years ago because he was indicted for a list of murders longer than your arm."

"Do tell."

"O'course, that's all blown over now," said Washington. "You've got the same old rebels back in charge, keeping the coloreds down. Dixon could go back home, but he lost everything. His roots are here now. He likes being the big frog in a small pond. I guess

157

we're stuck with him."

"Maybe," said Slade.

And maybe not.

In parting, Jabez Washington gave Slade a list of people he could trust in Last Resort. Slade didn't put the names on paper, trusting in the memory that had secured him victory through countless poker games to keep the list in order, names matched with the businesses they ran.

Leaving the barbershop with the same hair he'd taken in, Slade crossed the street on a diagonal to reach the town's newspaper office. It was called the *Clarion,* and Washington had named its owner-editor, one Caleb Greeley, as a citizen of Last Resort who did not bow to William Dixon.

" 'Course, you wouldn't know it from the paper," Washington had said. "Man's gotta eat. He needs those ads to stay in business, and the night riders would likely burn him out if he wrote anything the boss man didn't like."

So, Slade was cautious as he stepped into the office, smelling ink and newsprint. Overhead, a cowbell jangled to announce him.

"Be with you in just a minute," someone called out from another room, in back.

Slade waited thirty, forty seconds, then a young man fairly bounded into view, smiling from ear to ear. He wore small wire-rimmed spectacles beneath a mop of curly auburn hair, vest over shirtsleeves that were rolled up to his elbows, hands spotted with printer's ink. His eyes caught Slade's badge first, then rose to scan his face.

"Excuse me if I don't shake hands, Marshal. You've caught me setting type. I'm Caleb Greeley."

"Jack Slade. Have you got a minute?"

"For the law? Of course!" He waved Slade toward a pair of wooden chairs facing a smallish, cluttered desk. "Please, have a seat."

Slade sat. When Greeley was ensconced behind the desk, he asked, "How can I help you, Marshal Slade?"

"I was referred to you," Slade said, "by certain folk in town who say you have an independent mind."

"I like to think so," Greeley said, but he had lost his smile. "What's this about?"

"I'm working on a case from Enid, and it's led me here," Slade said. He briefly sketched the circumstances of the Monday shooting and that morning's incident, omitting names of the intended victims.

"Damn it all!" said Greeley, when he'd

finished. "I've been worried it might come to this. Not with your judge, of course. God only knows what that's about. But with the homesteaders, I mean."

"What can you tell me about William Dixon?" Slade inquired.

Greeley glanced toward the office door, as if he thought someone might be there, listening, then said, "He's forty-nine years old, a Mississippi native. Comes from wealthy stock, a planter's son. Slaves built their fortune up, before the war. He fought for the Confederacy, lost two older brothers: one at Shiloh, one at Gettysburg. Meanwhile, the old plantation went to ruin in the siege of Vicksburg. Dixon comes home after Appomattox, finds his parents destitute or damn close to it, and he blames whoever's handy. Carpetbaggers, scalawags, Republicans, the Negroes. Same story that you've heard a thousand times before."

"I understand he didn't take it lying down," said Slade.

"Oh, no," Greeley replied. "He's proud of that. Yes, sir. You get some whiskey in him, and he'll tell you all about how he and others like him helped 'redeem' the South. Of course, the damned Yankees got quarrelsome about it, slapped him with a raft of murder charges, and he's been in exile ever since. Doing quite nicely from it, I would say."

"And has he given up the night riding?" asked Slade.

"I can't prove anything," Greeley replied. "I'd tell myself I'd print it, if I could, but who knows anymore? Marshal, the sad truth is that I'm no better than our sheriff or the other folks in town. I don't like Dixon, or the things he does, but I've done nothing to oppose him, either."

"Why not?"

"Do you want the whole list? First, I didn't know or understand exactly what was happening. Then, by the time I *did*, I had to think about survival. On a good month, I break even with the paper, and the good months aren't that common. As it stands, opposing Dixon, I would run a risk of losing everything — my life, included — or escaping Last Resort with nothing but the clothes I stand up in."

"So, you're afraid," Slade said.

"Damn right. Tack on *ashamed,* and that's me, in a nutshell."

"Fear's a normal thing," said Slade. "What matters is the way you deal with it."

"I don't," Greeley replied. "I look the other way and make believe it isn't there."

"Still not too late to change."

The newsman frowned at him and asked, "What did you have in mind?"

When he was finished at the *Clarion,* Slade moved on to the dry-goods store. The store was about to close when he walked in, but the proprietor still met him with a smile of welcome.

"Marshal! Always good to see a new face here in Last Resort. What can I do for you?"

Slade introduced himself and learned the owner's name was Marcus Tucker. Midway through their handshake, Tucker's wife emerged from a back room, and Tucker introduced her as Lurleen.

"No kind of trouble, is there?" she inquired.

Slade spoke to both of them at once, but focused on the husband. He was thirty-odd years old, his hair thinning on top, and compensating for it with a pair of mutton-chop sideburns. He hadn't gone to fat from good home cooking yet, but Slade could see the warning signs beneath his chin, and at his waist.

"I'm asking certain folks in town if they have any information on some men I'm looking for," Slade said. "A couple of your neighbors mentioned that you might be helpful, but I won't hold you to anything."

"What's it about, Marshal?" asked Marcus Tucker.

Slade briefly described the shooting of Judge Dennison, explained about the Southern Star matchbox, and passed his photographs to Marcus. Tucker's wife insisted that she see them, too, then grimaced and retreated while her husband studied them.

"The face-shot one, it's hard to say," Tucker replied at length. "I've definitely never seen the other two."

"Well, it was worth a try," Slade said. "And there's another thing."

"What's that?"

He sketched the morning's incident, again without naming the Jacksons, but the Tuckers caught on instantly. Lurleen seemed genuinely close to tears as she said, "Those poor people! Will it never end?"

"I hope to end it, ma'am," Slade told her. "But I may need help. Supporting testimony, evidence. Whatever you can tell me would be helpful."

They stood and stared at one another for a long moment, Marcus sliding an arm around Lurleen's shoulders, before the storekeeper replied.

"Lurleen is right. It needs to stop. But you must understand that anything we say could put our home, our business, and our very

163

lives at risk."

Slade said, "I won't be sharing anything you say with anybody else, unless I get sufficient evidence for an indictment and a trial. If that happens, the court can make arrangements to protect you."

"Can it?" asked Lurleen. "We're dealing with a vicious man. A *rich* and vicious man."

Slade nodded. "Yes, ma'am. I'm familiar with the type. They go down hard, sometimes. But they go down. His men are going down already."

"I'm afraid you haven't even scratched the surface, Marshal," Marcus Tucker said.

"How's that?"

"You know what Dixon was, in Mississippi?"

"I've heard mention of the Ku Klux Klan."

"I had an uncle who went down to Alabama, back in '69. He was a Presbyterian evangelist, connected somehow to the Freedmen's Bureau. He was called to preach and run a school for the ex-slaves, all ages underneath one roof. Did you know that before the war, teaching Negroes to read and write was treated as a crime?"

"I've heard that," Slade replied.

"My uncle wasn't down there long, before the Klan came calling. First they sent him

164

warning letters. When he didn't leave, they came for him one night and whipped him. Fifty lashes. Then they poured hot tar into his wounds and cut —"

"Marcus, please don't," his wife said.

"He was *mutilated*, Marshal. He survived, somehow, but he was broken, both in mind and body. Two years later, back at home in Pennsylvania, he shot himself."

"I'm sorry for your loss, sir."

"I'm not telling you to get a 'sorry,' " Marcus said. "You need to know the kind of men you're dealing with, before you start."

"Too late," Slade said. "I'm into them for eight, already."

"Then they won't rest till you're dead, or until you've killed them."

"About Dixon . . ."

Tucker released a weary sigh.

"After the Abernathys and the Jacksons filed their homestead papers, Dixon's foreman — he's a piece of scum named Jesse Stoner — came around to tell us that we shouldn't sell them anything. When I ignored him, Dixon came himself. Tried acting friendly, while he told me things could get *unpleasant* if I didn't toe the line."

"And have they?" Slade inquired.

"We had our window broken, shortly after that. I sent Dixon a bill. He never paid it, so I went around, talked to some other people, and we made a kind of pact to watch out for each other, if we could. It isn't much, I know, but at the time —"

"Did he retaliate?"

"We've lost his business," Tucker said. "That hurt, at first, but we can live with it. Some others in the town don't speak to us, these days. Reckon I never liked them much, to start with."

"I'd appreciate it," Slade said, "if you wrote down what you've told me, plus whatever else you may remember as you go along. Any details, or something else that comes to you. I need all I can get to make a case."

"And then, what will you do with it?" asked Tucker.

"See how hard a big man falls," Slade said.

"You all know why we're here," said William Dixon. "Let's get down to it."

He sat behind his desk, inside his office at the Southern Star. Three chairs in front of him were occupied by Sheriff Galen Evans, Reverend Hiram Locke (red-faced as all get-out to find himself in a saloon), and Jesse Stoner. Dixon's foreman had received one tongue-lashing already, for his failure to uproot the Jackson tribe, and it was clear he didn't relish any further heat.

"Sheriff," Dixon stressed the title as if it was an insult. "What all do we know about this U.S. marshal in our midst?"

"Well, he's from Enid, named Jack Slade," Evans replied. "And like I told you earlier, he's looking into something happened to Judge Dennison, a couple days ago. I don't know anything about that, Mr. Dixon."

"You don't *want* to know."

"No, sir."

"What else?"

"He talked about some trouble with a bunch of shooters, coming into town. From what I understand, he got the best of them."

The sheriff cut a sidelong glance toward Stoner, who was shifting restlessly in his hard wooden chair.

"He killed five men," Dixon replied.

"Yes, sir. That's what I understand."

"And did you question him about that fact, by any chance?"

"No, sir. For one thing, he's a lawman, federal. Plus, you always have me say that anything outside of town's —"

"Beyond your jurisdiction. Yes, of course. Did you, perhaps, ask where the *bodies* were, so they could have a decent Christian burial?"

The sheriff blushed. "No, sir. I didn't

think of it."

"And by *not* thinking of it, you give Marshal Slade a reason to believe that you already *know.*"

"Oh, Jesus!" Evans flicked a look at Locke and muttered, "Sorry, Reverend."

"Now, Preacher," Dixon said, moving around the circle. "You've told me the marshal mentioned me by name."

"That's right."

"Concerning photographs he's carrying of three dead men?"

"Yes, sir. And their tattoos. He said they might have worked for you in some capacity."

"And how did you respond to that?"

"What *could* I say? I'd never seen the men before. I don't know *who* they may have worked for when they were . . . alive."

"Thank heavens for small favors," Dixon said. "Sheriff, *you* didn't drop my name, by any chance, when he was showing you his pretty pictures?"

"Hell, no!" And again the hasty side glance. "Sorry, Reverend."

"Then," Dixon said, "I think we can assume he heard it from the niggers. Jesse, can you tell us why they're still alive and talking?"

"Mr. Dixon, sir, we had 'em covered. They

were history, for sure. But then *he* rode in out of nowhere, shootin' everything that moved. Next thing I know —"

"You had your ass smack in a saddle, galloping for home."

"Aw, now, he killed five of my boys!" Stoner protested.

"Meaning you still had him, two to one."

"Well, I —"

"You ran. That's it. We need to go from where we stand right now."

"I don't know if the preacher and the sheriff want to hear this," Stoner grumbled.

"We're in this together," Dixon told him. "Sink or swim. Does anybody disagree with that? If so, speak up right now."

Grim silence answered him.

"All right," he said. "Here's what we need to do."

Crossing the lobby of the Empire Arms, Slade pinned the clerk with stony eyes. Joe Eddie. Could that be a human's full-fledged name? He thought of strolling over to the desk and thanking Mr. Eddie for his tip-off to the sheriff, but the young man had a nervous look already.

Slade decided it was best to let him sweat.

He climbed two flights of stairs, slowing as he approached the landing for the second floor. It seemed unlikely that he'd find an ambush waiting for him in his room, so soon after arriving, but he couldn't rule it out.

Just take your time, Slade told himself.

And drew his Peacemaker.

He had already marked the hallway's squeaky floorboards on his first trip and took care to step around them now. It wouldn't cover his approach entirely, but if there *was* someone waiting for him in his rented room, Slade wanted all the edge that he could get.

To that end, he produced his key and held it ready in his left hand, tightly clutching it so that the key and metal fob had no chance to produce a clanking sound. At the same time, he thumbed back the Peacemaker's hammer, making it ready to fire.

Slade reached his door and crouched to one side of it while he slipped his key into the lock. A shot fired from inside might still find him, but hotel walls were generally thicker than their door panels, and lowering his height would waste a bullet aimed chest-high.

The key turned with a clicking, grating sound that set his teeth on edge, then Slade was pushing through the doorway, sweeping left to right around the room with his six-gun.

Nothing.

He didn't feel the least bit foolish, standing there. Fools were the ones who took their lives for granted, let their guard down in the midst of hostile territory, and were taken by surprise. Slade didn't mind embarrassing himself a thousand times, if it kept him alive.

Besides, he had no audience.

He closed and locked the door behind him, double-checked the window latch and shut the curtains tight, then lit the single lamp provided for his room. It offered light enough to read by, if he'd had something to read, but Slade used it to finish checking out his room.

Specifically, he opened the freestanding chifforobe, then checked behind it, making sure it didn't hide some kind of entrance to the room next door. With that resolved, he shed his gunbelt and his clothes, half filled the ornate washbowl from its matching pitcher, washed and dried his face, and then climbed into bed.

He slipped the Colt beneath his pillow, hammer down, and squirmed around until he found a place that fit him on the sagging mattress. He had slept on worse and doubtless would again, sometime, if he got through the next few days.

As busy as his mind was, Slade's fatigue won out and pulled him down into the dark.

7

Bobby Shelton shifted awkwardly in his hard wooden chair. The cracked ribs pained him when he moved, and the scabbed-over stripes on his back wouldn't let him relax. He gulped his glass of whiskey for relief and hoped a refill would be coming soon.

Across the bunkhouse poker table, Jesse Stoner stared at him and said, "The Dragon's giving you another chance to prove yourself."

Shelton was tempted to reply that he'd already had his punishment for anything he might have done or failed to do to earn the Dragon's wrath, but he was smart enough to know that mouthing off would be a grave mistake.

Next time the hooded brethren came for him, they might be carrying a hanging rope.

Whatever Stoner was about to tell him, it would not be a suggestion.

It would be an order.

"Anything that I can do," Shelton replied, needing that whiskey more than ever now.

"He knew you'd feel that way," said Stoner. Reaching for the bottle Shelton didn't dare to touch, he topped off Shelton's glass. "You heard about the marshal that's in town."

Not asking. Taking it for granted.

Shelton nodded, didn't feel the need to speak.

"You know he came from Enid, looking for whoever pinned a target on the judge."

Another nod. Saving his breath in case the foreman ever got around to asking questions.

"Well, the way the Dragon sees it — how we *all* see it — that marshal wouldn't be here if the job had been done right, to start with. There'd be no pictures of dead men, and he wouldn't have these questions about tattoos or a matchbox from the Southern Star."

Shelton had almost choked on that, first time he'd heard it. He remembered giving Number Four a light, the evening they had met, and telling him to keep the matches. It was nothing but a common friendly gesture — less than nothing, when you thought about it. But the goddamned matches had come back to haunt him now.

"I understand," he said, having to force the words out of his tightened throat.

"It's good you recognize the problem," Stoner said. "But now, you need to put it right."

"What did you have in mind?" asked Shelton, almost croaking.

Stoner refilled his glass and said, "The marshal needs to go. He's got his damned nose sticking in where it's not wanted, asking questions nobody can answer without winding up in jail, or worse. We want him gone."

"By 'gone,' you mean . . ."

"That's up to you, Bobby. Part of your challenge is to use your wits. Show some initiative."

"Can't lay a false trail," Shelton said, thinking aloud. "He's already mixed up in helping Jackson and the other niggers, right?"

"Seems like it."

"So, we need to stop him cold. Make sure nothing he's heard or figured out gets back to anybody else."

"I'd say that's accurate."

"You know, o' course, that when he's dead, they'll just send someone else."

"We'll be prepared for that," Stoner replied. "Have all our ducks lined up in a nice tidy row. No one knows anything. We'll have our little darky problem solved by then, and no loose ends."

"So, what about the others?" Shelton asked.

"What *others?*"

"Them in town who stand against the Dragon. I can think of half a dozen who —"

"Suppose a couple of them spread some crazy rumor," Stoner said. "So what? *If* they're alive to meet a second marshal, where's the evidence supporting anything they say? Tattoos? We wear 'em out of loyalty to the spread and to the best boss any of us ever had. Next question?"

"But the field hands . . ."

"Number one, I doubt that any marshal's gonna ask some cotton-picking nigger if he knows who shot a judge in Enid. Which they *don't* know, by the way. If one of them gets brave and claims he's being held against his will, we've got the paperwork on each and every one to prove they're working off a legal fine or money that they owe the boss."

"I guess, but —"

"What you need to do right now," said Stoner, interrupting him, "is think about *your* problem. Which, as I've explained, is getting Marshal Jackass Slade once and forever off the Dragon's back. Can do?"

"I'll think of something," Shelton said.

"Think of it now," Stoner replied. "You're doing it tonight, and I'll be supervising."

Shelton swallowed hard. Said, "Right. Can I have one more shot of whiskey, then?"

"One for the road, Bobby. Time's wasting, and you haven't got much left."

"Why can't you run a story on it, stir things up a little?" Marcus Tucker asked. Lurleen clung tightly to his hand, giving a small squeeze of encouragement.

"What could I say that wouldn't leave me stuck between a rock and a hard place?" asked Caleb Greeley. And before his hosts could speak, the newsman started answering himself. "I can't say that the marshal's planning to arrest Dixon for anything. I can't say Dixon has committed any crimes, because we have no evidence. I can't —"

"Caleb, you *know* he's guilty," Lurleen interjected. "We *all* know it!"

They were seated at the Tuckers' kitchen table, curtains tightly drawn, talking by candlelight, their voices hushed.

"Knowing and proving are a hundred miles apart," Greeley replied. We *all* know *that.* If I print anything that can't be proved in court, all Dixon has to do is slap me with a libel charge and shut the paper down. I'd have to search the territory for a lawyer, pay him every cent I've got, and I'd *still* lose, for want of proof."

"But if you *had* the evidence," Marcus began.

"Huge 'if,' " said Greeley, stopping him. "I've just said that I don't."

"But if you *did,* he couldn't sue you, right?"

"Unfortunately, wrong. In this great nation, anyone can sue for anything. Unless the allegation is dismissed, the case will go to trial, and from day one, both sides are paying lawyers. *They* get fat, no matter what. Suppose I had the evidence — which I do not — and won the case. What, then? I've spent my last dime proving that I published a true story, while Dixon is only out some petty cash. He *still* wins, since the only people who'll have read my paper are a bunch of locals who already know the truth, to start with."

"What you need," Lurleen suggested, "is a wider audience."

"Now, that's the truth," Greeley replied, beaming a smile at her. "If only each and every soul within the Oklahoma Territory bought a copy of the *Clarion,* my problems would be solved."

"You're making fun of me," she chided him.

"In no sense, ma'am. I'm simply pointing out the cold reality: I print a local paper, read by *maybe* half the folks in town. The rest just cut it up and hang it in their privies."

"Suppose somebody took the story to that Oklahoma City paper," Lurleen asked him. "What's it called, again?"

"The *Daily Oklahoman*," Greeley answered. "Run by Samuel Small. I met him once, about a year ago. But —"

"Wouldn't he be interested in a story about murder, slavery, and who knows what all?"

"He's a bigger fish than I am, granted," Greeley told her. "But he still needs proof for anything he publishes. The law applies in Oklahoma City, just the same as here in Last Resort."

"What law?" asked Marcus, nearly snorting his derision. "Galen Evans? Is there any doubt he does whatever Dixon tells him to? What kind of law is that?"

"Which brings me to my other point," said Greeley. "Dixon wouldn't have to sue me. All he has to do is point a finger and I'm gone. His men could burn me out, kill me. Who'd raise a hand against them?"

"I would," Tucker said, his backbone stiffening.

"Now, Marcus —" Lurleen cautioned him.

"Your darling lady's right," said Greeley, letting Tucker off the hook. "Why sacrifice yourself for a lost cause? And why should I? If I save up and live on beans for six or eight more months, I should be able to afford a wagon, for the printing press."

"You're *leaving?*" asked Lurleen. She sounded horrified by the idea, which gave Greeley a warm feeling inside, against his better instincts.

"I've been thinking of it for a while now," he admitted.

"Where would you go?" Marcus asked.

"Well, since you mentioned Oklahoma City, I've been thinking Mr. Small could use some competition. Keep him honest, you might say."

"And leave us in the lurch," Marcus responded, sounding angry.

"You're asking me to risk my life or bankruptcy for Last Resort, when no one else will lift a finger against Dixon? When I have no evidence to prove that he's done anything illegal? Where's the sense in that?"

"Why not report what Marshal Slade's already found? You've got the Jacksons under fire, with raiders killed. If you identify the men and they're on Dixon's payroll, wouldn't that be worth a headline?"

Greeley frowned, thinking it over. "Anyway," he said, "they're likely in the ground by now."

Marcus smiled at that. "You may recall I run the dry-goods store. You need a shovel, Caleb, I'm your man."

The first time Bobby Shelton tried his fast draw, practicing, he nearly dropped his pistol in the dirt. Between his cracked ribs and the fresh cuts on his back, the movement didn't flow. And honestly, he'd never been that fast, to start with.

Shelton liked to have the odds on his side when he faced a man — or didn't face him, as the case might be. Back-shooting didn't bother him a bit; in fact, he favored it. There was less risk that way, and he could choose his moment without thinking about sweaty palms or sunlight in his eyes.

On those occasions when he absolutely had to face an enemy, Shelton preferred to have a couple dozen of his best friends from the Brotherhood around him, suitably disguised, dragging their man out of his bed at midnight with a noose around his neck.

He wouldn't have that luxury with Marshal Slade, but Shelton figured he still had a chance to catch his man asleep — or, at the very least, with weapons out of reach. He'd have a passkey to the lawman's hotel room and go in shooting, keep it up until his man was dead beyond a whisper of a doubt.

No messing up this time, like with the judge.

He planned to lead off with a cut-down ten-gauge, using special shells loaded with dimes. They stacked flat on the cartridge wadding, but when fired, they spun like tumbling razor blades and sliced the hell out of a target. If he played it right, Slade wouldn't even wake to find out he was dying.

But it did no harm to try the not-so-fast draw just a few more times.

In case something went wrong.

Stoner had promised he would be around when Bobby made his move, whatever that meant. Shelton wasn't counting on him for assistance if his first try didn't put Slade down and out, but maybe Stoner would step in if it began to fall apart. Better for him to help than go back to the Dragon with the news that yet another plan had failed.

Of course, by that time, Shelton reckoned, he would probably be dead.

He hadn't seen this marshal work in Enid.

God knew that he'd been too busy getting out of town, scrambling to save himself. But Slade had killed five of his friends that very morning, maybe with some help from Colin Jackson, but they'd all been decent hands. Not Wild Bill Hickok fast, but good enough.

Or so he'd thought.

So Shelton didn't plan to duel with Slade, unless he had no other choice. A shot or three in darkness, while the marshal slept, was more his speed.

If only he could pull it off.

With that in mind, Shelton replaced his six-gun in its holster, hoping it would stay there. Turning to the ten-gauge shotgun, he made sure that both barrels were loaded with the proper ammunition, then slipped four spare shells into his vest pockets.

The extra bit of weight was comforting, somehow.

Shelton consulted his old pocket watch and saw that it was nearly midnight. He decided on the spot to give his man another half hour in dreamland. That would let him make a leisurely approach, spy out the land for any traps Slade might have laid, and still be done in time to get himself a good night's sleep.

He hoped that killing Slade would end it. If the federals sent someone else to take his place, Shelton would have to think about fleeing from Last Resort. And that, in turn, would mean leaving the Brotherhood.

The very notion gave him pause.

The Brotherhood was powerful; its reach was long. Could he escape it, even if he tried? Where would he hide that others could not find him? Was there any place on Earth where he'd be truly safe?

Don't think about it now, a small voice in his head advised.

There would be time enough to think of running if he blew his last chance to redeem himself and reclaim the Dragon's favor.

And if that happened, he'd probably be dead in any case.

If any of his hooded brothers sought to punish him on top of that, they'd have to follow him to Hell.

Galen Evans gulped his double whiskey and immediately poured another, while the liquor scorched its way down to his stomach. He swallowed a sour belch and rocked back in his chair. It took him two tries to prop his feet up on the edge of his desk.

Not drunk, he thought. *Just getting old.*

And forty-seven *was* old for a lawman in the Oklahoma Territory. Old for anywhere on the frontier, when he considered it. But he still had a few good years left in him yet.

Good years?

That might be stretching it. On second thought, make it a few *fair* years, if he was careful and stayed out of trouble, didn't push his luck with any hair-trigger badmen or back any losers.

Which brought Evans back to his current problem.

He was bought and paid for at the moment. William Dixon held the deed, and he could call the tune as he saw fit, expecting Evans to dance on command. The fact that it might put Evans in conflict with a U.S. marshal wouldn't trouble Dixon. After all, where he'd come from, the state and local law was constantly at odds with Uncle Sam, to the point of collusion in wholesale murder.

It would be nothing for Dixon to demand that Evans deal with Slade, assuming that his own men failed at their assignment for the evening. And if Evans died trying, Dixon's only regret would be for one more failure. Nothing else would cross his mind.

Evans did not deceive himself about his place in Last Resort. He knew some of the locals feared him as another pair of eyes and hands employed by Dixon, while the rest dismissed him as a stooge. There'd been a time when Evans would have rankled at that judgment, but he'd learned to live with it, as long as no one spoke the words aloud, in front of him.

What other choice was open to him?

After all, it was the truth.

He'd been a fairly decent lawman once, in Kansas, spending time in Dodge City and Wichita. He'd known the Earp brothers in Dodge, briefly, when their association with Doc Holliday earned them a reputation as "the fighting pimps." In those days, Evans was inclined to look at them with something close to scorn, asking himself how lawmen could involve themselves in gambling and prostitution on the side, using their badges to harass red-light competitors, but times had changed.

These days, he marveled at his own youthful naiveté and wondered how he'd even lived to reach his present age. And even as the question formed, he knew the answer.

He had stayed alive by making deals, accepting the reality that every town was basically corrupt, with wheeler-dealers operating everywhere behind the scenes. When realistic lawmen promised to "clean up" a town, they meant disposing of the riffraff: drifters, drunkards, independent tinhorn gamblers, and the like. They were supposed to deal with bank robbers, not think about the bankers who were robbing common folk behind closed doors.

In short, a lawman went along to get along, and if one of the drifters he confronted was a faster gun, the grateful city fathers would commemorate him with a stylish funeral. Ashes to ashes, dust to dust.

Amen, the sheriff thought and took another drink.

Jack Slade's problem was thinking he could change the world. If he'd been smart, Slade would've settled for the shooters who'd been killed in Enid. Maybe try to find the fourth man, then give up after a day or two. But coming into Last Resort — hell, killing five of Dixon's men before he even got to town — was tantamount to suicide.

And Galen Evans knew his job description didn't cover saving people who were bent on self-destruction.

A part of Evans wished the silly bastard luck, but he would never voice that wish aloud. He wouldn't lift a finger to protect the marshal, but he'd make a show of looking for the killers.

Ten or fifteen minutes ought to do the trick.

Evans refilled his glass and raised it in a toast.

"See you in Hell."

Reverend Hiram Locke was not a drinking man. He found no solace in the bottle, but the Bible wasn't offering him much tonight, either. He had tried praying to his Savior, but it simply wasn't working out.

Locke had always regarded himself as a man of principle. His father was a minister before him, and a leader of the movement that had split the Baptist Church when northern abolitionists declared that Jesus hated slavery. The proof that they were wrong was there for anyone to see, in Exodus 21, Leviticus 25, on into the New Testament from Luke to Ephesians and Timothy. Who could deny it and still claim salvation?

Locke had been raised to believe his Maker shaped man in His image — and clearly, that had to mean *white.* Africans were the children of Ham, cursed by Noah to be "servants of servants" for all time. It made no difference what the Yankees thought, or how they twisted scripture to serve their own ends. God's word was eternal.

Locke himself had been ordained to

preach the Word two years before his native Alabama finally seceded from the Union. As a strapping Southern youth, he'd longed to serve in uniform and crush the heretics who sought to undermine God's holy scheme of things, but he'd been relegated to a noncombatant chaplain's role, doing his best to comfort dying heroes at Round Mountain, Fort Henry, Fredericksburg, and other places he'd endeavored to forget. A sniper's shot had grazed him at Chancellorsville, the same day Stonewall Jackson fell to friendly fire, but Reverend Locke endured.

Tonight, he wondered how much longer that could last.

After the war, he'd prayed for strength while carpetbaggers looted Dixie, leading the illiterate ex-slaves to vote for candidates they didn't even recognize by sight. When young war veterans had organized to purge the land with blood, Locke had resumed his chaplain's post, but this time in the service of the Ku Klux Klan. He'd never swung a whip or fired a shot himself, but he had prayed for Jesus and the Holy Ghost to bless the night riders who fought for Dixie's honor, risking everything the tragic war had left to them.

And in the end, they'd won.

Dixie had been redeemed for white home rule. The freemen were disfranchised and returned to the subservient position God ordained for them, restricted in their movements and the places they could live. Locke's world should have been perfect, but the Devil threw a stumbling block into his path and brought him down.

Her name was Sara Monaghan, and she was married to a brutal drunkard who had made her live a veritable Hell on Earth. She'd come to him at first for guidance, as a member of his church, and Locke had done his best to counsel her. But he'd been weak, and she'd been willing. Oh, so willing after years of spite and cruelty at home.

It had been sweet, dear Lord, like a foretaste of Heaven, if such things could spring from sin. And when her husband had found out, by chance, the outcome was predictable.

Locke still recalled that night, although he'd spent the better part of ten years trying to forget. He'd gone to Sara's house, thinking her husband had a wagonload of cotton to deliver in Mobile, and found him home instead, sitting beside Sara's dead body in a rocking chair. Her throat was cut, blood everywhere, and Locke had seen the long knife in her husband's hand as he rushed forward to collect another pound of flesh.

Locke should have died that night. Over the years since then, he'd often wished that it had gone the other way, that he'd been weaker, clumsier, and failed to grip the drunken bastard's wrist *just so,* turning the knife around by pure dumb luck and driving it between his adversary's ribs.

The court had called it self-defense, of course, for such it was. But Sara's husband had already shared his intimate suspicions with a group of worthless friends, and gossip travels faster than wildfire in rural Southern towns. Within two weeks, Locke's congregation melted down to nothing, left him preaching to an empty church, and there was nothing he could do but slink away to someplace where nobody recognized his shame.

And he'd wound up, quite fittingly, in Last Resort.

He'd been surprised when William Dixon recognized the tattoo on his arm, one afternoon while Locke was working on his new church with his sleeves rolled up. Before Locke knew it, he had been invited to a meeting of the Brotherhood, then drafted as its chaplain.

And the rest, as someone wrote, was history.

He'd closed his eyes to much of what was happening in Last Resort, but murder would be done this night and Locke was an accessory before the fact. How would he square that with his Lord, on Judgment Day?

Tears brimming in his eyes, Locke bowed his head and offered up another fervent prayer.

At first, Slade thought it was a nightmare. Then he guessed it was the beans he'd had for dinner. *Something* had disturbed his sleep, and lying in his narrow sagging bed, he tried to work it out.

The dream was muddled, nearly lost as Slade opened his eyes into darkness. He'd been chasing someone — one of his more common themes, since he'd become a lawman — but he couldn't see his quarry's face or close the gap between them, even when he sprinted like a logger trying to escape a forest fire. Reaching for his six-gun, Slade had found an empty holster slapping at his thigh.

On balance, though, he didn't think the dream was strange enough to wake him. That opinion was supported by the grumbling in his gut.

Beans, then.

He lay on his left side and waited for the gas to shift, thinking about what he had learned so far in Last Resort. The town was clearly split between Dixon supporters and opponents, though he gathered that dissenters were in the minority, discouraged from speaking out by peer pressure or worse. Slade didn't know if any of the anti group would help him, in a pinch, but he'd have been a fool to count on it.

More to the point, Dixon appeared to have the sheriff on his side, which meant that he could get away with damned near anything he wanted to, if he could do a halfway decent job of covering his tracks. The town's lone preacher also seemed to be in Dixon's camp, another handy tool for keeping folks in line, but Slade had sensed a certain weakness there that still might be exploitable.

If he could only —

Damn it!

Grimacing at yet another cramp, Slade knew he couldn't stay in bed and wait it out. Cursing, he sat up and found the bedside lamp, lit it, and turned the wick down to provide the least light needed for the chore of dressing.

If the Empire Arms had offered guests indoor amenities, at least Slade wouldn't need his boots. But as it was, the trek downstairs and out to reach the privy meant he might be walking over stones — or rattlesnakes, for all he knew.

Despite a sense of urgency, Slade took the time to draw his Colt from underneath his pillow, holster it, and buckle his gunbelt. He didn't strap it on, but draped it over his left shoulder, where the Peacemaker was handy if he needed it.

Now get a move on!

Picking up the lamp and his room key, Slade first unlocked his door, then stepped into the hall and closed it, locking it again behind him. Carrying the dim lamp in his left hand, he proceeded toward the stairs, making an effort not to clomp his way along and trouble any other sleeping guests along the way.

The clerk was absent from his check-in counter, maybe dozing in the back, as Slade descended to the ground floor, turned hard left to put the lobby at his back, and passed on through an exit at the rear, into a kind of courtyard where the privy stood alone. The hinges on its door squeaked like a field mouse as he entered, shut the door again, and latched it for a bit of privacy.

Slade checked the place for spiders, still remembering a childhood story that his uncle told, about a drover who had squatted on a nest of fat black widows in Cheyenne. When he was satisfied that there were none in residence, Slade hung his gunbelt on a wooden peg and sat down to relieve himself, placing the lamp between his feet.

His thoughts came into focus on a man he hadn't met, whom he suspected of conspiring to assassinate Judge Dennison. It seemed appropriate to think of him in this place, with its noisome smell.

You stepped in something, boy, Slade thought. *And you don't even know it yet.*

8

Bobby Shelton felt conspicuous as hell on Main Street, walking to the Empire Arms. It seemed to him as if the whole town must be watching from behind the curtains drawn on darkened windows, following his progress on the wooden sidewalk from the Southern Star to the hotel. Even knowing as he did that most of them were fast asleep, it didn't help.

He didn't have a clue where Jesse Stoner was, except that he'd been told the Dragon's foreman would be close by if he needed help. That might explain the prickly feeling on the back of Shelton's neck, but he supposed that most of it was simply nerves.

He'd been granted a second chance, and now he was afraid of failing as he had in Enid, with the move against Judge Dennison. Shelton had managed to escape that time, and while he'd suffered punishment for letting down the Brotherhood, at least he was alive.

So far.

Tonight was different. If Shelton failed this time and somehow wriggled out of it without the marshal killing him, he'd have no place to run and hide. Stoner and Dixon wouldn't shelter him after a blunder in their own backyard. If anything, they'd likely put a bullet in his head and plant him somewhere on the Dragon's spread, to spare themselves embarrassment.

So, do it right.

Shelton carried the ten-gauge shotgun at his left side, underneath a knee-length coat, thus doubly shielded from potential witnesses. The night was cool enough to justify the coat, but so far he'd seen no one on the street who might have questioned it.

No one to help him, either, if his plan disintegrated.

Where in hell was Stoner?

Never mind.

A half block from the Empire Arms, Shelton began to slow his pace and tried to act more casual. He didn't need it for the clerk, of course. The fix was in on that score, anyway. But passing from the street into the hotel's lamp-lit lobby made him ill at ease.

The clerk was doing something in the office as Shelton approached his counter. He could hear the young man shuffling papers, muttering to himself as if he'd lost something. Shelton stood there for a moment, then reached out and rapped his knuckles on the counter for attention.

The clerk came out to greet him, frowning slightly, not at all a face to welcome customers. In fact, he looked a little surly, something Shelton didn't feel inclined to tolerate.

He had a job to do, and Shelton didn't need some little weasel looking down his nose at him, as if working a hotel desk at night was some big deal.

The clerk — what was his name? Shelton couldn't remember, and he didn't give a damn — approached the counter cautiously, not rushing it. He flicked a glance around the lobby, as if making sure that Shelton was alone, before he spoke.

"Yes, sir?"

A little bit of attitude, but Shelton let it go.

"You got something for me," he said, not making it a question.

"Sorry?"

If Shelton's ribs hadn't been paining him, he might've swung a fist across the counter. As it was, he took his time and spelled it out in no uncertain terms.

"The passkey. You were told to have it ready."

It was nice, watching the color drain out of the snotty little bastard's face. Maybe he'd managed to convince himself that someone higher up the line had changed his mind and nothing bad would happen on his graveyard shift.

Well, guess again.

"The passkey. Um. Yes, sir."

The clerk turned to retrieve it from a rack of keys behind him, choosing one that wasn't numbered. Shelton made a mental note of where it hung, in case he ever felt the urge to come around sometime and help himself. Snoop through the rooms or something. Maybe drop in on a lady visitor and give her a surprise.

He palmed the key and asked, "This fits 'em all?"

The clerk's head bobbed in affirmation.

Shelton left him standing there and moved off toward the stairs.

The best thing about outdoor privies, Slade decided, was the chance he got to catch up on his reading. Normally one-holers offered cut-up squares of newspaper that always left you wondering how stories ended, but the privy in the backyard of the Empire Arms featured pages of a catalog from something called the R. W. Sears Watch Company, which sold mail-order jewelry and watches guaranteed to run without a hitch for six full years.

What was the world of commerce coming to?

Yawning, Slade hoisted up his pants, buttoned his fly, and took his gunbelt from its wall peg, slipping it over his shoulder once again before he bent to grab the lamp. From force of habit, he peered through the standard half-moon cutout in the privy's door and scanned the yard before he stepped outside.

Nobody lurking there.

Slade guessed he might be overdoing it, but you could never tell when you were working a strange town, poking around in search of answers to important questions that the local boss would rather not have answered. Last Resort wasn't the first place Slade had felt his life might be at risk, and in the past his judgment had been proven valid.

Not the first, he thought.

But might it be the worst?

If what he'd heard from Colin Jackson and a handful of the folks in town was accurate, then William Dixon hadn't simply tried to kill Judge Dennison. On top of that, he should be standing trial for peonage. The top-end penalty for that was twenty years on each count proved in court, meaning that a defendant holding ten slaves could be locked up for two hundred years, and so on. Add attempted murder of a federal judge and sundry homesteaders, you might as well just throw away the key.

And would a man of Dixon's background kill to hide his crimes, to stay at liberty?

There was no question in Slade's mind.

By now, he took for granted that the man in charge of Last Resort must know he was in town and asking questions. The survivors from the morning's raid would've briefed Dixon on their losses, so he'd have another reason to hate Slade.

Logic dictated that the question wasn't *if* he'd make a move, but rather *where* and *when.*

Slade crossed the moonlit courtyard, checking out the darker shadows as he passed. He kept the lantern in his left hand, with his right arm crooked to bring the hand across his chest, a short reach for the holstered Peacemaker.

But nothing moved. No sound disturbed the night except his own footsteps on sand and gravel.

Slade reentered the hotel and softly closed the back door, trying not to rouse the clerk. He didn't trust the hotel staff, knowing that Dixon owned the place and they kept tabs on guests for Sheriff Evans. Any small evasion of surveillance he could manage was a victory of sorts.

Slade reached the bottom of the stairs and surveyed the lobby and the registration desk without sighting a living soul. He heard a floorboard creak, somewhere above him, but he couldn't place it and he knew that any building taller than a single story made noise all night long. It could be someone turning over in his sleep, even a couple getting busy in the midnight hour.

Maybe a ghost.

Another moment passed with no sign of the clerk. Pleased with himself, Slade quietly began to climb the stairs.

The plan was simple. Any idiot could pull it off. Pick up the master key and find the marshal's room. Be extra quiet when you turn the lock, then bust in on him shooting while he's trying to wake up.

Dead lawman. Problem solved.

At least, until another marshal came along.

There was a built-in limitation to the plan that Mr. Dixon didn't seem to recognize, but Jesse Stoner wasn't paid to contradict the boss. His job was to obey and get things done, not argue back or mess up like he had at that morning's business at the Jackson place.

Stoner had been a poor sharecropper's son in Georgia, lost two older brothers in a war he didn't really understand while it was going on, except to hear his daddy say that Jewish bankers and Republicans were telling Southern white men how to treat their nigras. Then the carpetbaggers came to steal whatever they could carry off, and Stoner's daddy fought to drive them out. For that, he'd been arrested, tried, and hanged. Something about killing a tax collector and a sheriff who foreclosed on farms.

It was enough to make you hate the men responsible for breaking down your family. And if you couldn't find them, if you didn't really know who gave the orders, you could still hate those you had to see and deal with every day: the carpetbaggers, scalawags, and darkies pretending they were citizens.

Stoner had been too young to fight when people like his daddy were redeeming Dixie for home rule, but he had learned from their example and he never missed an opportunity to put a black man in his proper place. Force those he hated to remember where

203

they'd come from and where they would be again if he had anything to say about it.

And since Stoner couldn't do it all alone, he had been pleased to find a place serving the Dragon and the Brotherhood. Except that now, it meant he had to babysit for Bobby Shelton on a job that anyone could do with one eye closed.

Or, maybe not.

Stoner had spoken to Joe Eddie at the Empire Arms, told him that someone would be coming for a passkey around midnight, and that he should hand it over without asking any questions if he meant to keep his job. Joe Eddie, being yellow for the most part, hadn't argued.

Stoner's plan, having arranged for Shelton to receive the key, involved sneaking around behind the Empire Arms and coming at it through the courtyard. Slipping in that way, unseen, he'd be in a position to support Shelton if anything went wrong.

And now, by God, it had.

Stoner had barely set foot in the yard when he saw someone exit from the privy, moving off toward the back door of the hotel. Someone who'd dressed for the occasion with a gunbelt draped across one shoulder, ready for a cross-hand draw.

Okay, he couldn't see the midnight rambler's face, and moonlight wasn't all that great for judging shirt colors, but wasn't that the goddamned marshal there in front of him? The one whom Bobby Shelton was supposed to be surprising in his bed, right about now?

Stoner experienced a fleeting thrill of panic, seeing in his mind how it could all go wrong and leave him standing in the Dragon's office, hat in hand, explaining how another brilliant plan had blown up in his face.

Not this time, he decided, as he drew his pistol.

It would be so easy, aim and fire from the shadows and call it a night, but Stoner caught himself short of cocking his six-gun.

If something went wrong and he missed, or just wounded the lawman and then couldn't finish the job, he'd be worse off than ever with Dixon. Better to wait and follow the target inside, then be ready to help out if Shelton couldn't handle him.

He watched the tall, slim figure pass through the hotel's back door, gave him enough time to have reached the stairs, then followed at a jog.

Bobby Shelton's legs were trembling as he climbed the stairs, silently cursing himself as a coward. His job should be easy, his target sleeping. So what in hell was he worried about?

Plenty.

When the Dragon had picked him to handle Judge Dennison's murder in Enid, it had been a colossal promotion. Before that, Shelton had been little more than an overseer on Dixon's plantation, supervising the darkies and wielding a lash when they got out of line, maybe showing some muscle to merchants in town when their payments of tribute were slow in coming. He'd taken his orders from Stoner, rarely direct from the boss.

The Enid contract would've set him up for good, if he'd succeeded — but, of course, he'd blown it. Barely made it out of town alive with bullets whispering around his ears, and then came home to learn the judge was still alive, despite the hits he'd taken while Shelton stood watching.

The Dragon had punished Shelton for that failure, but whipping wasn't the end of it. Now, he had to deal with the damned U.S. marshal, possibly the same one who'd tried to kill him in Enid.

Repaying the favor, he thought, but the joke didn't fly.

The stairs topped out at one end of a corridor that ran the full length of the second floor. The marshal's room, he knew, was all the way back, overlooking the hotel's backyard.

Shelton paused on the landing to check his shotgun, dropped his key in the process, and winced as it clattered across the floorboards. Frozen there, half expecting the marshal to open his door and start blasting, Shelton cursed himself again in whispers until he ran out of breath.

When no one killed him on the spot, he stooped, reclaimed the key, and put it in a pocket of his coat. He went ahead and broke the shotgun open then, already feeling stupid, and of course the shells were right there in both barrels, where he put them in the first place.

Idiot!

Closing the shotgun's breech, he made another sharp metallic sound that no one who had handled guns was likely to mistake. Shelton was close to weeping at the depth of his own foolishness as he began to move along the hallway, toward the last door on his left.

He paced it off, walking with measured strides and praying that the floorboards wouldn't play a squeaky tune to wake his enemy. He'd been in the hotel before, of course, but hadn't gone upstairs. Its smell and wallpaper were new to him.

Halfway between the staircase and his destination, he remembered to extract the passkey from his pocket, nearly dropping it again. That would've been the last straw, might have sent him fleeing to the street and almost certain death, but at the last split second he had caught it, clutching it as if it were a snake trying to bite him.

I'd be safer with the snake, he thought and pushed it out of mind.

At last, he stood before the marshal's door, passkey extended in his left hand, ten-gauge cocked and weighing heavy in his right. He didn't dare to breathe while he was angling the key into the keyhole, desperate not to miss and scrape across the brass faceplate. He got that right somehow, then had to turn the key slowly and silently.

Please, Jesus, make it quiet!

By the time he felt the tumblers turning, Shelton's lungs were aching and his vision swam with swarms of tiny half-transparent gnats. He drew a breath, steadied himself, then turned the knob and pushed his way inside, letting the door swing wider on its own, his left hand coming back to brace the sawed-off's stubby barrels.

His first blast thundered in the bedroom,

echoed down the hall behind him like the clap of doom. A dozen buckshot pellets ripped into the bed and made it jump, sent feathers flying from a comforter or pillow, maybe both.

He squeezed the second trigger half a heartbeat later, holding on the same mark as he fired. Some of his pellets hit the wall behind the bed this time, as if it mattered. Two blasts at a ten-foot range were the equivalent of twenty-four shots from a .32-caliber pistol.

And dead was dead.

He crossed the smoky room, drawing his pistol just in case the marshal might be clinging to the last grim breath of life. He prodded at the ripped and riddled bedspread with the six-gun's muzzle, whipped it back, and saw —

Nothing.

He'd killed a goddamn empty bed.

Spinning around too late, Shelton covered the room behind him, waiting for a shadow shape to take its turn and drop him where he stood. When nothing moved, he started thinking, wondering how he'd explain his latest failure to the Dragon.

Wondering exactly where in hell the marshal was.

Shelton retreated through the open bedroom door and got his answer. Marshal Slade was standing in the hallway, twenty feet in front of him.

"Looking for me?" the lawman asked.

Slade hadn't seen the gunman opening his door. He'd reached the second floor just as the first explosion rocked the sleeping Empire Arms and saw the muzzle flash inside his room. And he'd been moving forward, footsteps covered by the echoes, when his would-be killer fired the second blast.

A ten-gauge, by the sound of it, and as the nervous-looking shooter cleared Slade's doorway, he could see it was a double-barrel, not another Winchester repeater. There'd been no time for his adversary to reload the shotgun, but the prowler had a pistol in his hand.

"Looking for me?" Slade asked, primarily to throw his enemy off balance. As he spoke, though, something clicked inside his mind. He recognized the half-familiar face.

From where?

Enid. It had to be.

The one who got away.

The gunman didn't answer, though he hesitated long enough to weigh his options. He could either drop his guns and raise his hands or try to fight his way past Slade.

In fact, he did a bit of both, dropping the empty scattergun and bringing up his newly freed left hand to fan the hammer on his six-shooter, slamming three shots at Slade in rapid-fire.

It was a decent move and might've saved him if they'd been six feet apart, instead of twenty. As it was, the fanning simply spoiled his aim and sent his bullets off the mark, slapping into the ceiling and the left-hand wall.

Slade took a heartbeat longer, aimed, and put his bullet more or less dead center through the nameless shooter's chest. The .45 Long Colt's impact lifted his target off the floor and bounced him off the doorjamb on his way to landing in a boneless heap.

Slade took no chances with the dead or dying gunman, making his approach both slow and cautious. When he came within reach, he kicked the shooter's pistol clear of twitching fingers, but a closer look told him that it was just a dying muscle spasm, not a last attempt to raise the gun and fire.

A door opened behind him, bringing Slade around with pistol at the ready, but he saw no menace in the sleepy female face regarding him with shock and fear. The tousle-haired woman ducked back out of sight, slammed her door, and locked it.

Slade glanced into his room, saw that the bed was shot to hell, then closed the door on drifting clouds of gunsmoke and used the prowler's key, still in the lock, to secure it.

Someone had used a sharp object to scratch the word MASTER across the key's clover-shaped bow, which told Slade he should have a word with Joe Eddie, the hotel's helpful clerk.

He took the dead man's pistol, shoved it down inside his belt, against his spine, and stalked back toward the stairs.

Stoner was at the bottom of the staircase, one foot on the first step's tread, when Bobby Shelton fired the first blast from his ten-gauge, somewhere overhead. It seemed to shake the whole damned building and echoed in the stairwell, making Stoner grimace.

"Jesus! What was that?" a frightened voice demanded, coming from behind him.

Stoner turned to find Joe Eddie standing in the middle of the lobby, hands clenched in front of him with fingers interlaced, as if he was preparing to recite a prayer in church.

The second blast seemed even louder than

the first. Joe Eddie flinched and did a little backward two-step, eyes wide in fright.

"You want to go and have a look?" asked Stoner. "I could wait down here. You check it out, then come on back and fill me in."

"Nuh . . . nuh . . . no!"

"Then maybe you should just get lost."

He didn't wait to see Joe Eddie mind him. Didn't give a damn, in fact, whether the clerk stayed where he was or ran home to his mama.

Stoner had a job to do.

It wasn't good enough for him to wait downstairs and hope that Shelton had discovered Slade was missing from his room, then set a trap to take the marshal down. There had been time enough for him to use the passkey, slip into the lawman's room, and wait there, but just barely. If he'd dawdled on the way. . . .

Three quick-fire pistol shots cracked through the ringing silence, catching Stoner halfway up the stairs. Another came, no more than half a heartbeat later, then the silence fell once more.

The smell of gunsmoke made his nostrils twitch.

Stoner supposed that Shelton must be dead. Clearly, he had accomplished nothing with the shotgun, or the pistol would've been superfluous. Hit someone with a double load of buckshot from a ten-gauge, and you didn't need a Colt to finish him.

Three rapid shots, then one. Bad news.

Stoner could picture it unfolding in his mind. Shelton had used the master key as planned, barged into Slade's room shooting, and bagged nothing but his linens. By the time he recognized his error, Slade was there and Shelton must've botched another chance to drop him, fumbling with the scattergun, then firing too fast with his sidearm for a hit.

The last shot, Stoner knew as sure as anything, would have been Slade's.

Now Stoner had a choice to make. He could take off and blame the mess on Shelton, risk putting his own neck on the Dragon's chopping block, or he could make it right.

Which boiled down, finally, to no damn choice at all.

He climbed another step with leaden feet, then stopped himself. Why blunder into Slade and get his head blown off, when he could wait in ambush on the stairs and catch the lawman coming down to find Joe Eddie and report the killing?

It was perfect.

Stoner thumbed back the hammer on his

pistol, eased his left shoulder against the wall, and settled in to wait.

Slade was picturing his fingers clenched around Joe Eddie's throat, pinning the little rodent up against a wall, or maybe shaking him until his back teeth rattled and the truth came spilling out of him. No bruises, mind you.

Not unless the prick resisted.

Slade had no doubt as to who'd given the order for his execution, but he doubted that the boss man would've come to the hotel himself, soiling his hands with something so mundane. There'd be a go-between, and when the clerk had named him, Slade would wrap his hand around that throat, in turn, and so on up the line until he had his man.

It might not qualify as great detective work, but at the moment he was more concerned about results.

And just a pinch of sweet revenge.

Slade was ten feet from the staircase leading to the lobby when a new thought stopped him in his tracks. Dixon had sent four men to kill Judge Dennison and seven to attack the Jackson homestead. Why should Slade assume that only one was sent for him?

And if the corpse he'd left behind had

reinforcements, where would they be waiting? Where was Slade certain to go if no one rallied to the sound of gunfire on the second floor?

Downstairs.

He backtracked, not quite tiptoeing, to reach the dead man lying at the doorway to his room. Slade played a hunch and patted down his coat pockets, then tried his vest. Found four spare shells for the ten-gauge, distributed two on each side.

Slade took all four, then broke the shotgun and ejected its two empties. He reloaded, closed the breech and pulled back both hammers, then put the extra cartridges into his own vest pocket, within easy reach.

He took it easy, walking back down to the stairs. No one had come up yet to check on all the ruckus, so he figured that Joe Eddie must've flown the coop, or else someone was keeping him downstairs. Whichever it turned out to be, Slade didn't think the clerk had guts enough to face him with a gun.

And if he did . . . well, he could bleed the same as anybody else.

Slade reached the stairs, imagining shooters crouched somewhere below, ready to fire as he descended. They'd expect him to be standing up, but Slade wasn't required to play by anybody else's rules.

Not when his life was riding on the line.

He sank slowly to hands and knees, then bellied down along the springy hallway carpeting. Crawling around the corner seemed an awkward proposition, so he braced himself, shoved off, and rolled onto the landing, ending with his gaze and borrowed scattergun aimed down the staircase.

He'd expected two or three men, but saw only one — and sure enough, the shooter had his pistol aimed somewhere around chest-high for Slade. The stranger cursed and tried to bring it down, but Slade was disinclined to wait and give him the first shot.

He squeezed one of the shotgun's triggers, rode its bruising recoil, narrowing his eyes against the storm of plaster dust and crimson spray that filled the air down range. His target may have screamed as he was falling backward, but it was impossible to say for sure with thunder in his ears.

Slade saved the other barrel, just in case, but no one else popped out to challenge him as he descended to the lobby, moving past his second corpse kill of the evening. No need to check for this one's pulse, based on the damage he'd sustained to face and chest.

Slade walked around the check-in counter, scanned the little office tucked away behind it, and confirmed that Joe Eddie had fled. No matter. If he wasn't on a horse already, racing out of town, Slade trusted his ability to track the little bastard down.

But first, he'd have a word with Galen Evans and inform the sheriff that he had some late-night cleanup work ahead of him.

9

Slade woke in a new bed, with dawn's pale light breaking outside his window. The hotel's clerk had not returned after the shooting, so Slade had surveyed the rooms available and took the so-called bridal suite, which proved to be a slightly larger version of his former room, located at the southeast corner of the third floor, overlooking Main Street.

So much for the honeymoon.

Before he could switch rooms and shift his gear, Slade had to deal with Sheriff Evans. He'd thought the law in Last Resort might show up on his own, given the sounds of midnight battle in his sleepy town, but as it was Slade had to grab one of the neighbors who responded to the shots and send him off to fetch the sheriff.

Evans took the better part of twenty minutes getting there, and he smelled of whiskey on arrival. He had nothing much to say as Slade showed him the bodies, one sprawled in the hotel lobby, one upstairs. The climb took something out of Evans, almost winded him, but maybe that was just the liquor.

"Do you recognize them?" Slade inquired.

The sheriff nodded, clearly hating to admit it. "Yeah, I do."

"I'll need their names," Slade said.

"That's Bobby Shelton," Evans told him, looking at the corpse outside Slade's door. "And you've got Jesse Stoner down below."

"They live in town?"

"Not quite," Evans replied.

"So, let me guess. The Dixon spread?"

Another gloomy nod. "Jesse's his foreman. Was."

"He'll soon be running short of hands," Slade said.

Alarm flared in the sheriff's rheumy eyes. "You don't think Mr. Dixon sent them here, do you? He's a respected businessman. What kind of sense does that make, anyway?"

"Sheriff," Slade said, "your Bobby Shelton was the fourth man back in Enid, when they hit Judge Dennison. I saw him then, but missed my shot. This evening he was kind enough to let me have a second chance."

"Well, there you are," said Evans, sounding almost hopeful for a change. "He got mixed up in that, likely with Stoner, and they're both dead now. You've wrapped it up. Call it a job well done."

"I might, except it isn't finished yet."

"Come on, Marshal. You can't believe that Mr. Dixon —"

Slade cut through it, saying, "What I don't believe in is coincidence, Sheriff. So far today, I've got *seven* of Dixon's — and one of them his foreman — 'mixed up' in two separate attempted murders. Now this one" — a nod toward Shelton's corpse — "is linked back to Judge Dennison. That's *ten* dead shooters, all wearing the same tattoos. So what I *don't* believe is that your Mr. Dixon's ignorant and pure as driven snow."

At mention of the shared tattoos, Evans had glanced toward Shelton's body, fairly wincing when he saw shirt cuffs unbuttoned, sleeves drawn back.

"That's right," Slade said. "I checked while I was waiting for you. I've been thinking maybe I should have some other folks in town roll up their sleeves."

"There's no law against joining clubs or parties," Evans said, defensively. His eyes avoided Slade's.

"Not if they stay within the law," Slade

granted. "When they turn to plotting crimes, the courts call it conspiracy."

"You say that like I oughta know something about it," Evans grumbled.

"I'm just making conversation, Sheriff. Hoping no one else gets killed."

"What should I do about this?" Evans asked him, indicating Bobby Shelton's corpse.

"First thing," said Slade, "wake up the undertaker. Get him started on the preparations. He'll be glad to get the business. Then, you need to think about your own next step."

"Meaning?"

"Sometimes mistakes come back to haunt you," Slade replied, "unless you let them go and make amends."

"Supposing it's too late?"

"Some say there's hope as long as you're alive."

Evans was silent for another moment, then he shrugged. "What's your next move?" he asked.

Slade gambled, knowing it could be a critical mistake.

"Sometime tomorrow," he replied, "I'm riding out to see your Mr. Dixon."

Evans nodded, showing no surprise. "I was afraid of that," he said. "I haven't studied law much, but I know you can't just go out and arrest him or his men 'cause his men have those tattoos."

"Who said that I was going to arrest him, Sheriff?"

"But, I thought —"

"I'll need to meet him first. Talk to him. Maybe have a look around his place and see some of his other men. Law says that I need evidence for an arrest. I'm looking for it."

"You won't find anything," the sheriff said, without conviction.

"Not unless I try."

Evans seemed on the verge of saying more, but then he shrugged again and said, "I'll wake up Silas Diggs. He does the undertaking here in Last Resort."

"Must keep him busy," Slade told Evans's retreating back.

Now here it was, another day, and he'd be meeting William Dixon in a few more hours. After breakfast, that would be, and once he'd made a few more stops along the way. There was no point in rushing it.

Slade reckoned it was fifty-fifty, whether Evans would alert Dixon to his impending visit or stand back and keep it to himself. Whichever way the sheriff played it, Slade knew that he would be walking straight into the lion's den.

And hoped he would be ready for what-ever happened next.

As Galen Evans saw it, he was obligated to inform the Dragon that another couple of his men were dead. That didn't mean he had to ride out in the middle of the night, however, so he waited for the sunrise, had a few more drinks to stiffen up his spine, then started on the four-mile ride from Last Resort to Dixon's spread.

And hated every minute of it.

Not the ride, per se, although the lazy rocking of his palomino mare sent waves of dull pain rolling back and forth inside his whiskey-sodden head. Evans had washed up, shaved, and changed his clothes, then chewed some cloves that almost made him puke before he left, all hoping that the smell of liquor wouldn't follow him into his meeting with the Dragon.

If it did . . . well, then, to hell with it.

Walking a tightrope was enough to make a saint toss back a few, and Evans knew full well he'd never been a saint or anything close to it. If the Dragon didn't think that he was up to handling the bullshit that was thrown his way, then let him find somebody else to wear the badge.

And what would happen then?

Would he be cast aside, or planted in a shallow grave?

What difference does it make? a small voice in his head inquired.

Not much, maybe.

A rider came to meet him on the outskirts of the Dragon's property and rode back to the house with Evans, making small talk that the sheriff mostly managed to ignore. It didn't seem to hurt the lookout's feelings.

One of Dixon's darkies met him at the door, dressed up in fancy butler's clothes. The sheriff followed him along a hallway lined with mounted deer antlers, their points aimed toward the ceiling as if lifted to salute him.

Not damned likely, Evans thought, as he was shown into the Dragon's library.

Dixon was waiting for him, standing by the cold fireplace, smoking a long cigar. "Bad news brings you out early," he suggested.

"Yes, sir."

"Well, let's have it, then."

"It's Jesse Stoner and that Bobby Shelton," Evans told him.

"What have they been up to, Galen?"

"Mostly getting killed."

The Dragon didn't seem surprised. He

nodded thoughtfully, smoke curling from his nostrils like a true dragon of olden times, before he said, "The marshal?"

"Dropped 'em both, without a scratch on him," said Evans.

"That's too bad."

"Yes, sir. You might say that. He didn't have much trouble putting it together."

"With your help, by any chance?" asked Dixon.

"Didn't need it. He saw Shelton back in Enid, when they hit the judge. Then, once he checked 'em for tattoos, that nailed it down."

"And has he checked *your* arms, Sheriff?"

"Not yet. He may, before much longer."

"What will you do then?" asked Dixon.

"Nothing much I can do. Like I told him, having a tattoo's not criminal, but he's got notions about claiming a conspiracy."

That put a frown on Dixon's face.

"He used that word?" the Dragon pressed.

"As we were standing over Bobby Shelton's body. Yes, sir."

"Well, we can't have that. Can we?"

"I can't help what he thinks," Evans replied. Then, without warning from his traitorous tongue, added, "Besides, he's not far wrong."

Dixon regarded him as if he'd dropped

his pants and shat on the library floor.

"I didn't say that he was *wrong*," the boss said, when he found his voice again. "I said we can't allow it."

"I've tried to see a way around it," Evans said, "but I keep coming up empty. Even if you kill him, they'll just send another marshal, and another after that one. Kill 'em all, they'll send the army. You can string it out awhile, but I don't see a happy ending."

Dixon smiled and said, "There are no happy endings, Galen. In the end, we're all worm bait."

"No need to rush it, then, is all I'm saying."

"It's important," Dixon told him, "that we stand for something while we live. You would agree with that, I'm sure."

Evans, who couldn't think of anything he'd stood for recently, nodded and shrugged at the same time.

Dixon pressed on, saying, "It had been forty years since the Confederacy made its stand on principle. The goddamned Yankees thought they had us beaten, back in '65, but they were wrong. The carpetbaggers thought that if they dressed a bunch of monkeys up in human clothes and called them citizens, they'd rule the South. And *they* were wrong. The bastards learned their lesson from the rope and lash. Then damned Ulysses Grant thought he could crush the Brotherhood with nigger troops, and *he* was wrong! We're still alive and kicking. Here to stay!"

It was the longest speech Evans had heard the Dragon make without a mask over his face, and from the sound of it he had to wonder if the man had lost his grip. Instead of saying that, he nodded, muttered, "Yes, sir," and prepared to take his leave.

"Is the marshal coming out to see me?" Dixon asked, when Evans was halfway to the door.

"Sometime today," Evans replied.

"Perfect," said Dixon, as he turned away. Smiling.

Slade stopped for breakfast at the Southern Belle — fried eggs with crispy bacon, cubed potatoes roasted to a golden brown, flapjacks, and coffee strong enough to make his hair stand up on end — before he walked down to the livery. The dun mare seemed relieved to see him, even more so to be heading out of town.

I know the feeling, Slade thought, as he rode through Last Resort.

A few more people stared at him this

morning than had watched him yesterday, when he'd arrived. Slade guessed that word of last night's shoot-out would've made the rounds by now, allowing everyone in town to choose up sides.

How many stood with William Dixon of their own accord, without arm-twisting, bribes, or any other kind of interference? How many were strong enough in opposition to the Big Man that they'd stand against him when — not *if* — push came to shove?

Slade wouldn't know until it happened.

And by then, there wouldn't be a damned thing he could do about it, except look out for himself.

As usual.

He didn't ride directly out to Dixon's spread but detoured past the Jackson place to see how they were holding up. As he approached, Colin Jackson stood waiting on the front porch, with a rifle in his hands.

"Marshal," he said, when Slade was close enough for conversation, "I was hoping you'd still be alive today."

Slade had to smile at that. Dismounting, he told Jackson, "Some in town may find it disappointing, but I'm not done yet."

"Mayzie's been praying for you," Jackson said. "I'm not much good at it, myself."

Never religious on his own account, Slade let that slide and asked, "Have you had any trouble since the business yesterday?"

Children spilled out onto the porch, followed by Jackson's smiling wife, as Jackson said, "No one's come back to claim their leavings. I suppose the guns are mine, now."

"Best to keep them handy, just in case," Slade said.

Jackson nodded. Said, "It's nice of you to check on us again. I know you've got your hands full as it is, in Last Resort. We're much obliged."

"Fact is," Slade said, "I'm headed out to Dixon's place this morning."

Mayzie Jackson gave a little gasp at that. Her husband frowned and said, "Marshal, with all respect, I'm bound to say that doesn't strike me as a wise idea."

"You may be right," Slade granted. "But I have to meet the man and talk to him, at least, before I file charges."

"You'd actually *charge* him?" Mayzie asked, sounding as startled as if Slade had said there was a colony of fairies living in her barn.

"Yes, ma'am, if I can bring the court sufficient evidence. Nailing his men's no problem, but they all keep dying on me. What I need is proof that Dixon gave their marching orders when they came out after you and tried to kill Judge Dennison."

"Those rats won't give him up," Colin replied. "Alive or dead, they hang together."

"There's a chance I may not need them," Slade replied. "You may already know that some folks back in town don't care for Dixon any more than you do."

Mayzie blurted out, "There's Mr. —"

"Mayzie!" Colin cut her short, then told Slade, "I don't like passing names around. Don't want friends hurt for being decent to us."

"Understood," Slade said. "I've met some of your friends in Last Resort. I'm hoping to meet more. If some of them will testify that Dixon pressured them to freeze you out or sent his men around to pressure *them,* it may be all I need."

"That still leaves them he rents from Sheriff Evans, for his cotton fields," Colin replied.

"I'm working on the sheriff, too," Slade said, "but I don't need him, necessarily. If I can bring the people he's arrested into court and let them tell their stories, he and Dixon might wind up sharing a prison cell."

"Wouldn't *that* be a hallelujah morning," Mayzie said.

"So, first things first," Slade said. "I

thought I should tell someone where I'm going, just in case something goes wrong. It's what, another hour from here to Dixon's spread?"

"About that," Colin granted.

"And I'm not expecting much, in terms of hospitality," said Slade. "All things considered, I suppose I should be passing back this way in four, five hours, tops."

"You'll need to stay for supper, then," said Mayzie, without asking Colin. "We insist!"

Colin could only smile, adding, "I might see if the Abernathys want to come. Martin will be disturbed he missed you, as it is."

"I don't want to impose," Slade said.

"We'll hear no more about it, then," said Colin. "Take care in that nest of vipers, and we'll hope to see you soon."

"I'm looking forward to it," Slade replied, and couldn't help but smile.

Slade thought of Faith as he was riding from the Jackson homestead out to William Dixon's property. He didn't know what waited for him there — or back in Enid, where Faith was waiting to have their heart-to-heart talk.

There'd been times, in the not-so-distant past, when Slade had wondered if his heart was even functioning. It moved his blood around all right, but on the other hand it never seemed to yearn for home, a family, or any other "normal" thing that most people appeared to take for granted.

Then he had received the telegram announcing that his brother had been murdered, and his world turned upside down. It seemed that he'd been sucked into another kind of life entirely: one with roots, responsibilities, and something he'd begun to think might be the thing called love he'd heard so much about.

Or, maybe not.

One thing was sure enough. They wouldn't have that talk if Slade got careless with his enemies.

And how reckless was Dixon, really?

Slade was convinced that he'd dispatched the shooters who had nearly killed Judge Dennison and —

Slade stopped short, as if his thoughts had run headlong into a stockade fence. It struck him that he didn't know if Dennison was still alive or not, whether he was investigating an *attempted* murder or a certified political assassination. Dennison's condition had been critical when he'd left Enid, with Doc Hauser saying it could still go either way.

So, which way had it gone? Was Dennison's survival still in doubt, or had he passed on to whatever end awaited humans when they died?

And was there anything beyond this life at all?

Slade's personal acquaintance with religion had been severed when he left home in his youth. He knew what preachers said about the afterlife, rewards in Heaven versus punishment in Hell, but knowing and believing were two very different things.

He'd sent his share of men off to what some folks called the "Other Side," but they'd been adversaries bent on killing him, and Slade's feelings on that subject were limited to sweet relief when he survived. Of course, he'd thought about the subject after learning that his twin brother was dead, but Slade had come to no conclusions.

And what difference did it make?

If what the preachers taught was true, he'd find out soon enough. If they were wrong, he'd learn that, too — or *wouldn't,* if nothing whatsoever lay beyond his time on Earth.

In either case, Slade didn't want to rush his shuffle off the mortal coil. And when he went, assuming he was *pushed,* he meant to take the pushers with him if he could.

If that made him unworthy of a mansion in the sky, so be it.

Slade knew when he was nearing Dixon's spread because the air changed. Cotton does that, when it's planted in long rows, irrigated, and left to steam beneath a hot sun all day long. There was a smell about the cotton fields, as well, that told Slade he had almost reached his destination.

But the riders found him first.

They came from the northeast, approaching at a gallop with their rifles at the ready. Slade considered drawing his but then thought better of it, choosing not to risk the provocation. When they saw his badge, the pair relaxed and put the long guns back into their saddle boots.

"Marshal," the taller of them said, "we've been expecting you."

Slade wasn't sure if that meant Sheriff Evans had revealed his plans to visit Dixon, or the boss man simply took it as a given that he'd have to meet with Slade. In either case, it hardly mattered. He'd arrived now, and the planter's men weren't shooting at him.

Yet.

"You're my escort?" Slade inquired.

"Looks like it," said the spokesman for the duo.

"No point in wasting time, then," Slade replied.

He didn't argue when they flanked him, just made sure that neither of them rode within arm's reach. Slade was prepared to kill them both, or try to, if it felt that either one was on the verge of making a false move, but they surprised him. Sitting easy in their saddles, barely speaking, they conveyed him past one of the sprawling cotton fields toward Dixon's home.

Scattered across the field, Slade counted twenty-odd black men and women stooped beneath the sun, hoeing and weeding in a ragged line that stretched from east to west. A few of them glanced up as Slade rode past with his bookends, but none were brave enough to make eye contact.

Their reserve was evidently prompted by a third rider, who sat off to one side, watching them work. The overseer wore twin pistols on his hips, carried a rifle braced across his lap, and had a bullwhip coiled around his saddle horn. The last piece of equipment told Slade all he had to know about the state of life for William Dixon's field hands.

He was coping with a morbid sense of dread as they entered the yard of Dixon's home when Slade obtained his first view of the man himself.

Slade had never seen Dixon before in his life, but who else could it be on the boss man's front porch, dressed up like a Kentucky colonel and puffing on a fat cigar? The planter's eyes tracked Slade through his approach but they revealed nothing. For all the life they showed, Slade thought they could've been glass orbs inserted by a taxidermist.

Slade dismounted without waiting for an invitation, tied his mare to a hitching post with its own water trough, and climbed the porch steps to stand level with his host. A glance from Dixon sent his escorts wheeling back across the yard and galloping away.

A third rider came out to join them, suddenly appearing from the east end of the rambling house, and Slade guessed that he knew how Dixon had been warned of his arrival. There'd been *three* scouts riding the perimeter, and one of them had left his pals to deal with Slade, while he raced off to rouse their master.

"William Dixon?" he inquired.

"The very same."

Slade introduced himself and Dixon offered him a soft hand, unaccustomed to labor, but his grip had power behind it, warning Slade that muscles lurked beneath the dove-gray tailored suit and starched white shirt. The planter's smile was neutral, uninvolved. It could as easily have been a carving on a totem pole.

"Come in, please," Dixon offered, leading Slade into his home. "I don't know why you're here, of course, but hospitality demands I offer you refreshments. If you'll step this way . . ."

They wound up in what some folk might refer to as a drawing room or library. Three walls were lined with bookshelves from floor to ceiling, while the fourth consisted of tall windows facing more of Dixon's cotton fields. Four hand-carved wooden chairs surrounded an ornate table at the heart of the room.

Dixon was saying, "Marshal, have a seat, by all means. What can I offer to cut the trail dust? Kentucky bourbon? Irish whiskey? Scotch?"

"I wouldn't mind a cup of coffee," Slade replied.

Dixon tugged on a bellpull near the door and waited for a black man in an ill-fitting butler's costume to arrive. He called the servant Amos, ordered Slade's coffee and bourbon for himself. The black man bowed, muttered, "Yes, sir," and left.

"Won't be a moment," Dixon said, moving to take a seat across the table from where Slade had placed himself. "Now, if you don't mind, Marshal, would you tell me how I come to have the pleasure of your company?"

Slade said, "There's not much pleasure to it, I'm afraid. A few days back, in Enid, four men tried to kill Judge Isaac Dennison."

"The hanging judge. I've heard his name, of course," said Dixon. "You say *tried* to kill him?"

"He's still alive," Slade said, compelled again to wonder whether that was true, "but not for lack of trying on their part."

"Outrageous," Dixon said. "What will they think of next?"

Slade fought an urge to lean across and slap the big man's face. Instead, he told Dixon, "Three men died trying. One escaped. I traced him back to Last Resort."

"May I ask how?"

"It's what I do," Slade said, refusing to elaborate, "On my way here, I interrupted seven men trying to kill some homesteaders."

"Lucky for them. The homesteaders, I mean."

"But not so lucky for the raiders. Five went down, two got away."

"You must be quite a hand," Dixon observed.

"I do all right."

"And then some, from the sound of it."

"It turns out that the shooters from the homestead worked for you," Slade said, stretching a point but feeling sure that he was on the mark.

Dixon's reply was cut short by the black butler's return. He bore a silver tray, supporting Dixon's liquor glass and Slade's coffee in an ornate cup with matching saucer. The servant delivered their drinks and bowed his way out of the study.

"*My* employees you say?" Dixon frowned, sipped his bourbon, and set the glass down. "Well, anything's possible. I have considerable turnover among my hands, of course. Many who try the job for size can't follow orders to my satisfaction."

Forging onward, Slade told Dixon, "Then, last night, a couple more guns tried to take me down at the hotel, in town."

"The Empire Arms?"

"That's it."

"How do you like your room?" asked Dixon.

"I prefer it without bullet holes."

"Of course. Please, do proceed."

Slade drank some coffee, then said, "As

you see, they didn't pull it off. It was a funny thing, though."

"What was?" Dixon pressed.

"One of the shooters was the fourth man from the ambush on Judge Dennison."

"Do tell?"

Slade nodded. "And the sheriff tells me that his sidekick was your foreman."

"Jesse Stoner?" Dixon wore a startled face.

"The very same," Slade echoed Dixon's comment from the porch, mere moments earlier, and watched a hint of color tinge the planter's cheeks.

"Well, I'm astounded," Dixon said. "I haven't seen Jess yet, today."

"You want to visit him, he's at the undertaker's, back in town."

"Sounds like you've had a busy week, Marshal."

"It isn't over yet," Slade said.

"What's next?"

Slade took another sip of coffee and replied, "Let's start with you explaining what your men are up to, riding over half the territory, killing folks or trying to. The last I heard, that wasn't part of growing cotton."

"I'm a man of many interests, Marshal."

Slade had a response in mind, but it eluded him somehow. And when he tried to speak, he couldn't seem to form the words that he was groping for. In fact, it seemed he couldn't really manage any words at all.

A wave of dizziness washed over him, followed by anger at his own stupidity. His left arm swept across the table, sent the tainted cup of coffee flying, as his right groped for the Peacemaker.

Christ, it was heavy! Anchored in its holster somehow, not about to budge.

Slade struggled to his feet and found his legs had turned to rubber. Mouthing garbled curses as the whole world slid away from him, he caromed off the polished table and collapsed. The floor rushed up to meet him, smashed into his face, and Slade was gone.

10

Slade's dreams were bad, but waking up was hell. His mouth was desert dry and tasted as if something small and furry had crawled down his throat to die, about three days ago. His head ached viciously, reminding Slade of once when he'd been pistol-whipped, but there were no specific sore spots, just a brutal throbbing everywhere inside his skull.

Beyond that, as he struggled back to consciousness, Slade found that he was sitting upright, more or less, bound to a straight-backed chair. Keeping his eyes closed for the moment, Slade tested his bonds and found that rope encircled his chest and waist, as well as his wrists, fore-arms, calves, and ankles.

In short, he wasn't going anywhere.

Slade cracked his eyelids next, regretting it as soon as dim light made the short trip from his pupils to his optic nerves. Vision was blurred at first, though whether from the pain inside his head or some residual effect of being drugged, he couldn't say. It cleared by slow degrees, revealing that his prison was some kind of storage room, illuminated by a lamp somewhere behind him, burning with its wick turned low.

So, he'd been drugged instead of poisoned, which had been his last coherent thought before he hit the floor in Dixon's library. A *poison* strong enough to take him down in seconds flat wouldn't wear off and leave him with a simple — if atrocious — headache.

Hell, it wouldn't leave him breathing.

As to *what* they'd slipped into his coffee, Slade had no idea. He couldn't even guess how long he'd been unconscious, but it struck him that his enemies could easily have killed and buried him — or buried him alive, for that matter — while he was out.

That meant the boss man wanted him alive.

At least, for now.

A voice from somewhere at his back told Slade, "You're wondering what hit you. It was chloral hydrate."

Dixon moved around to stand in front of him. Slade recognized him from the gray trousers and didn't risk a worse headache by leaning back to eye the bastard's face.

"So, we'll consider this your full confession, then," Slade said.

"I'm not a Catholic," said Dixon. "And if you're referring to a criminal confession, it won't do you any good. You've seen your last courtroom."

"It wasn't my trial I was thinking of," Slade told him.

"If you think I'll be tried for something, you're delusional," Dixon replied.

"It doesn't end with me," Slade said. "No matter what you tell yourself, there'll always be another marshal. And another after him."

Dixon retreated from his field of vision, then came back dragging a second chair. The grating sound drove spikes of pain into Slade's head. Dixon reversed the chair and sat down straddling it, arms folded across its top rail.

"That's better," he said, as his eyes locked with Slade's. "It makes me nervous when you're talking to my crotch."

"You should be nervous," Slade advised him.

"All those other marshals coming to avenge you?" Dixon answered, not quite mocking him. "You may be right. My good friend Sheriff Evans thinks there may be soldiers coming."

"That's another possibility."

"I'll cross that bridge when I come to it," Dixon said. "I've seen the face of war, my friend. It doesn't frighten me. I'd rather die fighting than lying in my bed, with some disease eating me from the inside out."

"Why not save time and shoot yourself right now?" Slade asked.

Dixon *did* laugh at that. Then said, "You've got some nerve, I give you that."

"What have I got to lose?"

"Another point." After a pause, Slade's captor said, "You must be curious about all this. The reasons for it? Why I sent those men after your precious judge?"

"Because you're crazy?" Slade suggested.

"Some might think so," Dixon answered. "But they have no sense of honor, duty, or responsibility. I'm guessing you were too young to have served during the war."

"Sorry I missed it," Slade replied. "Maybe I could've killed you then and saved some time."

Dixon ignored him, saying, "And I guess you don't know anything about what happened afterward, across the South. The so-called Reconstruction that was just a damned excuse for looting Dixie, ruining and raping anything the goddamned carpetbaggers couldn't carry off."

"I guess you miss your slaves," said Slade.

"Not anymore. Of course, we had to fight again, after the war, to keep from going under. Those who didn't fight were drowned in filth or swept away. Good riddance to the weaklings, anyhow."

"Sounds like you've got night riding with a bag over your head mixed up with military service," Slade remarked.

"It was a different uniform, that's all," Dixon replied. "Our enemies were still the same. They never change."

"Judge Dennison?"

"He was among the worst. You should've seen him, strutting in his finery, lording it over men who'd built plantations from the ground up over generations, telling them how they should treat their niggers. Sending decent men to prison or the gallows for defending their own race."

"That must've been a shock," Slade said. "Somebody saying that you couldn't run around and whip or kill someone because you didn't like the color of his skin."

"You think I hate niggers?" Dixon inquired. "You think the Brotherhood hates them? We don't, I promise you. We *love* them, in their proper place."

"Would that be chopping cotton free of charge and putting money in your pocket?"

"And why not?" Dixon demanded.

"Weren't we kind enough to bring them over here from Africa, give them a roof over their heads, clothes to wear, and three square meals a day? Didn't we save their heathen souls from Hell by introducing them to Jesus? What else do they want, for Christ's sake?"

"Maybe freedom," Slade suggested.

"To do what? Fall back into their old ways, living in mud huts and picking lice out of their hair until they starve from pure damned laziness?"

"Why wait this long to try for Dennison?" Slade asked, changing the subject.

"Circumstances put us out of touch," Dixon replied. "I never thought I'd hear his name again, but then Fate intervened. Of course, it took some preparation, planning."

"And your people screwed it up."

"You know the saying, Marshal. If at first you don't succeed . . ."

"It should be interesting, when you stand before the bench and hear him sentence you."

"I'll never take the gallows walk," Dixon assured him. "As for you . . ."

"You didn't set a certain time for supper?" Martin Abernathy asked. "Like six o'clock or something?"

"How am I supposed to know how long the marshal's business with the man is gonna take?" Colin Jackson replied.

Abernathy inhaled the rich aroma of roasting venison and felt his mouth begin to water. "I'm just wondering out loud," he said. "Not knowing when we ought to start in worrying."

"Too late for that," said Jackson. "I've been worried since he told me he was going out to Dixon's place. What good he hoped would come of that, I couldn't say."

"He likely feels a need to meet the man he's up against," said Abernathy. "You know how that goes."

"I haven't met the man," Jackson responded, "but I know he's rotten to the core and you can't trust a thing he says or does."

"Unless he's killin' you," said Abernathy. "I'd trust that."

Jackson wanted to check his pocket watch, find out what time it was in fact, but what would be the point? He hadn't fixed a time for Slade to sit down with his family and dine but . . .

"He said four, five hours, tops," Jackson remarked.

"Oh, yeah? How long ago was that?" asked Abernathy.

"Half past eleven, give or take."

Martin pulled out his own watch, then, opened its face, and frowned at what he saw.

"It's goin' on five forty-five," he said.

"Still lots of daylight left," Jackson replied.

"Man say that he'd be coming back at night? That doesn't sound like four, five hours. More like six or seven."

"He was guessing, Martin."

"Based on distance and the time he meant to spend with Dixon."

"Right."

"So, if you work it out, two hours was the very most he planned to stay there."

"We don't know that anything's gone wrong."

"Not knowing is the part that makes it dangerous," said Abernathy.

That was true, Jackson admitted to himself. He'd rather *know* gunmen were coming for him than to sit around and wonder all night long. Dixon and others like him thrived on mystery, did their best work when they could strike from ambush, taking someone by surprise. Strip off their masks and face them in the light of day, it turned out they were just trash waiting for a broom to sweep them all away.

Jackson had hoped that Marshal Slade might be that broom. But now . . .

"We need to do something," said Abernathy.

"Such as what?" Jackson inquired.

"Go looking for him, maybe."

"Up at Dixon's place?" Jackson was forced to smile at that. "You need a bigger hat, Martin. The sun's cooking your brain."

"I mean it, Colin. What if he's in trouble?"

"Well, what of it?" Jackson challenged him. "How many men does Dixon have? Thirty? Forty?"

"Less seven, thanks to Marshal Slade," Martin reminded him.

"Well, that makes all the difference." Jackson hated his mocking tone, but couldn't seem to curb it. "We'll just ride in there, the *two* of us, and say, 'Now, Massuh Dixon, don't you hurt dat mahshul none! He be our friend!' "

"Knock off that shit!" snapped Martin, angry now. "I'll never call another white man 'Master,' even if he has a *hundred* men with pistols pointed at my head."

"It doesn't take a hundred, Martin. Thirty's more than ample. We've got families to think about, if you recall."

"And what becomes of them if Dixon figures he can kill the law and get away with it? You reckon that'll make him more inclined to leave us all in peace? Because I don't."

"What could we do?" Jackson inquired.

"For one thing, we could have a look around, all sneaky-like. Look for the marshal's horse, that dun mare. If it's gone, then maybe he had other business after Dixon's, and he couldn't spare the time to come and tell you."

"Or he just forgot," said Jackson.

"I can't speak for anybody else," Martin replied, "but if I had a supper invitation to a place where I killed five men yesterday, I wouldn't just forget."

Jackson was silent for a long moment, then said, "You know we can't risk it by daylight."

"No," Martin agreed. "We'll have to wait another little while."

"Whiskey?" asked William Dixon.

Rafe Hollister considered it, as if it might be a trick question, then replied, "Yes, sir. Thank you."

Dixon poured two fingers of bourbon, passed the glass to Hollister, and watched its contents disappear in one quick gulp. He didn't offer seconds.

"I suppose you wonder why I called you in," said Dixon.

"Yes, sir. But if it's somethin' I supposedly did wrong —"

"Nothing like that," he interrupted Hollister before the younger man began to lie about some incident that Dixon neither knew nor cared about. "You've heard about poor Jesse, I suppose."

"Well, sure. That law dog kilt him."

"So he did. And now, I have that very dog penned up, downstairs."

Hollister shot a glance down toward his boots, as if the floor might open and reveal the scene to him, but then his eyes snapped back to meet Dixon's.

"You want me to take care of him?" asked Hollister.

"That's part of it," Dixon replied. "How do you feel about advancement, Rafe?"

"Say what?"

"Promotion," Dixon translated.

"Um, well . . ."

He almost reconsidered, but then forged ahead with it. "I want you to replace Jesse as my foreman, if you think you're up to it."

"Foreman?" A dumb-ass grin split Hollister's long, slightly lopsided face. "Well, sure. Yes, sir! And thanks a million!"

"We both know it doesn't pay that much."

Rafe laughed obligingly at Dixon's little joke, then nodded to confirm his understanding, adding, "No, sir."

"And you'd be taking Stoner's place as nighthawk, too."

It was the rank below his own Grand Dragon's post within the Brotherhood. Rafe Hollister seemed suitably impressed and grateful.

"Yes, sir! Thanks again, sir!"

"You're conversant . . . that is, do you understand the nighthawk's duties?"

"Carry out your orders," Hollister replied, "and supervise the others when they're takin' care of business. Help you lead the ceremonies."

"That's correct. Think you can handle it?"

"Yes, sir!"

"Your first order of business *will* be dealing with the marshal, as you mentioned."

"Glad to do it, sir. I'll have him out of here in two shakes."

"Not so fast," said Dixon. "Anything worth doing is worth doing well, don't you agree?"

"Well . . . sure."

"I'd like to make a real example of this nosy marshal, not just take him out and drop him in a hole somewhere. Know what I mean?"

Rafe thought about it for a moment, then replied, "Like what we did with Bobby Shelton, only make it permanent?"

"That's more like it," Dixon said.

"No problem, sir. I'll set it up and pick a team to do it right. You want the boys all gathered for the show?"

"Why not? Of course, we'll need a few on guard, to watch the field hands."

"Right. Yes, sir. Sure thing."

"I'll leave the preparations in your hands, then," Dixon said. "You have my every confidence."

"Okay," said Hollister, already on his feet, raring to go. "And thanks again, sir. For the opportunity and all."

"Just make me proud," Dixon replied. "That's thanks enough."

"I will. Yes, sir!"

"Maybe we ought to have a cross, this time."

Rafe grinned at that. "I'm on it, Mr. Dixon. Right away!"

"Good man."

Alone once more, Dixon allowed himself another glass of bourbon to relax his jangling nerves. It wasn't like him to be anxious, most particularly when his enemies were kneeling at his feet, but he was well aware that much remained undone, if he was going to preserve the small empire he'd built in Oklahoma.

First, he had to silence one Jack Slade and

make him disappear forever.

Second, he would have to send another team to Enid and complete the job that Bobby Shelton and the rest had bungled.

When that was done, there'd be no link connecting Dixon to the judge's death, except whatever thoughts Slade might have shared with others prior to leaving Enid. Ramblings about a matchbox and tattoos wouldn't mean anything, once Slade was gone for good and Dennison was silenced for all time.

Thy will be done, the Dragon thought. And whispered to himself, "Amen."

He had a chance to save it, after all, despite the clumsy errors that his men had made so far. He might even decide to lead the second team in Enid personally. Not to pull the trigger, mind you, but to supervise and make sure no one got cold feet.

If you want a job done right, do it yourself.

Slade strained against the bonds that held him fast and got nowhere. There wasn't any slack, no wriggle room, and whoever had tied the knots was smart enough to place them well beyond Slade's reach.

Okay, he thought. *Now what?*

There was no doubt in Slade's mind that he would be dead before sunrise unless he found a way out of the trap he'd stumbled into. Raging at himself for being foolish didn't help; in fact, it wasted precious energy that would be better used . . . well, *how*, exactly?

Bitterly, he ticked off things he *couldn't* do. Untie his bonds. Break them by sheer brute strength. Cut through them. Run and slam the chair against stone walls until it fell apart and freed him.

No, no, no.

He'd thought of tipping over sideways, falling to the floor, but finally decided that it would accomplish nothing beyond adding bruises to whichever side he fell upon. The chair was stout and solid and wouldn't shatter from a simple tip over, nor would the fall loosen his bonds.

He'd been disarmed completely while unconscious, couldn't even feel the small jackknife he always carried in his right-hand trouser pocket — which the ropes binding his arm wouldn't have let him reach, in any case.

Having dismissed all possibility of an immediate escape, Slade tried to think ahead. He didn't know what kind of death his captors had in mind for him, but if it was a simple bullet in the head, they would've finished it by now.

So, something else. Some kind of spectacle for Dixon's boys?

Slade sifted through his meager knowledge of the Ku Klux Klan. He knew the members dressed in funny costumes and adopted silly titles, though he couldn't think of one offhand. They hated blacks and anyone who stood up for them against racist whites, keeping a list of targets to be terrorized at night, when darkness cloaked their cowardice.

What else?

Dixon had spoken of a "gallows walk," and Slade recalled that Klansmen sometimes hanged their victims. Most of those were blacks who tried to vote or were accused of petty crimes, but he supposed they might string up a white man if it suited them.

Call that one riddle solved.

Slade knew they wouldn't hang him in the farmhouse basement, where a man of average height could touch the ceiling without reaching far above his head. Slade hadn't seen a proper scaffold, riding in, but there were trees aplenty on the Dixon spread, and he supposed his would-be executioners might have a special one they used for such occasions.

Meaning that they'd have to take him

outside, somewhere, for the necktie party. And unless they planned to tote him in his chair, trussed up, he'd be untied and marched out under guard.

How many guards?

Slade couldn't guess, but he supposed there would be two or three, at least, to cover him and guarantee delivery wherever he was going. Others would be waiting there, he guessed, to marvel at the spectacle.

Slade was a bit surprised to find that thoughts of hanging didn't frighten him, per se. He'd seen hard men reduced to tears and wailing as their time approached in Enid. One had begged Slade to be merciful and shoot him, claiming an escape attempt. Others were dragged or carried to their deaths, reduced to moaning semiconsciousness.

For Slade, the mode of dying wasn't terribly significant. A broken neck or bullet in the head: what difference did it really make? Of course, he would prefer a minimum of pain, perhaps a gliding into dreamless and eternal sleep when he was old and gray, but Slade had never reckoned that was in the cards for him.

He'd been a gambler all his life, in one way or another, and that hadn't changed when he put on a U.S. marshal's badge.

Each time he faced a fugitive, knocked on a door that might conceal a felon, Slade was gambling with his life.

This time, he'd made a stupid bet and lost his freedom. But he hadn't lost his life.

Not yet.

As long as he could breathe and think and move a muscle, he was in the game.

So, when they came for him, his first job was to weigh the odds against him. Count heads, check their weapons, see if he had any chance at all. He obviously wouldn't try to take them in the basement, where he could be bottled up forever by a single gunman covering the stairs.

But outside, in the house or yard . . .

It might be possible — and if he failed, at least he would've tried. Better to go down fighting than submitting to his enemies. A fusillade of bullets might be quicker than a noose, and if it hurt . . . well, it would all be over in a minute, maybe less.

Slade smiled and let himself relax a bit, saving his strength, slowing his respiration and his heartbeat. What he had in mind wasn't a fancy plan, but it was all that he could manage in the circumstances.

And with any luck at all, it just might do.

"You can't be doing this," said Mayzie Jackson. Colin thought she sounded desperate.

"I have to," he replied. "*We* have to."

"Why?" she challenged him. "Because the lawman stopped those men from killing us? Colin, I bless him for it, too, but that's his *job.* It's what they pay him for. He goes all over Oklahoma helping folks. He's not your special friend. He's not your family."

"No, ma'am, he's not," Colin replied. "But if he hadn't helped us yesterday, there'd *be* no family. We'd all be dead, most likely nothing but a pile of ashes in what used to be our home."

"You'd leave us here alone and unprotected, to ride off and help a stranger," she accused.

Feeling a flash of anger, he replied, "First off, he's not a stranger. I admit he's *strange,* a white man helping colored stay alive, but that's all the more reason to help him stay alive. Second, you're *not* alone. With Martin's brood, there's eight of you. And thanks to Dixon's men, you've got more guns than you can use. If anyone but me or Martin comes back to the house, think of the kids and shoot to kill."

"Colin —"

"Mayzie, I love you. You know that. You and the children are my life. But I still have to be a man. That's one reason we pulled up stakes and came here, in the first place. If I turn my back on Marshal Slade without at least going to see if we can help him, then I'm worse than useless. I'm no good to anyone at all."

Tears overflowed her eyes and glistened on her cheeks.

"Promise you'll watch yourself," she said.

"You know I will. And I'll have Martin watch me, too."

"If Marshal Slade's already dead, or you can't find him, or the odds are just too great against you, Colin, please, *please* give it up and come on home. Don't chase your pride into a grave for no good reason."

"I most certainly will not," he said.

She kissed him softly, then with greater passion, but remembered where they were and who was watching, backing off before it went too far. Her eyes flashed as she turned to Martin Abernathy, telling him, "I'm trusting you to bring my Colin home."

"I plan to bring us both home, Mayzie," he assured her.

"Don't plan, Martin. Do it!"

Abernathy bobbed his head, received a chaste kiss from his wife, Corina, then stood watching as the families retreated into Jackson's house.

"I'm having second thoughts about this,"

Martin said.

"Just *second* thoughts?" asked Jackson, smiling. "I'm already up to sixth or seventh."

"Mayzie's right, you know. There's only so much we can do against a gang like Dixon has."

"And we won't know what that is till we try," Jackson replied.

"I'm with you, Brother," Abernathy said. "But it would help me if I thought we have some kind of chance."

Dusk had already overtaken them, and night was swiftly coming on. Jackson mounted his gelding, staring down at Abernathy when he spoke again.

"We're going in to have a look around, Martin. If we see Marshal Slade's already dead, we slip back out and come on home. One of us can ride into Enid later, and report what happened."

"What if he's alive, though?" Abernathy asked.

"We can't plan that without judging the numbers and the layout of the place. I don't feel like committing suicide, even if I *do* owe the man my life and all that I hold dear."

Martin mounted his mare and slipped his Winchester into its saddle boot. When he was settled, he replied, "I know you, Colin.

You've been looking for a chance to settle with the Man since you were knee-high to a polecat."

"And I haven't found it yet," Jackson admitted. "But that doesn't mean I want to throw my life away on a lost cause."

"So, if we *can't* help, we lay back and get word to the other law in Enid, right?"

"That's what I said. And if it comes down to it, we agree to testify in open court against that bastard Dixon and the scum that rides for him."

"Oh, Colin —"

"Either that, or we can save some time and just start packing now. Move out of here and leave the land to Dixon, like he wanted in the first place."

"Now, I didn't say —"

"Because unless he's gotten rid of, one way or another, this will never truly be our home. You know that, don't you, Martin?"

Slowly, with reluctance, Abernathy answered.

"Yeah. I know that, true enough."

"Well, then?"

"We'd best be on our way, before it gets too late. Those Kluxers could be up and puttin' on their sheets by now."

"One thing about those white robes, if they wear 'em," Jackson said.

"What's that?"

"They make fine targets in the dark."

Laughing together, they rode north, toward William Dixon's spread and whatever was waiting for them there. Jackson almost glanced back once more to see his house, but fearing that it might turn out to be his last glimpse of the place, he changed his mind.

He knew that grim work lay ahead of him. And he was ready to begin.

11

Slade didn't have a clue what time it was when he heard footsteps on the basement stairs, somewhere behind him. Time enough had passed for his headache to fade somewhat, though it still pulsed behind his left eye. Slade thought he was as fit as he would ever be, for what was coming next.

Four men surrounded him a moment later, three with pistols drawn, the fourth holding a bowie knife unsheathed. All four were hooded and wore knee-length robes or nightshirts made of white muslin, with gunbelts strapped around their waists outside the robes. The end result made their outfits resemble belled skirts, but he didn't feel the slightest urge to laugh.

The knife wielder circled around behind Slade, pausing long enough to let him think the blade might find his throat, but Slade was past that. If they meant to butcher him, they wouldn't do it in their boss's cellar, where Slade's blood would soak into the earthen floor.

A moment later, he felt tugging at his bonds, behind the chair, and then the bowie's blade was freeing him, one set of wrappings at a time. His arms and legs were saved for last, then one of those with pistols leveled at him said, "Get up."

Slade did as he was told. There was no point in getting knocked around or wounded in the basement, when his goal — like theirs — was to escape it and find his way upstairs and out of Dixon's house.

Slade's escort marched him to the wooden stairs, two men ascending first, the others following behind him as he climbed. A scuffle followed by a cross fire on the stairs might take out some of them, but Slade wouldn't survive to reap the benefits of Dixon's men shooting each other in the melee.

Scratch that plan.

Slade's keepers surrounded him at the top of the stairs, prodding him with pistols through unfamiliar rooms and corridors of Dixon's home until they reached an exit he had never seen. Outside, they crossed an open yard between a barn and paddock where a half dozen sleek horses watched them pass. Wherever they were taking Slade, they clearly planned to walk.

Counting his steps and waiting for a chance to make a move, Slade noted that they'd traveled some four hundred yards from Dixon's house before he heard a murmuring of voices up ahead. Another moment and they topped a gentle rise that overlooked a pasture lit by torches. Twenty-odd robed figures clustered on the open ground below, with a great oak tree in the background.

And a wooden cross roughly three times as tall as any man who stood before it.

What the hell?

Eyeing the crowd, Slade knew he should've tried his luck when there were only four Klansmen around him, even with their pistols drawn. With their arrival at the hanging tree, his chances of survival had just plummeted to somewhere in the neighborhood of zero.

Still, he thought, there was a chance to take some of them with him. Anytime before they bound his hands again, he could attempt to seize a pistol, fire into the crowd at random — or at Dixon, if the bastard stood out somehow in the hooded crowd — and make the others gun him down, instead of hanging him up like a side of beef.

Why not?

A pistol prodded him, and Slade suppressed an urge to spin and seize it, see what happened next. As long as he was bound to die, he might as well wait for the moment when he stood among his enemies with targets close on every side, impossible to miss.

Six shots, six kills — at least in theory, and whatever happened after that, he'd leave them with a bitter, tainted memory of their pathetic ritual.

As Slade approached, surrounded by his guards, he saw that burlap had been wrapped around the wooden cross, anchored in place with strands of wire. Up close, it reeked of kerosene.

A man robed all in red stepped forward from among the others, flanked by one in black. These two would be in charge, Slade guessed, and when the red-robed Klansman spoke, he recognized the boss man's voice.

"Light up the cross!"

A torchbearer obeyed, leaning in toward the base of the cross and applying his flame to the burlap. Within seconds, the cross was a tower of fire. Slade supposed it would be visible for miles, if there was anyone around to see it.

Dixon and his disciples stood for a moment, admiring the flames, then the red mask turned back toward Slade.

"Bring forth the infidel!" it said.

William Dixon scanned the ranks of identical masks ranged before him, eyes glittering by firelight through holes snipped in muslin. Behind him and to his right, the fifteen-foot-tall cross popped and crackled, enveloped by flames. Its radiant heat baked that side of Dixon's body, merging with the warmth of bourbon in his stomach.

He stood atop a flattened slab of stone, cast up from somewhere underground eons before, then weathered down until it made an almost perfect dais. Standing with his arms upraised, Dixon was three feet taller than the white-robed brothers who stood waiting for the spectacle to start.

On his command, two of his men muscled Jack Slade out of the crowd and hauled him before Dixon's stage. They remained at his sides, one man clutching each arm to restrain their captive.

"Brothers!" Dixon called out to one and all. "We're gathered here tonight to witness punishment of an intruder in our midst. An interloper who despises us for all that we believe and who'd destroy us if he had the power. One who has the blood of seven faithful brothers on his hands!"

Slade called out, from between his minders, "Don't forget Enid. I make it nine, so far."

That brought an angry rumble from the audience, with scattered curses clearly audible above the muttering. Dixon could only smile behind the red mask that denoted his Grand Dragon's rank within the Brotherhood.

"You hear him!" Dixon thundered. "Listen to the nigger lover boasting of his crimes. We know that he was sent by one who hates us, who was once a filthy carpetbagger preying on the decent people of the South, to make their lives a Hell on Earth. Belatedly, we had a chance to punish that transgressor, but the brothers that I chose to carry out that punishment were weak. They failed. And now we have the enemy within our very camp."

"And I won't be the last," Slade said. "Get used to it."

One of the hooded bookends tried to punch him, but it wound up in a scuffling match that needed two more Klansmen, just to hold Slade still. When he was pinned, Rafe Hollister stepped up and drove a fist into the lawman's face.

"You speak again," Rafe bellowed at him, "and you'll go to Hell without your tongue!"

Slade seemed to get the message — for the moment, anyway. Dixon stood tall and told his men, "You see the kind of trash we're up against. But we will persevere. Our ancient enemy, the so-called judge, will not escape his punishment. Another handpicked team will finish what their brothers started, and the honor of our native land will be upheld. As we restored home rule to Dixie, so we shall pursue justice for all the wrongs we've suffered over time."

Dixon looked down at Slade and saw the marshal spit a gob of blood into the grass. It wasn't strange, after the punch he'd taken, but it struck Dixon as a defiant gesture of contempt.

"Tonight," he said, "we shall impose upon this enemy the same sentence his master has inflicted on so many innocents, while posing as a man of law and justice. He will *hang,* Brothers! Prepare the rope!"

At that command, Rafe Hollister retrieved a coil of rope already knotted with a hangman's noose at one end. Dixon didn't have to count the tight turns in the knot. There would be seven, ready to be snugged behind Jack Slade's left ear.

To the condemned he said, "For killing *nine* of our sworn brothers, by your own admission freely given, you are now condemned to hang by the neck until dead. We take no pleasure in your fate."

That was a blatant lie, of course. Dixon had never met a Klansman in his life who didn't like a hanging. Most would rather hoist a black man — or black *woman,* after giving her their full attention for a day or so — but Slade would satisfy their blood thirst for the moment. And his death would energize whichever men were picked to finish off Judge Dennison.

Not Hollister, the Dragon thought. *He isn't smart enough. But —*

"No last words from the condemned?" asked Slade.

Rafe was already moving, reaching for his knife, when Dixon called out, "Stay, Nighthawk. He has the right to speak before he dies."

More rumbles from the crowd. Whatever Slade came out with now, it damn sure wouldn't help his case.

"You have one minute," Dixon told his captive. "Make the most of it."

Jackson was doubly thankful for the torches. First, they'd helped avert a grave mistake on his part, which could easily have doomed the man he'd come to rescue. Second, by their light and that provided by the giant burning cross, he thought he had a chance to do the job. He couldn't guarantee success, of course — or even know with certainty that he'd survive the next half hour — but at least he had a chance.

Jackson's mistake, the one he'd *almost* made, was telling Martin Abernathy that they ought to have a word with Dixon's field hands on the sly, find out if they'd seen Marshal Slade arrive that afternoon or knew what had become of him. That meant that he and Martin had to find a place to hide their horses, well out from the shabby barracks blocks where Dixon's prisoners were kept, then sneak in past the guards and have their conversations without rousing any white men.

Without getting shot.

It would've been a neat trick, not impossible but damned close to it, and they would've wasted all that effort if the field hands had seen nothing. As it was, though, they had seen the distant torches borne by ghostly figures and had ridden toward that light instinctively, knowing that it portended nothing good.

And here they were, both stretched out prone beneath a weeping willow roughly half the size of the oak tree that stood a hundred yards down range, where Dixon's

Klansmen were assembled with their prisoner. They'd seen Slade marched by guards from the direction of the farmhouse, and they'd watched the giant cross go up in flames.

"That looks familiar," Martin whispered.

From back home, he meant, when night riders who claimed they were descended from the Scottish Highland clans adopted fiery crosses — once a method of long-distance signaling at night, like smoke signals by day — to terrorize communities of former slaves.

A burning cross came first, often accompanied by hooded men who threatened violence unless the freedmen "remembered their place" and "mended their ways." If those warnings failed to achieve the goals desired, there followed whippings, arson, mutilation — and murder.

Not this time, thought Jackson, sighting down the barrel of his lever-action rifle.

Dixon had to be the man in charge, dressed up in red and needing only horns to make a perfect Devil. Jackson guessed his number two would be the man in black, ironic as it was. The rest were simple soldiers, gathered for the show.

From a distance, they heard Dixon whipping up his troops, picking out snatches of his words while breezes claimed the rest. Slade talked back to the man at one point and was punched because of it, the black-robed Klansman leaning in to threaten him with worse, from all appearances.

Martin was ready for his first shot then, but Jackson hissed at him to wait.

"Not yet!" he said. "We want him clear before we start."

Start what? an inner voice inquired.

Start shooting at a crowd of twenty-odd Klansmen, all armed and spoiling for a taste of blood? Tackle odds of ten or twelve to one, hoping to save a man he barely knew? A man who'd probably be shot first thing, as soon as he and Martin started firing?

But another voice, more recognizably his own, answered the question and prevented any more from being asked.

Start being a man, it replied — and commanded.

Across the dark and open ground, he watched the black-robed Klansman toss a rope over one of the oak tree's lower limbs. Dixon, in red, stared down at Slade, responded to some comment from the lawman, and Jack Slade began to speak.

"A minute's plenty," Slade told Dixon.

Turning toward his hooded audience, he

told them, "Every one of you is subject to the laws of the United States and *will* be punished for the crimes that you've committed. If you stop now, some of you may get away with prison time. Joining in murder means the rope. Think how that noose will feel around *your* neck and use your brains for once, instead of being pushed around by someone with nothing to lose. Your boss man's as good as dead, and he knows it. He —"

One of the Klansmen rushed Slade, snarling curses, and swung a right cross at his face. Slade ducked it, crouching, and whipped a fist into his enemy's gut, but somebody else struck from behind him, driving him down on one knee.

Slade braced himself, prepared to die fighting, but the next blow never landed. Instead, the whip-crack of a rifle shot rang out from somewhere to his right, and one of the assembled Klansmen squealed in pain.

Slade saw his chance and seized it. More precisely, he reached out and plucked a six-gun from the holster nearest to him, swung the barrel hard into its owner's mask, and felt a satisfying crunch of cartilage.

The phony spook went down, squealing, and Slade spun away from him, holding his crouch as more rifle fire cracked overhead. He didn't know precisely where the shots were coming from, much less who was behind them, but the spacing told him that there must be two rifles involved, firing at will, without trying to synchronize their fire.

And suddenly, Slade knew what people meant when they referred to all hell breaking loose.

Two Klansmen nearest to him had seen Slade appropriate their comrade's pistol. Both of them were snatching at their own guns, though disoriented by the bullets flying out of darkness to their left, and Slade already had the drop on them before their irons cleared leather. He shot both of them at point-blank range, his muzzle blasts scorching their robes before bright crimson covered up the powder burns.

Klansmen were scattering in all directions, cursing, shouting questions and commands that no one heeded, several of them firing their revolvers to the south, at targets none of them could see. Dixon had leaped down from his stony dais and was weaving through the frantic mob scene, angling back in the direction of the farmhouse.

Slade tracked Dixon with his pistol sights, was on the verge of squeezing off a shot, when he was flattened by a hurtling body and his gun discharged into the sod. He couldn't tell if his assailant had intended tackling him, or simply stumbled over him, but they were locked together now, punching and gouging as they grappled for their lives, each with a gun in hand.

The other man was taller, heavier, and he wound up on top, using his weight to bring the barrel of his piece around toward an alignment with Slade's face. Slade couldn't seem to stop him, couldn't break the grip that held his own right arm and forced his Colt off target. In another moment, if he didn't find some new reserve of strength —

Some say a man won't hear the shot that kills him, since a bullet travels faster than the speed of sound. Slade didn't register the shot that nailed his would-be slayer, either, but he witnessed its effects — and felt them, as warm blood surged from the dying Klansman's mouth, beneath the loose mask of his hood, and sprayed across Slade's face.

Cursing, he rolled the corpse aside, using a sleeve to clear his eyes, and struggled to his feet. Three rounds gone from his captured pistol, and he grabbed the dead man's, crouching with a gun in each hand now.

Across the clearing that was meant to be

his place of execution, Slade beheld the black-robed figure who had punched him in the face, running to join the others who were firing off into the night. A rifle bullet caught him in mid-stride and knocked him sideways, stumbling hard into the blazing pillar of the fiery cross.

It didn't take the Klansman's robe a heartbeat to ignite, and he was lurching, staggering, a screaming human torch. Slade gave a fleeting thought to shooting him, but then another target loomed, demanding his attention. He fired twice into the night rider who would've gunned him down, waiting to see his adversary fall.

And by the time Slade raised his eyes, the black-robed man was out of range, a shrieking comet blazing through the night, fleeing as if some part of him believed that he could outrun Death.

Good luck with that, Slade thought and focused once again on fighting for his life.

William Dixon whipped off his hood and ran for his life. When he'd covered a hundred yards without taking a bullet in the back, he paused and pulled his crimson robe over his head, flung it aside, and then ran on.

Jack Slade should have been dangling

from a limb by now, stone dead, while Klansmen passed beneath him with their torches to incinerate his corpse. Instead, the ritual had been reduced to screaming chaos, and the Dragon didn't have the first clue as to what in hell was happening.

Nor was he waiting to find out.

The questions swirling in his mind could wait. Escape was Dixon's first priority. He must survive the night, find some way to protect himself — or, at the very least, to hide — before one of his enemies lined up a lucky shot and brought him down.

Survival wasn't guaranteed by any means, he realized with something of a shock. He might be killed at any moment, running for his life, but what else could he do? He didn't have the stomach for a battle in the dark with unseen enemies.

But if he lived, if he escaped, there would be time enough to find out who had chosen to defy him, threatening his life and everything he'd worked for through the years since leaving Dixie for a fresh start in the West. He would repay them in the only coin that traitors understood.

With blood and fire and worlds of pain.

He tripped on something in the darkness, stumbled, sprawled, and cursed as rough ground flayed his palms. Fearing that someone might be closing in behind him, Dixon lurched and staggered to his feet, took time to orient himself after his fall, then set off running once again toward home.

It couldn't be much farther now. The hanging tree stood just a quarter mile from his doorstep, although you couldn't see it from the house. Rolling terrain concealed it, but Dixon could stand on his front porch and *feel* it there, waiting to receive another sacrifice.

Now, where in hell was his house?

It seemed impossible to Dixon that he could be lost, so close to home. Granted, the unexpected gunfire and confusion could have set him running in the wrong direction, but he still knew east from west. He'd put the hanging tree and fiery cross behind him, which could only mean that he was running eastward. Running home.

And yet . . .

He paused, crouching to make a smaller target of himself, and tried to catch his breath. Good living hadn't helped him stay in shape, by any means. His lungs burned, knees ached, and there was a sharp pain in his left side, just below the ribs, which felt as if a blade had been inserted there.

Behind him, at a distance now, gunfire still crackled, but he thought that it was winding down. That might be good news, or the very worst. In either case, he wasn't doubling back to find out how his men were doing.

They could take care of themselves.

Dixon needed to reach his house, rally the guns he'd left behind, collect some things, and get the hell away from there. Given the chance, he would ride into Last Resort and hole up at the Southern Star.

At least until he found out what was happening.

But where, in God's name, *was* the house?

Cursing, nearly sobbing in his anger and frustration, Dixon struggled to his feet once more and slogged onward. His pace had slowed, but he was moving forward, damn it. That was all that mattered, putting ground between himself and whoever had found the nerve to stand against him after all these years.

If asked, before the fact, he would've said that Jack Slade didn't have a friend in Last Resort or anywhere nearby. Unless, of course, it was the —

"Niggers!"

Dixon's sudden fury gave him new strength, helping him accelerate his pace. It had to be the black homesteaders. They already hated him, and Slade had given them a shred of hope that might embolden animals to turn upon their betters.

Fair enough.

Dixon had spent his whole life fighting for his race, and now it seemed he wasn't finished yet. He'd see them all die screaming for their impudence, if he survived the night.

A moment later, Dixon saw the lights of home.

Slade triggered his last two shots and watched another Klansman fall. He dropped the empty guns and was moving toward the nearest white-robed body and its weapons when another ghostly figure stepped into his path.

"Where do you think you're going?" asked the man behind the mask.

"My first choice," Slade replied, "would be your funeral."

"Think so?"

The Klansman wasn't wearing pistol leather, and the image jogged Slade's memory before he saw the bowie knife extended, firelight glinting from its twelve-inch blade.

"I should've gutted you back at the house."

That knife had cut his bonds in Dixon's cellar. Now, its point was aimed somewhere between Slade's heart and groin, passing in front of him from left to right and back again, almost hypnotic in its motion.

Which, he guessed, must be the point.

Knife fighters liked distractions, feints, whatever threw their enemies off balance, made them vulnerable for a killing thrust. Slade tried to cover everything at once — the blade, his adversary's free hand, and his feet — but it was difficult. One slip, and he'd be skewered, bleeding out before he had a chance to land a telling blow.

Slade circled to his right, taking the Klansman with him, keeping several yards between his soft flesh and the restless bowie. Every now and then, his enemy would grunt or hiss and scuttle forward, lunging, forcing Slade to back away. Around them, Slade was conscious of the gunfire dying off, but he could not have said which side was winning.

Hell, he didn't even know who else was on his side.

The knife was all that mattered now, this moment. If another one of Dixon's men was lining up a shot at him from somewhere on the sidelines, there was nothing Slade could do about it. He could only focus on the man in front of him, the fire-lit blade that wanted to invade his body, savage it, and leave him writhing on the ground in mortal agony.

Slade was aware of bodies scattered here and there around him, white robes stained with dirt and blood. All of them had been armed before the shooting started, but he couldn't stop and scrutinize their corpses, couldn't spare the time to duck and snatch a gun from lifeless fingers.

If he looked away, his adversary would be on him in a heartbeat, slashing, thrusting. Slade knew he must concentrate and —

He had missed the nearest body somehow, stumbled over it as he was backing up, and felt his balance go. Slade reckoned he was dead as he began to tumble over backward, cursing silently.

The Klansman rushed him, as expected, knife extended for the kill. Slade landed on his back and got his feet up somehow, felt the bowie graze his left boot, then his heels were buried deep in the night rider's gut and he was lifting, straining, gasping as the ghost took flight and soared over his head.

Slade heard his enemy touch down, grunting on impact, but he didn't wait to catch his own breath. Turning swiftly, scrambling to all fours, he threw himself headlong at the Klansman, both hands reaching out for the hand that still clutched the long bowie.

Slade landed on his adversary upside down, secured the straining arm an instant before it drove the blade toward his face, and then they were rolling together, kicking and cursing in the dust, the Klansman's free hand hammering Slade's shoulder and his ribs without precision. Slade hung on for dear life, waiting until he was once again on top, then drove his forehead hard into the night rider's white mask.

His enemy slumped underneath him, lost his focus long enough for Slade to turn the bowie knife around and throw his weight behind it, grimacing as all twelve inches of its blade sank out of sight between the Klansman's ribs. He rode the thrashing corpse until it stilled beneath him, then rolled clear and started looking for another gun.

"Thought we might have to help you out with that one," a familiar voice remarked.

Slade spun to face it, smiling wearily at the sight of Colin Jackson with a rifle in his hands. Behind him, Martin Abernathy used his own Winchester as a prod to check another sheeted corpse for signs of life.

"You helped me plenty," Slade replied. "I'm in your debt."

"I'd call it even," Jackson said. "But we're not finished yet."

Scanning the field, Slade saw close to a dozen white robes stained with red, but no all-crimson costume.

"Dixon got away," he said.

"He ran back toward the house," said Abernathy, finished with his prodding now. "I couldn't make the shot in time."

"He'll likely have more people there," Slade said.

"And lots of ours," Jackson reminded him. "He might decide it's time for cleaning house."

Slade moved among the dead and dying, scooped up two more six-guns for himself and checked their loads.

"No time to lose," he said. "Unless you want to get back home."

"I start a job," Jackson replied, "I try to finish it."

"I'm in," said Abernathy.

"Right," Slade said. "Let's go."

12

Dixon was gasping by the time he reached his house, unable to respond at first when two of his men found him slumped on the porch. They helped him up and listened while he stammered out a warning.

"Ambush . . . somebody . . . rifles . . ."

"We heard the shooting, Boss," one of them said.

"Thought it was you all sending off the lawman," said the other.

"No. Ambush," Dixon repeated. "Maybe niggers . . . could be coming here."

"Jesus! I'll get the others," one man said and sprinted off into the night, leaving his friend behind.

Dixon knew all his men by name, but this one was eluding him. His lungs weren't burning quite as badly, now that he'd stopped running, but his thoughts were still chaotic, jumbled, going off in all directions at the same time.

If he could just start small . . .

"Danny?"

"Yes, sir, that's me," Danny O'Keefe replied. "What can I do for you? You hurt at all?"

"Not wounded," Dixon said. "Just winded. We need everybody here, right now."

"Yes, sir. I reckon Billy's fetching them. They'll be here any second."

Billy Goodrich, Dixon thought, nailing the second name. He'd left nine men in all to watch the house and barracks where the field hands slept. It wasn't much, considering what he'd already lost, but it would have to do.

But if they couldn't do the job . . .

"I need my horse," he told O'Keefe.

"You're leaving, Boss?"

He thought fast, knew he shouldn't make his people think that he was running out on them. Above all else, they needed confidence in Dixon and his leadership.

"I need to fetch the sheriff," he replied. "Get him to deputize some of the towns-people for reinforcements."

Danny blinked at that and asked him, "What about the other boys? Where's Rafe and the rest who went with you?"

"I *don't know* where they are!" snapped Dixon. "Damn it, I just told you we were ambushed! Halfway through the ceremony, rifles started firing from the dark and all hell broke loose. I saw men dropping right and left. Rafe —"

He stopped then, shook his head, couldn't describe the sight of Rafe Hollister running with his robe in flames and screaming like a banshee.

"You don't mean . . . Are they *all* dead?"

"Damned if I know. They were dropping right and left. I didn't have a goddamned weapon. There was nothing I could do!"

O'Keefe was staring off through darkness now, in the direction of the hanging tree. Dixon was suddenly aware that the gunfire had ceased.

What did it mean?

He could collect his nine remaining men, go back and check, but that would put his life at risk a second time. For what? The wise thing was to head for Last Resort, get Galen Evans off his lazy ass, and round up every man who owned a gun. If nothing else, they could secure his property while Dixon's trusted men went out to hunt for Slade.

Dixon couldn't let him get to Enid.

Come hell or high water, Slade had to die.

"My horse," he said again, but didn't dally waiting for O'Keefe to answer. Dixon found that he could walk now, even if he was a trifle shaky, and he headed for the stable, standing northeast of the house.

Billy Goodrich and the others met him halfway there. They milled around, obstructing Dixon, sparking fury in his gut. As anxious as he was to leave, he forced himself to pause and tell the story one more time, watching their faces as he laid it out.

"You think they's all dead, Mr. Dixon?" Toby Parmenter inquired.

"I hope not, but they could be," he replied. "That's why you should be getting ready *now*."

"But if they knocked off twenty," Festus Green chimed in, "what'n hell can *we* do?"

"Stand your ground," Dixon said. "Hold the line. Do your best, for Christ's sake! Are you Klansmen, or not?"

That stiffened them enough to keep the rest from asking any stupid questions. All of them looked shifty nervous, but they clutched their weapons, waiting for instructions.

"Danny here's in charge," said Dixon. "I'll be riding into Last Resort for reinforcements, bringing back the sheriff and as many men as we can raise."

A couple of his shooters nodded, but the rest did not seem optimistic. Dixon left

O'Keefe to sort them out and moved off toward the stable where his horse was waiting, and his last, best hope of living through the night.

Slade had been delayed while his rescuers fetched their horses from the darkness and returned, mounted, to join him on the killing ground. Jackson had offered him a ride behind him, on his buckskin gelding, but Slade had declined in favor of stretching his legs.

Ready for anything but failure, he retraced his steps through darkness, homing in on the ranch house where he'd been held prisoner. Jackson and Abernathy held their horses to a walking pace and sat with rifles ready, both freshly reloaded since the turkey shoot around the fiery cross.

I should be dead, Slade thought and shrugged it off. He'd caught a lucky break, but couldn't count on any more of them tonight. Whatever happened next, he must be mentally prepared for it and strike his enemies wherever they appeared.

Slade smelled the barracks well before he saw it, nostrils twitching at the reek of bodies long unwashed. Long moments later, when they'd cleared another fifty yards, he crouched with his companions in the shadow of a long, low building that could probably house thirty occupants if they slept close together. Farther to the north and east, upwind, a second barracks of the same size crouched in darkness.

"What's the plan?" asked Colin Jackson, as he peered into the night, looking for targets.

"This is where we gamble," Slade replied, half whispering.

"What's that mean?" Abernathy asked.

"If Dixon's really keeping slaves, they should be glad to see us," Slade explained. "We break them out. They either side with us, or at the very least confuse whichever men he still has left. But if the story's wrong, and they're just hired hands loyal to Dixon . . ."

"I believe he's holding them against their will," Jackson replied. "I'd stake my life on it."

"Okay," Slade said. "That's just exactly what we're doing."

"Suppose they're guarded?" Abernathy asked him.

"That's another risk we take."

"I hope they are," said Jackson. "One more goddamned redneck bites the dust."

They crept along the back side of the barracks, Slade in the lead, on alert for any evidence of guards in place. He knew that Dixon should've made it home by now, and if he had, he would be rallying whatever troops remained with him.

Whether that lightened the security around the barracks or increased it, only time would tell.

Slade reached a corner, peered around it, then proceeded, holding both guns up and ready. If they met a sentry, he would weigh the situation in whatever time he had available. Strike silently, if that was possible, or shoot to kill if circumstances ruled out stealth.

Another corner coming up. This time, they would be facing toward the farmhouse when they cleared it, though the darkness might conceal them. But if Dixon's thugs were out in force, Slade had to be prepared.

He took a breath and held it, then stepped out into the open.

Colin Jackson followed Slade around the corner, feeling Martin Abernathy almost on his heels. There was no guard outside the one and only barracks door, but it was fitted with a hasp and stout padlock.

"You mean to shoot that off?" asked Martin, whispering.

"I'd rather not," Slade answered, "if

you've got a better way to do it."

"I just might, at that," Martin replied. He set his rifle down, leaning it against the barracks wall, and drew a short knife from a belt sheath. "Keep an eye out for those peckerwoods," he said, "while I dig out these nails."

"Be quick about it," Jackson urged his friend, then joined Slade where he stood, facing the house. They couldn't see the front porch from the barracks, but his ears picked up the muffled sound of voices over there, although he couldn't make out any words.

"They sound excited," Slade observed.

"Sounds like there's plenty of them, too," Jackson replied.

"I'd bet we've seen the worst of it," Slade said. "Dixon wanted an audience to cheer him while he strung me up. He'd only leave a few lookouts behind."

"How many do you reckon is a few?"

The marshal smiled and said, "We won't know that until we see them, but I'd guess he took two-thirds of his men to the hanging, at least."

"So, you're thinking he's got anywhere from five to ten more guns on tap," Jackson suggested.

"Well, you pegged the number about forty, starting out. Subtract the seven I already shot, then twenty-odd who fell or fled to-night."

"You make me wish we had more men on our side," Jackson said.

"We might," Slade told him, "if we beat these locks."

"I'm working on it," Abernathy muttered, and a rusty nail squealed shrilly as he pried it from the wooden door frame.

"Much more noise like that, we may as well just shoot the locks," Jackson replied.

"Excuse me all to blazes," Martin said. "I didn't bring my oil can."

"Listen, if they see us —"

Jackson bit his comment off in mid-sentence, punctuating it with a whispered curse as two armed men appeared at the northeast corner of Dixon's ranch house. Others were close behind them, all advancing toward the barracks.

"Well, that tears it," Slade observed.

"I've almost got it," Martin told them. "Last nail coming out . . . right . . . now!"

There was another squeal, and then a sharp metallic clacking as he pushed the hasp and lock aside, reached out, and yanked the barracks door open. Jackson slanted a glance toward the interior, but it was pitch-dark in the bunkhouse, and he couldn't see a thing.

"You'd better get them moving, Martin," he advised.

Martin was on the top step, leaning in and talking to the darkness. "Hurry up, now!" he was saying. "Anyone who's tired of slaving for the man had better make a move *right now,* before his shooters get here!"

Jackson heard a sound of feet shuffling on floorboards, muted voices asking questions, but he could no longer focus on them. Staring off at Dixon's house, he counted nine men visible and moving toward the barracks now, most of them toting long guns in addition to the pistols on their hips.

"I'd say we're out of time," Jack Slade remarked.

"I'd say you're right," Jackson agreed.

He raised his Winchester and found a target in the front rank of the group advancing toward him. One of them was shouting now and pointing toward the barracks.

Jackson heard the white man shouting, "Niggers!" as he aimed and fired.

Dixon flinched at the fresh sounds of gunfire, crackling outside the stable. He couldn't place the source exactly, but from how it stung his ears, he knew it must be close.

Too close.

He fumbled with the cinches on his saddle, cursing bitterly under his breath. For years now, hired hands had performed those tasks for Dixon. He was out of practice, clumsy when dexterity was critical. The cinch connecting the strap nearly defeated him, but finally he got it right and stepped back, wiping clammy perspiration from his forehead with a sleeve.

Dixon had everything he needed. Money from the safe. Two pistols and a rifle. Men in Last Resort who would obey his orders under threat of being cast adrift, turned out of jobs and homes. A small, poor army, granted. But if he could whip them to the proper frenzy, they might serve him well enough.

And if they failed him, too? Then, what?

Then, nothing.

He was too old for starting over in a new place, trying to rebuild what had been stolen from him twice. He'd never find the proper climate or the necessary group of men who shared his view of how things ought to be. Not in a world where U.S. marshals claimed that all men were created equal, with the right to liberty.

That kind of nonsense undermined the very premise of civilization. There had to be masters and servants, or else you had chaos.

White men who pretended otherwise were lying to themselves, in Dixon's view, and they would rue the day when those they'd liberated rose against them.

Dixon hauled himself aboard his nervous stallion, settled in, and snugged his boots into the stirrups. In the yard outside, gunfire was escalating, and a stray round hit the north wall of the stable, adding to his horse's agitation.

It was now or never. Flee, or stand and fight.

He fled.

It was a straight run through the open stable doors and past the back side of his house, then over open country to the road that serviced Last Resort. Pushing the stallion, he could be in town by midnight, easily. Drag Galen Evans out of bed — his own, or someone else's — and begin to organize the town's last-ditch defense.

Against what?

Slade. The shooters who had rescued him. Maybe some townspeople who had opposed Dixon in little ways from the beginning, waiting for an opportunity to bring him down.

Housecleaning time.

But first, he had to make it past the guns outside.

He whipped the stallion forward, bending low over the saddle horn to make himself a smaller target. In another second, they were through the open doors and Dixon had a fleeting glimpse of what was happening outside.

His men had formed a skirmish line across the yard and were advancing toward the nearer barracks, firing as they went. Down range, two or three men were answering that fire, while others streamed out of the barracks block.

All black.

He spurred the stallion, turned his back on everything he'd built, trusting the night to cover his escape. But even darkness failed him.

"Thar he!" someone shouted, audible above the crack of gunshots. Dixon didn't know which of his captive laborers had seen him — why should he take time to learn their names? — but now that he was spotted, Slade would know where he was going.

If Slade lived.

There was a chance the lawman would be killed, of course. Maybe his friends would fall, as well, with odds at nine to three. But who would put the genie back inside the bottle? Who would round up Dixon's field hands, shackle them, and put them back to work on his behalf?

No one.

So be it. If his world was crumbling, let it. If the last vestige of happiness had slipped beyond his reach, he would accept it.

And he'd take the bastards with him when they met again, in Last Resort.

Most shots fired in the average gunfight are wasted. The more guns involved, the higher the number of stray shots will be. Precision shooting rarely happens in a life-or-death emergency, where marksmanship is complicated by a moving target that shoots back.

Or *nine,* in this case, charging toward the barracks from the big house, ducking, dodging, rapid-firing as they came.

Slade wasted two shots on the night before a bullet whispered past his face and sent him scrambling for cover. In this case, that meant a narrow crawl space underneath the barracks, which was raised some eighteen inches off the ground on sturdy posts.

Slade wriggled through the dust and cobwebs under there, calling to Jackson and to Abernathy, but he got no answer. They were caught up in the moment, furiously fighting for their lives and for the strangers they had liberated from captivity.

For how long?

Some of them had already been hit by fire from Dixon's men. Failing to drop their primary opponents, it was easier to fire into the crowd of milling bodies, knowing that you almost had to hit *someone*. Curses and cries of pain accompanied the sounds of gunfire, the chaotic effort to escape.

Where could they go? Where had they come from, in the first place?

Slade dismissed those questions from his mind and focused on survival, here and now. Lying beneath the barracks, he took time to aim a pistol shot and was rewarded when his target crumpled, clutching at a wounded leg.

Better.

But sniping from the shadows while his two companions stood and faced their adversaries didn't suit him. Wriggling on his stomach, eating dust, he reached the back side of the barracks and emerged once more into the clean night air. Rising, he took advantage of the darkness, running in a crouch to flank his enemies.

And he was still on the move when a rider burst out of the nearby stable, galloping past Dixon's men, around behind his house, and off into the night. Slade recognized him on the fly but didn't have a chance to track him with the dead men's pistols he was carrying.

Damn it!

If Dixon hoped to find a hiding place in Last Resort, there still might be a chance for Slade to overtake him. If he simply kept on riding, though, the odds got whittled down somewhere from slim to none.

The wasp's whine of a bullet past his ear brought Slade's mind back to more immediate concerns. One of the fleeing Klansman's shooters had already spotted him and missed his first shot, but he wasn't giving up. A headlong rush carried him forward, shortening the range.

Slade dropped into a crouch, right hand extended as he quickly aimed and fired. His bullet caught the runner high up, on the left side of his chest, and spun him like a whirling dervish from a storybook. He went down hard, yelping with pain, but didn't waste a moment struggling back to hands and knees.

Slade saw the shaky pistol swinging back in his direction, knew he couldn't give the wounded man a second chance. He raised the pistol in his left hand, sighted down its barrel in the time it took to draw a breath, and fired again. This time, his target's hat went flying with a portion of his scalp and skull inside. The dead man dropped without a whimper, sprawling facedown in the dirt.

And that left eight.

Martin Abernathy led the runner with his rifle sights, held his breath, and squeezed the trigger lightly without jerking it. Down range, his target seemed to stumble over something, tumbling through a dusty somersault before he came to rest.

"Good shot!" said Colin, somewhere to his left and on the move, ducking bullets as the line of Dixon's men advanced.

The white men kept up steady fire, something they may have learned from fighting in the war for all he knew, though most of them looked too young to have served. In any case, it wasn't like the first engagement of the evening, where they'd been hidden in the dark and shooting at an enemy exposed by firelight.

This could get a person killed.

As if to make him doubly conscious of that fact, a bullet nearly parted Abernathy's hair. He could've sworn that he felt muzzle heat against his scalp, and nearly raised a hand to see if any of his hair was singed, but that meant letting go of his Winchester, which might be the last mistake he ever made.

He looked around for Colin Jackson, couldn't see him anywhere, and felt a surge of something close to panic. Marshal Slade had disappeared, now Colin was gone somewhere, into the night. All that remained were Dixon's men and the field hands he had released from their confinement in the barracks.

Abernathy fired another shot and missed, distracted by a sudden problem nagging at his mind.

Too many field hands.

He had freed about two dozen, but he now saw twice as many swarming in the yard around him, ducking bullets, shouting back and forth to one another with their angry, frightened voices. Glancing backward, toward the second bunkhouse, Abernathy caught a glimpse of Jackson standing by another open door and saying something to the captives who emerged.

Too bad they don't have guns, he thought.

But then he realized that some of them were running *toward* the weapons held by Dixon's straggling line of men, not fleeing *from* them. It seemed crazy at a glance, but they were charging at the men who'd held them prisoner for God knew how long, working them without a hope of liberty or payment. Even some of those who had been running for their lives a moment earlier were turning now, and joining the attack.

It was a sight for sore eyes, watching Dixon's men begin to waver, wearing shocked expressions on their faces. They kept firing, dropping human targets here and there, but half their shots were wasted as they rushed them. Now, incredibly, he saw the skirmish line dissolve and watched the gunmen turn, fleeing.

Too late.

Abernathy saw the black tide overtake and engulf them, dragging them down, one by one. They fought for life but couldn't hold it, falling underneath a storm of fists and feet and bludgeons snatched up on the fly, pummeled and battered into shapes barely recognizable as human.

Martin Abernathy stood and watched them die, wondering why he couldn't raise a smile.

There came a tense moment when Dixon's former captives turned on Slade, thinking that any white man within reach must be their mortal enemy, but Colin Jackson interposed himself between Slade and the mob's blood fury, talking fast to save his life.

It worked.

Some of the newly liberated slaves moved off to ransack Dixon's house for food, clothing, whatever they could find, while those who'd tackled Dixon's last few men were rinsing bloody hands with water flowing from a short hand-operated pump. Slade took advantage of the lull, drawing Jackson and Martin Abernathy off toward a nearby corral.

"Dixon's long gone," Jackson declared, before Slade had a chance to speak. "I saw him riding off toward Last Resort."

"I know," Slade said. "I need to follow him, as soon as I can find my horse and gear."

"You had the dun mare, I recall," said Abernathy. "I can check the stable, but I wouldn't recognize your saddle."

"I appreciate it," Slade replied. "I need to look for something in the house, then I'll be right behind you."

Abernathy moved off toward the stable, while Slade started for the house. Jackson fell into step beside him, saying, "Maybe I should tag along and keep you out of trouble, Marshal."

"Maybe that's a good idea," Slade granted.

Dixon's house already looked as if a tornado had swept through its principal rooms, breaking glassware and toppling the furniture, ripping art down from the walls. More than a dozen men were clustered in the large kitchen, raiding the cabinets and cracking eggs into large skillets on the stove.

"They'll likely burn the place before they're done," said Jackson.

Slade thought, *Maybe it should burn,* but kept it to himself. He made a beeline for the library, where tumbling, thrashing sounds came through the open doorway. Standing on the threshold, he found three men tearing books from Dixon's shelves and flinging them about the room, while one stood guzzling whiskey from a bottle and the fifth was buckling a gunbelt.

It was Slade's.

"That's mine," he told the fifth man, glad to hear no tremor in his voice.

The dark face showed him wild eyes, as the lips drew back from teeth so white they dazzled.

"Maybe useta be," the smiler said.

"Still is, if he says so," Jackson remarked, and cocked the hammer on his Winchester for emphasis.

"Whose side you on?" the would-be gunman asked Jackson.

"The right side, every time," Jackson replied.

There was a moment's hesitation, when Slade knew that it could still go either way, but then the former captive slipped the gunbelt off and set it lightly down on Dixon's desk. Slade took a forward step, retrieved it, buckled it in place around his hips.

"Thank you," he said. "You'll likely find no end of guns around the place, if you keep looking."

"I'll look into that," the black man said. "And, Marshal? Thanks back at you."

They found Abernathy in the stable, standing by a stall where Slade's mare shifted restlessly, then whickered greetings when she recognized his face. His saddle lay atop a bench, against the stable's western wall. His long guns, both the rifle and repeating shotgun, were secure inside their saddle boots.

When Slade was nearly finished saddling the mare, Jackson told him, "I reckon we should ride along with you, as far as town."

"That's well out of your way," Slade said. "I'm sure you have some worried people waiting for you."

"I just hate to leave a job half finished," Jackson said. "You know the feeling, I expect."

"It's not your job, though," Slade reminded him. "You've both gone way beyond what anyone expected of you, as it is. I won't forget it."

"That's the point, you see," said Abernathy, cutting in. "It's not about what you or anybody else expects from us. It's what *we* expect from ourselves, in order to feel like free men."

Jackson was nodding as he said, "So, if you've got no strenuous objections, Marshal —"

"Make it 'Jack,' " Slade said. "And there's no law that I can think of saying free men can't assist a marshal in performance of his duty. Just like there's no law saying they *have* to."

"Well, then, as long as we're agreed," said Jackson, "I suppose we'd best be on our way."

13

Galen Evans woke to someone hammering his door and bellowing his name. The voice sounded familiar, but he had some trouble placing it, between his hangover and the grim nightmare that his visitor had interrupted.

Running through dark alleys with an empty holster slapping on his thigh, chasing — or fleeing from — a heavy-breathing monster he could never glimpse, but recognized because it smelled like death.

Still fully dressed, except for boots, he struggled upward from the rumpled jail-cell cot where he was known to sleep from time to time, when work or liquor kept him overnight away from home. Evans considered putting on his boots, but then the caller started pounding on his door again, each blow driving a lance of pain between his bleary eyes.

"I hear you!" he responded, trying for a

shout and settling for a raspy croak. "No need to wake the dead."

"Hurry!" the disembodied voice commanded, and he recognized it now.

Well, shit!

Evans unlocked his office door and stepped aside as William Dixon jostled past him, muttering, "You weren't at home."

"You woke me up to tell me that?"

"And you've been drinking. I can smell it on you."

"So?"

Evans knew there were worse smells, like the ones that haunted him in dreams.

"I need you wide awake and fit for action," Dixon said. "And I mean *now.*"

"What kind of action did you have in mind?" Evans inquired.

"Slade and a gang of niggers hit my place tonight. Most of my men are dead or wounded," Dixon said. "I think they're coming here, next."

"Who? Your men?"

"Slade and the rest of them, goddamn it! Is there something wrong with you, besides the booze?"

"I hear you," Evans said. "But you're not making sense. Slade didn't come with any deputies, much less a bunch of blacks. Where would he even *find* them, hereabouts?"

"I'm telling you what happened," Dixon snapped. "He started out with two or three, I guess, but now he's got my hands riled up, and they —"

"Your hands?" said Evans, interrupting him. "You just said most of 'em were shot."

"My *black* hands! Pay attention, for Christ's sake!"

Evans began to get it now. If Dixon wasn't lying through his teeth — a possibility that couldn't be discounted out of hand — something had happened at his spread to liberate the work force he'd collected over time, with help from Evans. Simple logic told him they'd be mad as hell and out for blood. If they should find their way to Last Resort . . .

God help us all.

"You got away, I see," Evans remarked.

"And I could just as easily have kept on riding," Dixon told him, "but I knew I had to try and save the town."

"That's mighty white of you."

"You think this shit is funny?" Dixon challenged.

"Nope. That's not the word I'd use," Evans replied.

"I hope not."

" 'Tragic' comes to mind."

"I don't need any smart-aleck remarks from you, damn it!"

"Then tell me what you *do* need, Mr. Dixon."

"Get together all the men and guns you can, as fast as possible. Slade and his niggers could be on their way right now."

"Suppose they don't show up at all?" asked Evans.

"I would rather be prepared and waste the effort than to be caught napping. Wouldn't you?"

Weary, the sheriff nodded. "I can't promise you we'll raise too many soldiers," he replied.

"These people owe me," Dixon said. "Half of them would be living out of tents and begging for their supper if I hadn't set them up in business."

"What about the other half?" asked Evans.

Scowling, Dixon answered, "Keep a list of those who turn their backs when I'm in need of help. I won't forget them. When we're done with Slade and his trained monkeys, I will personally supervise their punishment."

"A list. I hear you."

"So, get on with it! You're wasting time!"

That said, the planter stormed out of the sheriff's office, leaving Evans in his stockinged feet, door standing open to the night.

"Just what I need," he told the empty room. "Another goddamned civil war."

"So, when we get to town," said Martin Abernathy, "what's the plan?"

"Find Dixon," Slade replied. "Arrest him, if he'll stand for it."

"And if he won't?" asked Colin Jackson.

"Take him down, regardless."

Slade had deputized both men before they rode away from Dixon's spread. He had no badges for them, but he'd testify that they were duly sworn if it should ever go to court.

Assuming he was still alive.

A lifelong gambler, Slade believed in luck. He took for granted that he'd stretched his to the breaking point this night and figured he was on his own, with nothing more than guts and gristle to support him.

That, and two new friends.

The right thing would've been to order them back home, but Slade sensed they were sick and tired of taking orders. William Dixon had insulted and harassed them both, the latest in a long line of antagonists who thought the color of their skin made them superior. He'd pushed Jackson and Abernathy past their breaking point, and there were dead men who had paid the price for Dixon's arrogance.

Before the sun rose, Slade assumed, there would be more.

"He won't be on his own, you know," said Jackson.

"I suppose not," Slade replied.

"Some of the folks in town are on his payroll. Others are in business with him, and I'll bet they feel the same way Dixon does toward colored folks."

"You're right," Slade said. "But others don't agree."

"Agreeing's one thing," Abernathy interjected. "Standing up to fight is something else."

Slade nodded, said, "We'll have to wait and see how many back him. I gave up on reading minds."

"Figure the sheriff's with him, anyway," said Jackson. "Him and them that runs the Southern Star, at least."

"That's where I'd start to look for him," Slade said. "I'm told he has an office there, and likely there'll be guns."

"If not, he'll get some from the so-called law," said Abernathy.

"The main thing's to be careful," Slade reminded them. "Don't get excited and rush into anything. If we can come up on his blind side, I'm all for it."

"That's no problem," Jackson said, "unless he's got the whole town posted doing lookout duty. We're old hands at going in the back door."

"That's God's honest truth," said Abernathy. "Half the stores in town won't sell us anything, and we don't like to advertise the ones that will."

"Avoid Main Street completely," Jackson said. "Just like a normal market day."

"You know the way, I take it," Slade replied.

"We never tried it after dark," said Jackson, "but I reckon we can find it, right enough. With any luck, we ought to come in near the back side of the dry-goods store."

"That's Marcus Tucker's?" Slade inquired.

"The very same," Jackson agreed.

"Sounds good to me," Slade said.

He estimated that they had another forty minutes before they saw the lights of Last Resort. More time for Dixon to prepare a welcome at the Southern Star, or somewhere else. Enough time for the people who supported him to arm themselves, find vantage points, and turn Main Street into a shooting gallery.

Slade wished that he could ride on past the town and back to Enid, but he still had work to do. And by the time he finished, instinct told him, there'd be blood enough to go around.

And then some.

Caleb Greeley was awake and brooding when a subtle rapping on his back door distracted him. His pocket watch lay open on the desk in front of him, informing him that it was half past midnight.

He remained immobile for a moment, waiting for the knock to be repeated. When it was, Greeley removed a small revolver from his top desk drawer and rose from his swivel chair, passing between his printing press and trays of type to stand beside the door.

"Who is it?" he demanded, through the slab of wood.

"Jabez," the caller answered, in a kind of hissing whisper.

Holding the revolver down against his thigh, thumb on its hammer, Greeley unlatched the door left-handed, opened it, and peered into the anxious face of Jabez Washington. The barber stepped around him, moving well into the room as he instructed, "Close it quick!"

Greeley complied, then asked his unexpected visitor, "What brings you out so late?"

Washington spent a moment staring at the pistol in his hand, then said, "You haven't heard? I thought . . . it looks like you're prepared."

"Prepared for *what?*"

"Dixon rode in a while ago," said Washington. "He's over at the Southern Star right now."

"He owns the place," Greeley replied. "I don't see —"

"He rode in *alone,*" the barber said. "When did you ever see him going anywhere without at least a couple of his boys?"

"A man's entitled to his privacy."

"That's not it," Washington insisted. "I was over there. I heard —"

"Hold on, now," Greeley interrupted him, half smiling. "You were at the Southern Star, this time of night? What for, pray tell?"

Jabez came close to blushing as he said, "I like a poke from time to time, the same as anybody. Will you listen to me, now?"

"I'm listening," said Greeley, still smiling.

"I heard him come in, talking to the bartender. That Roddy Doyle. Dixon was saying Marshal Slade attacked his place tonight, with nig — with coloreds helping him. Shot some of Dixon's boys, supposedly, and got some kind of riot started with the field hands."

320

Greeley was already framing headlines in his mind, but he would need more details for a story. And the last thing that he felt like doing in the middle of the night was riding out to Dixon's spread, particularly with a gunfight or a riot going on.

"So, what's he doing here in town?" asked Greeley.

"Rousting out of bed everyone who owes him favors and telling them to bring their guns. He claims Slade will be marching into town next, with what Dixon calls his 'nigger army.' He was whipping up the drunks when I slipped out."

"Good lord!"

"You don't believe it, do you?" Jabez asked him.

"What? That Slade attacked the place for no good reason, with a colored army? It's ridiculous. The only Negroes in the county, outside Dixon's field hands, are the families homesteading west of town. They wouldn't make an army, even if you count their kids."

"That's what I thought," said Washington. "But *something's* happened, sure as shit. If Dixon isn't careful, we could have a battle right out there on Main Street."

"Careful's not a word I normally associate with Mr. Dixon, when his temper's up," Greeley replied.

"I hear you. So, what should we do?"

Greeley considered it, then said, "Jabez, my job is to report local events. You are the town's best barber."

"I'm the *only* barber, damn it!"

"Even so. My point is that we're not gunfighters, and we never will be. Dixon's trouble with the marshal is between them. Why should we do anything? Where would we even start?"

"Growing a pair of balls might point you in the right direction," Jabez answered. "Jesus, man! You hate Dixon as much as I do. Or the Tuckers and some others I can name. Just yesterday, I heard you say you might be leaving Last Resort because you couldn't stomach his shenanigans."

"Leaving's one thing," Greeley replied. "Joining some kind of crazy feud is something else entirely."

"Sure it is. The something else takes guts."

"I try to do my thinking with my brain," said Greeley.

"How's that working for you?" asked the barber. Without waiting for an answer, he pressed on. "You think Dixon was bad before, imagine how he'll be after he's killed a U.S. marshal. Hell, first thing you know, we'll have the army in here gunning for him. By the time they're done, we may not even have a town."

"Is that so bad?" asked Greeley.

"What? Is it so —"

"Some towns don't deserve to live," Greeley cut in. "Lynch towns, and those where one man calls the shots for everyone. Who needs them, anyway?"

"Okay, you're young and ready to move on. That's fine, for you. But some of us have everything we've got sunk into Last Resort. If it dries up and blows away, we're done. There's no place left for us to go."

"Jabez, there's *always* someplace."

"Oh, sure. I can drift around from town to town, begging the other barbers that I meet for room to work. Kick back two-thirds of what I make on every shave and haircut. Spend what's left on hotel rooms and stabling a horse, which I don't own. Life's full of options when you're my age, son."

Greeley stared at the barber for another moment, then replied, "Tell me exactly what you have in mind."

William Dixon laid his matching pistols on the desktop, within easy reach from where he sat. They were Colt Thunderers, the double-action .44s that let you fire without cocking the hammer first. He could unload twelve rounds as fast as he could pull both triggers, and God help whoever happened to be standing in the line of fire.

The pistols reassured him, coupled with the lever-action rifle propped against the wall behind his chair, but Dixon couldn't shake the fear that had pursued him from his home to Last Resort. He knew Slade would be coming for him, if one of his gunmen hadn't made a lucky shot.

And even if the lawman *was* dead, Dixon's troubles weren't resolved. His plan for finishing Judge Dennison was shot to hell, along with his Klansmen. If he was forced to flee the territory, start from scratch, he'd never have another chance to punish Dennison.

Unless he did the job himself.

That was a thought. He could ride west to Enid, even start tonight, while Slade was busy hunting him in Last Resort. Dixon could be there well before Slade gave up searching and went home. No one in Enid knew his face, except for Dennison himself. Dixon could tell the local doctor they were friends, slip in to see him, draw a hidden pistol from beneath his jacket, and —

But that would mean giving his own life for the cause, something he'd never truly planned to do. There would be guards around the judge, no doubt. They'd either gun him down or hold him for a hasty trial that would result in Dixon dangling from a rope, blue in the face and twitching like a stranded fish.

The fear squirmed in his belly like a nest of worms. He tried to drown it with another shot of whiskey, but the sharp burn only lasted for a moment, then the worms were back, still wriggling.

In Dixon's world, the worst thing you could call a man was *coward*. Well, that wasn't strictly true, but it was second worst, after the dreaded *nigger lover*. He had never given anybody grounds to call him that, and never would.

But if they knew his secret shame . . .

He'd have a chance, when Slade arrived in town, to finally redeem himself. Or, at the very least, to play the leader's role as usual, directing those who'd do his killing for him.

And why not?

Rank had its privileges. He was a Southern gentleman of property and standing. Better still, he was a proud Grand Dragon of the Brotherhood.

And by God, William Dixon wasn't finished yet.

"Well, what are *we* supposed to do about it?" Marcus Tucker asked his uninvited visitors. He felt ridiculous, standing before them in his nightshirt, and he'd sent Lurleen upstairs to fetch a robe that might, with luck, preserve some measure of his dignity.

"Be ready," Jabez Washington replied. "That's all I'm saying."

"Ready for *what?* You come in here at — what? Twelve forty-five? — and tell me there may be a gunfight at the Southern Star. I sell dry goods, gentlemen. I'm not a doctor or an undertaker. What has it to do with me?"

"Marcus," said Caleb Greeley, "you have told me time and time again how much you wish that we were out from under Dixon's thumb."

"All right. That's true. What of it? Are you telling me the three of us should jump into the middle of a war between Dixon's army and this U.S. marshal?"

"That's the point," Greeley replied. "He doesn't have an army anymore."

"Says who?"

"I heard him," Jabez Washington chimed in. "Plain as day, he said that Slade and his . . . um, colored folk had taken out his people on the farm. That's why he's here in town, recruiting stand-ins."

"Which means he'll have the sheriff, everybody from the Star, and God knows who else lining up to help him."

Lurleen chose that moment to return and gave Marcus his robe. He struggled into it, somehow feeling more awkward than before.

"Figure a dozen people, tops," said Washington.

"Against the three of us," Tucker replied.

"And Slade. And anyone who's riding with him," said the barber.

"You believe this 'colored army' nonsense?" Tucker challenged him. "Dixon's obsessed with blacks. We all know that. He'd spin that story just to panic folks in town and bring them over to his side."

"All the more reason to oppose him," Greeley said.

"This is the marshal's business. I'm a shopkeeper, for God's sake, not a gunman! You're a *barber,* Jabez. Caleb, you're a *writer.*"

"We all have a stake in Last Resort," said Washington. "If we won't fight for what we have, I'd say we don't deserve to keep it."

Tucker felt Lurleen's hand on his arm. He

turned to find her watching him, wearing that look she got sometimes, when he'd gone off in a direction that she didn't think was sound.

"Marcus." Just that, and nothing more.

"Lurleen? You think I should run off and play soldier with these two, in the middle of the night? Are you prepared to be a widow?"

"Marcus, all they've said is that we should be ready. When the marshal comes. What's wrong with that?"

"Ready to get my head blown off, you mean."

But there was something stirring now, inside him. Something Marcus Tucker had forgotten he possessed. Was it a sense of pride, or pure damned spite?

All three of them were staring at him now. He closed his eyes, took one deep breath, and then released it.

"Well," he said at last, "I've got three rifles and two shotguns on the rack, there. Do you aim to help me load them, or just stand around and gawk all night?"

Most of the town was dark as Slade approached it from the northwest, following the path that Colin Jackson had suggested. An exception was the Southern Star saloon, which showed lights in the windows that were visible from half a mile away.

"That's where he'll be holed up," said Martin Abernathy. "Waiting for us with his men."

"Whoever's left to him," Jackson replied.

Abernathy said, "I'd figure half the town, at least."

"It may not be that bad," Slade told them, "but we can't go in assuming that his guns are all together at the Southern Star. After what he's been through tonight, I'm betting he'll have lookouts posted."

"I've been thinking," Abernathy said. "You deputized the two of us, okay?"

"That's right."

"Well, what if Dixon and his sheriff do the same? I mean, what's stopping him from deputizing everyone in town?"

"I wouldn't rule it out," Slade said.

"Well, there you go, then," Abernathy said. "It seems to me that if a bunch of deputies start killing one another, someone's bound to wind up stretching rope."

"Don't worry about that," Slade said. "Dixon's a felon and a fugitive from justice. Anyone who helps him to evade arrest becomes a criminal by definition, even if he wears a badge. Besides, Dixon's already tried to kill the only hanging judge in this part of the territory. You won't find him getting any sympathy in court."

But even as he spoke those words, Slade's mind replied, *If Isaac Dennison is still alive.*

Without him, who could say what might ensue from this night's bloody work?

Slade knew one thing, beyond a shadow of a doubt. The man responsible for Dennison's near miss with death — the same man who had tried to murder him and Colin Jackson's family, who had enslaved innocent men — was waiting for him up ahead, in Last Resort.

He wondered if another town had ever been more aptly named.

Whatever happened in the hours remaining before sunrise, Slade's account with Dixon would be settled. One way or another, whether Slade left Last Resort aboard his mare or laid out in a hearse, he would have done his best to finish it.

Beginning now.

They entered Last Resort through darkness, rifles at the ready, just in case. Avoiding Dixon's livery, they left their horses tied behind the barber's shop, all dark and silent now. Slade thought of Jabez Washington, considered waking him, then let it go.

He had a few allies in town, but they were peaceful souls trying to get along as best they could. Try as he might, Slade couldn't think of any rationale for dragging them into the middle of a shooting war.

There was a narrow alleyway between the barber's shop and a law office to the south, connecting to Main Street. When they had cleared it, lingering in shadows at the alley's mouth, Slade had a clear view of the Southern Star, standing some fifty yards away. The open ground between his hiding place and the saloon felt more like fifty miles.

Time's wasting.

"Here we go," he said. "Look sharp. Be careful."

"You don't have to tell us twice," Jackson replied.

Slade moved out of the shadows, scanning left and right along what seemed to be an empty street. Were hostile eyes observing him from darkened windows? Did a sniper have him framed in rifle sights already?

Shrugging off his hesitation, Slade stepped into Main Street, heard the others following behind him as he eased into a jog. A winking flash of light, somewhere above and to his left, made him recoil before he heard the gunshot's echo and a spout of dust rose at his feet.

Ambush!

Slade had a choice: go forward, or go back.

331

Cursing, he sprinted toward the Southern Star.

Sheriff Galen Evans was expecting gunfire, but he still flinched at the sound of the first shot. He nearly spilled the glass of whiskey poised before his lips, but Evans caught himself and downed it in one swallow, carefully replacing his empty glass on the bar.

Around him, men were jabbering and rushing toward the windows, cocking guns. He could have told them that it was a stupid waste of time to stand inside a lighted room and peer into the dark, but anyone with common sense should know that much, already.

Christ, but it was hard to work with morons.

Evans crossed the barroom, avoiding the windows and doors facing onto Main Street. There was an exit on the east side, granting access to an alley where the shadows would conceal him and allow his eyesight to adjust.

From where he stood with gun in hand, light spilling from the Southern Star's front windows lit a portion of the street. No one was visible, so far, but gunshots sputtered, ringing in his ears, and Evans saw a muzzle flash across the street, from what he took to be the doorway of the feed store.

Was it Slade? Had he brought someone with him for the showdown?

Evans didn't buy Dixon's story of a "black army" marching to raid Last Resort, but it was possible that Slade had found allies among the black homesteaders living west of town — or even in the town itself, among those who had bridled at the planter's efforts to control them. Evans couldn't think of any who would take up arms, offhand, but people could surprise you at times, when push came to shove.

More to the point, Evans wondered why he was still on Dixon's side.

A simple lack of courage might explain it. He'd grown used to following the path of least resistance, picking up whatever extra benefits he could along the way. It sure as hell beat chasing fugitives around the countryside, waiting to meet a faster gun or have some yellow bastard shoot him in the back.

Which, now that he thought about it, was exactly what he had in mind for Slade. Why else was Evans standing in a pitch-black alley, listening for footsteps in the night?

A feeling of revulsion gripped the sheriff, worsened by the fact that it was self-directed. Muttering a curse, he holstered his six-gun, reversed his steps, and let himself back into the saloon through its side door.

The so-called deputies he'd left behind, a motley collection of the town's worst lay-abouts and half a dozen men who should've known better, were still lined up around the door and windows, waiting for a skirmish line of targets to reveal itself. They didn't notice Evans as he crossed the barroom, climbed two flights of stairs, and found his way to Dixon's office.

"Sheriff?" Dixon seemed surprised to see him. "Why aren't you downstairs?"

"I'm not your sheriff anymore," Evans replied.

It was a second's work to pluck the tin star from his vest and toss it underhanded onto Dixon's desk. It bounced once, winding up between matched Colts that lay atop the desk, their muzzles angled toward the office doorway.

"That's a rash decision, Mr. Evans," Dixon said.

"Maybe," Evans replied. "At least it's one that I can live with."

"Are you sure about that?"

Evans saw the move coming, reached for his holstered gun, but there was no way he could beat the rising Colts. Incredibly, he felt a smile etched on his face as they exploded, driving sledgehammers into his chest, propelling him away from Dixon's desk and backward, into darkness without end.

14

The first and second shots missed Slade with room to spare. The upstairs sniper had a hasty trigger finger, jerking when he should have squeezed, or maybe he was just a piss-poor shot.

In any case, Slade made it to the south side of the street, clutching his rifle while the Winchester repeating shotgun slung across his back slapped at his ribs, and ducked into a shadowed doorway there. An alley stood between him and the Southern Star, as black as pitch.

The second-story shooter had no better luck with Slade's companions, but he scattered them. Jackson veered off and wound up two doors down on the far side of the Southern Star, while Abernathy doubled back and went to ground across the street. He was the only one among them with a fair shot at the sniper and he took advantage of it, trading shot for shot.

Someone inside the barroom had been waiting for a target, and a couple of them started firing through the bat-wing doors, pistols booming at Abernathy in the semi-darkness. There was nothing Slade could do to help him from his present vantage point, so he stepped out and edged into the alley, braced for anything that might be waiting for him there.

But nothing was.

It would've been a natural location for a shooter, maybe several, but the men Dixon had tapped for his last-ditch defense clearly weren't strategists. Slade moved along the alley. He passed a side door into the saloon that felt too risky and continued circling on around to the back.

The back door suited him much better, now that the saloon's defenders were distracted by a threat on Main Street. If they'd had their wits about them, someone would be posted at the rear of the saloon to watch their backs, but Slade was banking on the hope that Dixon's second-string defenders would be amateurs.

So far, so good.

He tried the back door, guessing that it would be locked, but felt the knob turn in his hand. Slade eased it open, inch by inch, letting his rifle's muzzle lead the way inside, his index finger taut around the trigger. If they had a shooter waiting for him, he could nail Slade through the door without risking a thing.

But no one fired.

Slade closed the door behind him, slowly, silently. He likely could've slammed it, with the gunfire blasting from the main barroom, but he decided not to take the chance. He was inside, and that was something, but it wasn't victory.

His next step was to locate William Dixon. It was even money, whether Dixon would be with his shooters on the firing line, or tucked up someplace where he felt secluded from the action. Based on Dixon's hasty flight from his own home, Slade guessed that Dixon would be hiding somewhere on the premises, but he had to be sure.

A curtain screened the Southern Star's main barroom from the hallway where Slade stood. Holding his rifle steady at his hip, he closed the gap and slowly drew the screen of fabric to one side.

It irritated Dixon that he had to move the sheriff's corpse himself. He hadn't minded shooting Evans — it had given him a sense of satisfaction, if the truth be told — but someone else should be assigned the dirty work.

No matter.

If you want a job done right, do it yourself.

With all the gunfire rattling around downstairs, he doubted whether anyone had even noticed two shots from the second floor. Killing the sheriff might've been a hard thing to explain, under the circumstances, but he wouldn't have to bother with that now. The deed was done.

He'd dragged the body by its heels, along the second-story landing, to a place beside the building's rear staircase. Dixon left it there, relieved to see that Evans hadn't left a blood trail on the floorboards that would show where he had died.

He could be anybody's victim. Dixon's hands were clean.

Returning to his office sanctuary, Dixon paused to scan the main floor of the Southern Star below him. Four of the locals whom he had dragooned into service were shooting at someone or something on Main Street, two of them taking turns at the swinging doors, two others dancing back and forth to fire through shattered windows.

Dixon might have thought they had been panicked into dueling with shadows, but then someone outside fired back. The bullet drilled one of his deputies, a shoulder wound that spun the man around and dropped him to one knee, blood pumping down his shirtfront. Someone else moved up to take his place, stepping around the injured man as if the damage might be catching.

Dixon retreated to his office, closed the door behind him, and secured its bolt. For good measure, he grabbed an extra chair and braced it underneath the doorknob, wedged in tight. The curtains on his office window were already drawn.

It was the best Dixon could do.

Whether Slade was alone or backed by an army, he'd have to get past Dixon's men on the ground floor in order to reach him. And if he managed that . . . well, then, he'd find out who the best man was.

In that respect, Dixon supposed he owed a debt of gratitude to Galen Evans. If the sheriff hadn't tried to kill him, Dixon might be cowering beneath his desk, instead of sitting tall and proud, replacing the spent cartridges from his twin Colts.

Killing the traitor had empowered him. Dixon felt like a new man, ready to take on the world.

Or, at the very least, a U.S. marshal who should already be dead.

He'd missed one chance to deal with

Slade, but he might have another. He could still eliminate the threat and buy himself some time.

When he'd finished reloading, Dixon rocked back in his chair and poured himself another double shot of bourbon.

"Ready when you are," he told the empty room. "What's keeping you?"

Colin Jackson was considering a rush down toward the Southern Star, to hell with consequences, when he heard someone moving around inside the shop whose doorway he had borrowed as a hiding place. The sound was anything but subtle, closer to a crash as something heavy fell and shattered on the floor.

He swung around to face the noise, noting that the shop's door was mostly made of glass. That helped him peer inside, but also made him vulnerable if the person who had caused the sound was one of William Dixon's partisans.

The shop was dark, except for faint light spilling down a stairwell at the back. Jackson supposed the stairs led up to living quarters on the second floor, a popular arrangement for the merchants he had met in Last Resort. If he could just remember who the owner was, what merchandise he carried . . .

Groceries. And it was one of Dixon's stores — or, rather, one of those he sanctioned and supported. Jackson's wife had tried to buy some beans and flour there, but the proprietor had told her that he didn't sell to coloreds. Jackson had been ready for a fight, but Mayzie had dissuaded him and now they ordered in from Mr. Tucker's dry-goods store.

High time to put things right, he thought, but didn't want to fire on anyone unless —

A shotgun blast shattered the top half of the door, showering Jackson with a storm of broken glass and splintered wood. He recoiled, cursing, and fired at the muzzle flash, praying for a hit without really expecting one.

The second shotgun blast was high and wide, perhaps thrown off by Jackson's shot. He took advantage of the miss by scrambling to all fours, cutting his left palm when he set it down on glass, and vaulting through the portal cleared by buckshot. Jackson nearly lost his rifle in the process, but he forged ahead, painfully conscious that his would-be slayer only needed seconds to reload his double-barreled gun.

Finding a target in near darkness was another problem, but his adversary helped, dropping a shotgun shell by accident. It clattered on the wooden floor, then started rolling, drawing Jackson's eyes and rifle toward the sound. A second later, he was sighting on a human form standing behind a counter where he knew produce was displayed.

Jackson fired once, then pumped the rifle's lever action, ready with another round in case he needed it. He was advancing at the same time, watching as his shadow target lurched backward, then sagged against the counter, still not going down. Jackson was about to fire again when gravity took over, and the figure crumpled out of sight.

It was a rush through darkness then, banging his left knee against something hard and painful, biting back the cry that welled up in his throat. Limping a bit, he reached the produce counter, swung around it, covering his fallen enemy.

Jackson couldn't see much by the dim light falling across the staircase, but he *heard* enough to know he wouldn't need to shoot again. The soggy gurgling noises coming from the figure sprawled before him were repellant.

They were sounds of death.

Noises upstairs drew Jackson's focus from the dying man, but he decided not to wait and see who else was spoiling for a fight. There was a back door close at hand, and it would grant him access to the Southern Star without returning to the Main Street battle zone.

He thought of Martin Abernathy, said a silent prayer that he'd stay safe, then started for the exit. Pausing only long enough to tell the almost corpse, "You should've sold me those beans."

Slade scanned the barroom, counting heads. There were eleven shooters on their feet and one slumped in a corner, bleeding out from what appeared to be a shoulder wound. The others made no move to help him, focused as they were on pouring lead into the street.

The only one among them whom Slade recognized was the bartender, still in his normal place, but carrying a sawed-off scattergun. The rest, Slade guessed, were townspeople who'd answered Dixon's call for reinforcements in his hour of need. As such, they were accomplices to any crimes he had committed and deserved no kid-glove handling.

Slade weighed his options. He would've liked to leave the barroom troops alone and go in search of Dixon, but he guessed that he would find his man somewhere upstairs.

And access to the stairs lay through the main room of the Southern Star. With that in mind — and the persistent threat they posed to his companions, somewhere in the night outside — Slade knew he'd have to deal with this lot first.

Damn it!

He stepped back from the curtain, stood his rifle upright in the nearest corner, and removed the lever-action shotgun from its sling. It held five rounds in its magazine, with one more in the chamber, and Slade carried extra cartridges in his vest pockets. There should be enough to do the job, if he was lucky.

If he lived that long.

Normal procedure called for Slade to warn the shooters, giving them a chance to drop their guns and raise their hands, but he decided that it wasn't in his own best interest to invite a volley from eleven guns before he'd fired a shot. With that in mind, he thumbed back the Winchester's hammer, braced its stock against his shoulder, and stepped back into the curtained doorway.

The bartender was closest and most dangerous to Slade, considering his stubby twelve-gauge. Slade gave him a blast from fifteen feet and saw the rag-doll figure airborne as he pumped the Model 87's lever action, swinging toward the gunmen lined up at the door and windows.

Some of them were turning as he opened fire, distracted from their mission by the shotgun blast behind them. Slade did not prioritize his targets, simply worked his way from left to right, unloading five rounds at a range that let his buckshot spread a foot or so in flight.

It was a given that he couldn't drop all ten that way. In fact, he only wounded half of them, and he supposed that two or three of those were merely hurt, not down and out. The rest were busy flipping tables over on their sides and dropping out of sight, turning their guns on Slade and peppering the doorway with a storm of lead.

Cursing, he rolled back out of range and started to reload.

"We need to get around behind the Star," said Marcus Tucker. "Maybe go out back, head north, and cross the street down by the livery."

"Sounds good," said Jabez Washington.

A silent nod from Caleb Greeley told them he was in.

Tucker couldn't have said why he appeared to be in charge, perhaps because he'd ponied up the rifles they were carrying. God knew he was no kind of military strategist, but common sense told Tucker that they couldn't approach the saloon along Main Street without drawing fire. Logic dictated that they find a safer way to cross and come at Dixon's people from the rear.

What logic *didn't* cover was the need for Tucker to involve himself at all. That came from somewhere else, defying rationality and all his fears. He simply knew that if they did nothing, if they stood back and watched while Dixon killed a lawman, Last Resort was finished as a civilized community.

Some might've said it never was one, in the first place, but in Tucker's mind and heart there lingered hope for better days. If that meant risking everything right now, instead of simply drifting with the tide and drowning later, he would take that chance.

Lurleen was tucked away upstairs, two loaded shotguns on the bed beside her, just in case. They'd kissed in parting, Tucker praying that it wouldn't be the last time, and he had pretended not to see her tears. It hurt now, stepping out into the night that smelled of gunsmoke, leaving her behind, but what else could he do?

Sometimes a man was forced to stand alone.

Or with two friends whose lives were also riding on the line.

They jogged along behind a line of Main Street shops, all dark and shuttered, even though he knew their owners had to be awake and listening to gunfire from the Southern Star. On second thought, he guessed that some of those, his neighbors, might be down at the saloon, defending Dixon from arrest and trial for all that he had done.

At least I'm not like them, thought Tucker. *If I die tonight, at least I won't be in the wrong.*

Or did that even matter?

He attended church each week, mostly to please Lurleen, but Tucker wasn't sold entirely on the concept of an afterlife. He hoped that there was *something* out there, somewhere, but the thought of mansions floating in the sky seemed ludicrous.

He smelled the livery before he saw it, slowed his pace, and stopped outside an alley separating Dixon's stable from the shop next door. Giving Jabez a chance to catch his breath before they moved again, Tucker turned down the alley, pacing off its length with care, afraid of running into someone he couldn't see.

They reached Main Street and stood there for another moment, staring at the Southern

348

Star. Gunfire still echoed all around it, but there seemed to be fewer muzzle flashes from the broad front windows. Now, more of the shooting echoed from within.

"Somebody got inside," the barber said.

"Sounds like it," Greeley answered.

"Then he needs us more than ever," Tucker said and left the safety of the shadows, jogging toward the killing ground.

Martin Abernathy reckoned it was time for him to move. He'd been pinned down at first, huddled and trading bullets with the second-story sniper, but whoever it had been up there, he must've given up. Minutes had passed without a shot from that direction, and the gunmen who had fired on Abernathy from the windows of the Southern Star now seemed distracted, too.

There'd never be a better time for him to make a break — but where should he go? He'd already lost track of Jackson and Slade, being stranded alone on Main Street in a town where he knew at least half of the white people couldn't care less if he died.

As for the other half, they were an unknown quantity. Some of them bucked the rules laid down by Mr. Dixon, but would any of them stand and fight against him?

Sick and tired of waiting, Abernathy

bolted from the doorway that had sheltered him. He ran across the street, meaning to join the fracas at the Southern Star if he could reach it. It was why he'd come to town, why he'd already risked his life to help the white lawman and liberate the slaves Dixon had penned up on his property.

He'd come too far to turn back now.

He was halfway across the street when someone shouted at him from an alley over there. "Whoa, nigger!" were the only words he heard, before a scrawny-looking white man stepped out of the shadows, leveling a rifle from his hip.

The stranger fired, and Abernathy heard the bullet sizzle past him as he hit the dirt, tumbled through something like an awkward shoulder roll, and wound up on his belly, sighting down the barrel of his Winchester from thirty feet. His target turned to track him, cursing bitterly, and dropped to one knee as he recognized the danger he was facing.

As it happened, that was the wrong move. Kneeling had the effect of raising Abernathy's sights from thigh-level to his opponent's chest. He saw the opportunity and took it, squeezing off before the stranger had a chance to fire again.

And thought he'd missed at first, until he

registered the dazed look on the white man's face, then watched him topple over backward, twitching as the life ran out of him and stained the dust of Main Street.

Abernathy didn't hang around to gloat. An instant later, he was up and running toward the Southern Star as if his life depended on it.

Which, in some way, he supposed it did.

The first barrage missed Slade because the barroom shooters were surprised to find an enemy behind them. Hasty shots rarely, if ever, found their target, but the storm of bullets wreaked havoc on the door frame and its dangling curtain. Huddled in a corner while the lead flew thick and fast, Slade concentrated on reloading his shotgun, then shifted his rifle to a more convenient spot for the inevitable switch off.

Everything came down to blood and thunder now. He wouldn't have a chance to pick his targets with precision. Instead he must hit hard and fast enough to daze them, maybe wound a couple more, and set them up for killing shots while they were trying to recover.

Thus, the twelve-gauge first.

He waited for a brief lull in the hostile fire, then craned around the bullet-riddled doorjamb, rapid-firing with the lever-action scattergun from right to left. There was no time to mark specific targets, but he registered the sight of buckshot ripping into tabletops, a runner sprawling as his legs were cut from under him, another vaulting through a shattered window when he couldn't find a better place to hide.

The shotgun's hammer snapped onto an empty chamber and Slade dropped it, scooping up his rifle as he bolted through the doorway, past the curtain all in tatters, scanning for a target on the move.

And saw two rising, far enough apart that Slade knew he could only handle one of them before the other took a shot. He picked the closer of them, going with the simple math, and put a slug into the stranger's chest from six or seven paces out.

The second shooter had him then, no question in Slade's mind as he went through the motions with his rifle's lever action, turning toward the man who was about to kill him, so at least he wouldn't take it in the back. Their guns came up together, Dixon's man with the advantage, leaning into it and bracing for the recoil.

When the shot came, Slade couldn't believe his enemy had missed. Thought that he must've lost his mind when red mist haloed his opponent's skull and sprayed the wall behind him.

Slade kept swinging through the turn, tracking the echo of that shot to find out who had saved his life, and there was Colin Jackson, standing in the doorway Slade had vacated mere seconds earlier.

"They should've watched the side door," Jackson said.

"I guess."

"Where's Dixon?"

"Still upstairs, I think," Slade said.

"You want to check it out, I'll finish up down here."

Slade bolted for the stairs, took them three at a time on his way to the second-floor landing, then stopped at the sight of a body sprawled out there.

Galen Evans hadn't made it to the main event downstairs. But who had gunned him down? And why?

No matter, now.

Slade moved along the second-story hallway, checking each door as he passed.

The lull in gunfire from downstairs put Dixon on alert. He downed a final shot of whiskey, set the glass down on his desk, and picked up his twin Colts. Their weight felt reassuring in his hands.

It wouldn't be much longer now, he understood. Whichever way the fight had gone below him, someone would be knocking on his office door. If Slade was dead, it would be one of Dixon's men, announcing victory.

If not . . .

Dixon was having second thoughts about his barricaded room. While it would hold his enemies at bay in theory, they could always starve him out — or burn the Southern Star around him, if it came to that. A sudden rush of panic at the thought of leaping flames made Dixon bolt out of his tall chair, snatching up his pistols from the desktop.

He began to pace the room, his agitation mounting by the second, fueled by liquor he'd consumed. Should he go out to face his enemies, instead of hiding like a trapped rat in his lair? Would it be suicide, or might his brave example tip the balance in his favor?

Or was the confusion down below a golden opportunity?

His mind flashed to the fire escape, located at the far end of the second-story hallway. It was just a ladder bolted to the Southern Star's east wall and served a double purpose when the roof needed repairs, but if Dixon could reach it and descend while his defenders kept the enemy distracted . . .

Knowing he could not afford to waste another moment, Dixon thrust his Colts into their holsters, grabbed his rifle on the fly, and hastily removed the chair he'd used to wedge his door shut. Fumbling at the lock in haste, he finally released it, threw the door open — and froze.

This was the risky part, the long run down the corridor to reach a certain window, open it, and clamber out into the night. His back would be exposed to anyone ascending the staircase from the saloon below.

Hurry!

He risked a glance back toward the stairs, saw no one there but Galen Evans sprawled in death, and bolted for the far end of the hallway. His escape route was so close that he could almost feel the ladder rungs clutched in his fist.

And he was almost there, one hand outstretched to throw the window's latch, when a familiar voice behind him called his name.

Slade was emerging from a hooker's crib, where he'd ducked into to check the closet and to peer beneath the sagging bed, when Dixon bolted from his office, three doors down. It startled Slade to see his quarry out and running, when he'd thought the planter would be holed up somewhere, waiting out the storm.

What did he hope to gain by running toward a window?

Did he mean to jump, or —

"Dixon!"

Slade's shout brought the slaver to a lurching halt, a few strides short of his apparent goal. Dixon froze for a moment, then spoke without turning.

"You're on the wrong side of this, Slade. Why not think of your race for a change?"

"I'm a human," Slade answered. "Can you say the same?"

"You're a white man, goddamn it! Made in God's image to master the beasts of the field!"

"It's too late for a sermon," Slade told him. "I'll ask you one time to drop the rifle."

And it took him by surprise when Dixon said, "All right, Marshal. Just let me set it down. I wouldn't want it going off by accident and have you shoot me in the back."

Slade watched as Dixon bent to his right, arm outstretched to set his rifle gently on the floor. He tracked the move, and he was almost ready when the planter spun around, crouching and whipping out matched Colts.

Almost.

Slade threw himself aside as Dixon's pistols roared. He fired as he was falling, felt a bullet pluck his sleeve but miss the flesh beneath. Slade knew his own shot would be high and wide, pumping his rifle's lever action as he fell against the wall and slithered toward the floor.

Dixon fired two more shots, his slugs ripping through wallpaper and wood a foot above Slade's head. Slade's shot in answer may have grazed his target, or perhaps Dixon just lurched away to save himself.

Firing again with his left hand, the planter whipped his other Colt around and hammered at the window glass behind him, furiously lashing out to clear the frame. It seemed incredible that he would still try jumping, under fire, but Slade was busy ducking bullets, rolling on the dusty carpet while the air was filled with lead and thunder overhead.

Dixon was halfway out the shattered window when Slade struggled to his feet, cocking his rifle as he aimed it hastily, then cursing as the hammer fell upon an empty chamber.

Dropping it, Slade snatched at his Peacemaker, then was forced to drop and roll again, as Dixon fired a parting shot that whispered past his ear. Rebounding as the planter dropped from sight, Slade sprinted for the window in pursuit.

When he was almost there, a voice he nearly recognized called out to Dixon in the darkness, from somewhere below. A pistol shot rang out in answer, then a rifle volley rattled through the alley's echo chamber.

Cautiously, Slade closed the gap and leaned out through the window, with his pistol at the ready. Twenty feet below, William Dixon's crumpled body lay sprawled before three men whose upturned faces Slade immediately recognized.

The barber, the dry-goods dealer, and the journalist.

All holding rifles pointed down at Dixon's corpse.

"Looks like we almost missed the party," Marcus Tucker said.

"Better late than never," Slade replied. And smiled.

EPILOGUE

The rest of it was cleaning up. Slade made his way downstairs, arriving just as Marcus Tucker, Jabez Washington, and Caleb Greeley entered through the bat-wing doors. They scanned the battleground with stricken faces, doubtless picking out the forms of men they knew.

Jackson and Abernathy had a couple of survivors covered in the barroom, while the rest of Dixon's makeshift troop were scattered where they'd fallen. Some of them were still alive and might remain that way if help arrived in time.

"Is there a doctor here in town?" Slade asked nobody in particular.

"I'll fetch him," Washington replied, sounding relieved that he'd found an excuse to put the scene of death behind him.

"And the undertaker," Slade called after him.

"I'll see to it," the barber told him and

was gone into the night.

Outside, Slade saw new faces peering through the shattered windows, men and women dressed haphazardly, deciding that they ought to find out what was happening, now that the guns had fallen silent. Some of them were pointing, whispering among themselves, as they recognized Dixon's fallen defenders.

"Who are these two?" Slade inquired, facing the pair who'd managed to emerge from the firefight unscathed.

"That's Harvey Wiggins on the left," said Tucker. "Dixon's partner in the Southern Belle. The other one is Rod Poteet. Sort of a handyman around the Belle and Empire Arms."

"Someone should probably escort them to the jail," said Slade.

"Now that you mention it, where's Sheriff Evans?" Greeley asked.

"Top of the stairs," Slade said. "Looks like he had an argument with Dixon and his contract was revoked."

"Jesus! I would've thought he'd toe the line."

"People surprise you sometimes," Slade replied.

"I see that," said Tucker. "Mr. Jackson, Mr. Abernathy, you're out late this evening."

"And we should both be getting home," said Jackson. "If we're finished here, that is."

"Seems like it," Slade responded. "I'll walk back with you and get my horse."

They left the Southern Star together, passing through a crowd of onlookers that edged away from them, as if the scent of death clung to their clothes. Some of the people on the sidewalk nodded to the homesteaders in greeting; others glowered at them with an animosity barely restrained.

When they were past the gawkers, Jackson said, "Maybe it hasn't changed, at that."

"They'll need some time," Slade said. "If nothing else, the loss of Dixon and his guns should keep them quiet for a while. Give it a chance."

"I will, if they will," Jackson said.

Slade nodded and left it there as they crossed Main Street and retraced their steps to reach their tethered animals.

Jackson untied his horse before he said, "I guess we won't be seeing you again."

"You never know," said Slade. "This was my first time here, but it's been memorable. I might make the trip again, if anybody needs me."

"We can always use another friend," said Abernathy, saddled now and ready for the long road home.

"You may have some already that you aren't aware of," Slade replied. "Without Dixon to draw a line and tell them where to stand, you might give them a chance."

"My mind's not closed," said Abernathy, "but I need convincing."

"Fair enough," said Slade.

Jackson was mounted now and looking down at Slade. He said, "At least when we have to come in town, from now on, we won't be worrying about someone riding out to burn our homes. We owe you that, Marshal."

"Not me," Slade said. "Without you, I'd be nothing but a decoration on a tree right now."

"I guess we helped each other, then," Jackson replied.

"That's how it ought to be," Slade said.

When they were gone, Slade walked his mare down to the livery and found an anxious hostler waiting in the stable's open doorway, staring toward the Southern Star.

"Sounds like they had a ruckus," he observed, as Slade approached.

"Be glad you weren't invited."

"Oh, I was," the hostler said. "One of the boss man's people came around and said he needed me. I told 'im I get paid to watch the horses, not run down to the saloon. Said he'd be comin' back to even up with me when the dust settled."

"I wouldn't give that any further thought," Slade said. "Your boss is out of business."

"What about the animals?" the frowning hostler asked.

Slade handed him a silver dollar, saying, "This is for my horse, tonight. Tomorrow, ask around and see if anybody's stepping up to handle the loose ends."

It seemed a long walk back to reach the Empire Arms. The scent of gunsmoke lingered in the air, strongest around the Southern Star, where Last Resort's mortician and a couple of assistants were removing shrouded bodies. Slade moved on and left them to it, trying to relax but checking shadows as he passed, alert for any stragglers from the losing team.

There was no clerk on duty when he entered the hotel. Slade wondered if Joe Eddie was among the dead and wounded, back at the saloon. He hadn't recognized the clerk while it was happening, but could have overlooked him in the midst of chaos.

Slade already had his key, in any case. He went upstairs, eased down along the hallway to his room, and listened at the door before he opened it with the Colt in hand. No rude surprises waited for him there, and he was pleased to shed his clothing, rolling into bed with the idea of putting off tomorrow until sunrise.

But it didn't happen.

There was too much going on inside Slade's head. He thought about Judge Dennison, wondered if he was still alive, then spun off into what he'd say in his report about the past few days. He wondered, too, about the fate of Last Resort. Would it survive without its warlord benefactor? Would the men he'd helped to free at Dixon's place go home, wherever that was, or continue roaming westward? Would the KKK, if it survived this night, put *his* name on a murder list?

Enough!

Slade knew he couldn't answer any of the questions tumbling through his mind tonight. Some might be easier to handle by the light of day, and others might evaporate entirely. As for masked assassins with tattoos, Slade reckoned he would take them as they came.

He overslept, which meant that it was half past six o'clock when Slade went downstairs, dropped his key off at the unmanned registration counter, and moved on to try the Southern Belle for breakfast. It was open, with the same waitress on duty, but he didn't recognize the cook who peered out through a hole cut in the wall between the kitchen and the dining room.

"New man today?" Slade asked the waitress, when she reached his table.

"Freddie didn't make it in this morning," she replied. "I guess there was some trouble overnight?"

Slade answered with a question of his own. "Is his replacement any good?"

"Oh, sure," the waitress told him, smiling hopefully.

Experienced or not, there wasn't much that he could do to ruin ham and eggs with fried potatoes on the side. Slade cleaned his plate and left a good tip for the waitress, who possessed the only smiling face he'd seen in Last Resort.

The ride back would allow Slade time to put his thoughts in order, maybe even think of ways to help the misbegotten town he'd torn apart. Given the circumstances, he supposed Judge Dennison might want to open an investigation and discover if the Klan was still a factor to be reckoned with.

He didn't want to think about the possibility that Dennison had passed while he was gone, or if the judge simply decided to retire. Slade didn't know who might be sent as a replacement, in that case, but he already questioned whether he could work for someone else.

He'd never meant the marshal's job to be for life. It had begun as a convenience, a one-time thing, but it had grown on him. And so had Faith.

That raised another host of questions in his mind, concerning their relationship. If he lost Faith *and* Isaac Dennison, would there be any point to staying on? Was he a lawman in his heart and soul, or was it just an outfit that he wore when he was on the job?

"I guess we'll see," Slade told his mare, as Last Resort slipped out of sight behind them.

And tomorrow, Slade supposed, would take care of itself.